UP ON THE WOOF TOP

UP ON the WOOF TOP

A CHET & BERNIE MYSTERY

Spencer Quinn

FORGE · TOR PUBLISHING GROUP
New York

UP ON THE WOOF TOP

A Forge Book
Published by Tom Doherty Associates / Tor Publishing Group
120 Broadway
New York, NY 10271

www.tor-forge.com

Forge® is a registered trademark of Macmillan Publishing Group, LLC.

The Library of Congress Cataloging-in-Publication Data is available upon request.

ISBN 978-1-250-84330-2 (hardcover)
ISBN 978-1-250-84331-9 (ebook)

Our books may be purchased in bulk for promotional, educational, or business use. Please contact your local bookseller or the Macmillan Corporate and Premium Sales Department at 1-800-221-7945, extension 5442, or by email at MacmillanSpecialMarkets@macmillan.com.

First Edition: 2023

Printed in the United States of America

0   9   8   7   6   5   4   3   2   1

For Jeff, Ann, Meggy, Anthony, and Catherine

UP ON THE WOOF TOP

One

Uh-oh.

Most perps turn out to be reasonable in the end. They know, for example, the moment a case is closed, namely when I grab them by the pant leg. Pant leg grabbing is one of my specialties at the Little Detective Agency, Little on account of that's my partner Bernie's last name. Do I even have a last name? I've never heard it, but if there's a change, I'll let you know. Till then just think of me as Chet, pure and simple.

Maybe you're wondering, but Chet, what about the unreasonable perps? I hope so, because that was exactly where I was headed with that uh-oh. Right now, we had a couple of unreasonable perps on our hands, although I myself have no hands, don't need hands, and wouldn't even know what to do with them. These unreasonable perps were the Burger boys, two brothers who'd hijacked a beer truck, now wrecked at the bottom of a box canyon they'd sped into in the hope of getting away from us—getting away in a wobbly truck from me and Bernie tailing them in the Beast, our brand-new, very old Porsche, can you imagine? A truck, by the way, that actually must have been hauling something un-beerlike, so unmistakably peanut oil from the aroma now hanging in the still air.

"What's that stink?" said a Burger brother, the one Bernie called Hammy. The Burger brothers did not look alike. Hammy was short and skinny with big round eyes. The other one, Cheesy, I believe, was huge with little slit eyes.

"I don't smell nothin'," Cheesy said. "And who cares? This is our chance, you moron."

Cheesy didn't smell the peanut oil? How astonishing was that? Every time you think you've hit bottom when it comes to what the human nose can't do they take it down another notch. There was nothing else to smell besides peanut oil, even for me who smells everything! I was about to feel sorry for them, or at least for Cheesy, when Hammy said, "Chance for what?"

"For hightailin' it—what else?" Cheesy said. "He'll be back any minute."

Possibly I should have mentioned that I was alone with Hammy and Cheesy, Bernie having climbed up to higher ground where maybe his phone would work and he could call into Valley PD. Was there room in the Beast for me, Bernie, Hammy, and Cheesy? Maybe just for me, Bernie, and Hammy, but we couldn't leave Cheesy out here in the desert all by his lonesome, his wrists cuffed in the pretty red, white, and blue plastic cuffs we used, just one of those touches that makes the Little Detective Agency what it is. The point I'm making is that Valley PD needed to come out here with the paddy wagon. I peered at the trail Bernie had followed up the canyon wall, a trail that took a sharp turn high up there, vanishing behind a jumble of red rocks, and didn't see him. But Hammy and Cheesy hightailing it, Bernie or no Bernie, was off the table. Hadn't the Burger brothers been grabbed by the pant leg, first Cheesy and then Hammy? The case was closed.

But Hammy and Cheesy weren't getting it. They'd gone from sitting peacefully on the ground to a sort of grunting struggle to stand, not so easy with their hands behind their backs.

Cheesy, despite being so enormous, was the first one up, a bit of a surprise to me. Then came a bigger surprise. He leaned over Hammy, chomped down on the collar of Hammy's shirt, and hoisted him up. Wow! A first in terms of what the human mouth is capable of, and I've been in the business for a long time.

"Let's go," Cheesy said.

"What about the dog?" said Hammy.

"No problem. If it comes close give it the boot, good and hard."

Excuse me?

Not long after that, Hammy and Cheesy were sitting nice and comfy on the ground and we were back to being buddies. I admit that their pant legs were no longer what you might call blood free, but the amount wasn't worth mentioning, hardly noticeable.

Bernie returned soon after, gave us all a close look.

"Was there a problem?"

None that I recalled, and Hammy and Cheesy were shaking their heads, the rhythm identical.

"But we were thinking you might cut us a break," Cheesy said.

"Why would I want to do that?" said Bernie.

Hammy snapped his fingers, a human thing for when they get a sudden idea, but amazing he could do it with his hands cuffed behind his back. "Isn't it Christmas time?"

"Next week, maybe?" said Cheesy. "Wednesday? Thursday?"

"Friday?" said Hammy.

They gazed up at Bernie, eyes open wide in a hopeful look like they were—oh my goodness!—begging. Didn't they know begging is a no-no? Also, Bernie had no treats on him. I keep close track of things like that.

"Do I look like Santa?" Bernie said, this whole little back and forth ending in total confusion, at least for me. But Valley PD arrived soon after, along with a nice lady from the peanut oil company, who gave Bernie a check. And we hadn't even been working the case, not until Hammy and Cheesy almost ran us off the road. What a day! The only problem was Bernie, sticking that check in the chest pocket of his Hawaiian shirt, the one with the dancing tubas. We'd had problems with checks and chest pockets in the past. I barked this low rumbly bark I have. Bernie got a look on his face, like he'd remembered something, and he transferred the check to the front pocket of his jeans, where it was nice and safe. If he wanted to think he'd done that remembering all by himself that was fine with me. Anything Bernie did was fine with me.

We've had Porsches in our career, maybe not out the ying-yang, but close. I can't tell you the actual number because going past two is an issue, but I can see all those lovely rides in my mind. The first one went off a cliff, then the one with the martini glass decals got blown up, or was that the one that ended up in a snowy treetop? It's hard to keep track. We have busy lives, me and Bernie. Here's the takeaway: all our Porsches have been old ones fixed up by Nixon Panero, our car guy, and the one we were in now, Bernie behind the wheel and me sitting tall in the shotgun seat—the breeze, not too hot at this time of year, ruffling my fur—was the oldest and best. It's all wavy black and white stripes, like a squad car rippling its muscles, Bernie says— who else talks like my Bernie?—and he calls it the Beast, on account of what's under the hood. Bottom line—if you're ever getting chased by us, just pull over. Whoa! I myself am black and white, specifically black with one white ear. And . . . and I can be something of a beast myself! Wow! For a moment I thought I knew all there was to know. Then the moment passed and I felt better.

"Something on your mind, big guy?"

Nope. Not a thing. Bernie looked at me. I looked at him right back. What a beautiful sight! Just his eyebrows, for example, not the namby-pamby kind of eyebrows you see all too often but eyebrows, amigo, that can't be missed. On top of that, Bernie's eyebrows have a language all their own. Right now, they were saying, Chet, you're something else. I placed my paw on his knee. We sped up, somewhat alarmingly, especially since we seemed to be bumper to bumper on the airport freeway, but Bernie hit the brakes and we were good. He laughed. Bernie's got the best laugh in the world. You can't miss it, and a woman in the next lane didn't. She glanced over, frowning at first, and then not.

Soon after that we were rolling down Mesquite Road, our street, the nicest in the Valley except for all the ones where the rich folks live. We pulled into our driveway and what was this? Action next door at the Parsons's house?

There hadn't been much in the way of action at the Parsons's house for some time. Mr. and Mrs. Parsons were old and not doing well, especially her. As for Iggy, my best pal, the Parsonses had never been able to figure out their electric fence—even though Bernie had checked it out and found it was working perfectly— so Iggy didn't get out much anymore. Mostly I just saw him through the tall window in their front hall, but he wasn't there now. Instead he was outside. They were all outside, Mrs. Parsons in her wheelchair and Mr. Parsons guiding the wheelchair with one hand and holding onto Iggy's leash with the other. Do I need to mention that Iggy was straining against that leash with everything he had in his tiny body, his amazingly long tongue flopping all over the place, and the look in his eyes at its craziest? I don't think so. You were probably picturing that already, plus the high-pitched yip-yip-yipping. But maybe you missed the little detail of Iggy's collar, not his normal plain collar but his Christmas collar with flashing red and green lights. The Parsons had bought one for me, too—this was sometime back—but I do not wear flashing light collars. I have black leather for dress up and gator skin for everyday, the story of me and a gator name of Iko and our trip to bayou country way too long to even start on. In the here and now, as Bernie likes to say, we had a taxi parked in the Parsons's drive-way and a taxi driver standing on the lawn, not in a good mood.

"The wheelchair? Plus that yapping little mutt?"

"We're prepared to pay extra," said Mr. Parsons.

"Yeah? Two hundred dollars extra?"

By that time, we were out of the car and strolling over.

"Hi, Daniel," Bernie said. "Where are you headed?"

Mr. Parsons turned to us, stumbling just a bit. Bernie took Iggy's leash in that smooth way he has, and Iggy went quiet.

"Oh, hi, Bernie," Mr. Parsons said, somewhat out of breath. "We're going to a book signing."

"Where?"

"Bookville. Dame Ariadne Carlisle is Edna's favorite author."

"She's so wonderful, Bernie," Mrs. Parsons said. "Have you read her?"

"Not to my knowledge," Bernie said.

"What luck for you! Imagine all the pleasure you've got in store. She's written ninety-nine novels, each one better than the last and all of them with Christmas themes."

"Oh," said Bernie.

"Hey!" said the taxi driver. "What am I? A potted plant?"

Bernie turned to him. I turned my nose to him, if that makes sense. Somewhat plantish, certainly, but in a special way you smell a lot in these parts, a combo of garlic plus weed plus mint mouth wash. Here's an interesting little fact: the mixture is never exactly the same. In short, I knew this guy.

And so did Bernie. "Two Bricks?" he said.

Ah, yes. Orlando "Two Bricks" Short, who'd had a scheme involving counterfeit watches, very good counterfeits if I remember right, except that he'd spelled a word—possibly Rolex—wrong on every one.

Two Bricks took a step back, raising his hands like Bernie was about to draw down on him. What a crazy idea! We weren't even carrying, plus we never draw down first on anyone. Still, I was suddenly in the mood for the .38 Special. Bernie can shoot spinning dimes out of the air, a lovely way to spend an afternoon.

"I ain't done nothin', Bernie," Two Bricks said. "I'm the most straight up dude in the whole Valley nowadays. Like, actually boring."

"Perfect," said Bernie. "So I assume you're going to drive this very nice couple to Bookville for the meter fare plus a boringly moderate tip. Chet and I will follow, with Iggy here in the back."

Some things in life start out nicely and then have a nasty twist at the end. This was one of those. Iggy on the little shelf in back? Iggy had never ridden in the Beast. The only member of the nation within—as Bernie calls me and my kind—who had was me. Why couldn't it stay that way? Was it possible to occupy both the shotgun seat and the little shelf? Why was this even—

"Ch—et?" said Bernie, in this way he has of saying Chet.

First time in a bookstore! The smells! I didn't even know where to begin. There were all kinds of human smells, which is what you get in crowd situations, and Bookville was packed with humans sitting on card table chairs and standing against the walls. No kids, though, so some of the most interesting smells were missing. Crowds are always better when kids are in them, if you want my opinion, and not just in the smell department. But forget all that. The most interesting smell—apart from the fact that a family of snakes seemed to be living under the floor—came from the bookshelves. So many books! Their smell was wonderful, somewhat like a very dry forest but a cozy, indoor one, if that makes sense, which it probably does not.

Even though there didn't seem to be room for us, meaning me, Bernie, and Mr. and Mrs. Parsons plus Iggy in her lap, a bookstore worker spotted her and wheeled her to a special section off to the side but up front, so that was where we all ended up, in our own little row with a good view of what I believe is called the podium. I know that from the time Bernie gave the keynote speech at the Great Western Private Eye Association conference. Everyone just loved his talk, although most of the audience had to leave early, probably for family emergencies.

A thin little guy wearing two sets of glasses, one in the normal place and the other on top of his head, was at the podium, speaking softly and reading from a note card.

"Merry, um, Christmas, Hanukkah, and uh, holidays." He looked up. "Only six book shopping days to go! Heh, heh." He glanced around, perhaps expecting some sort of reaction, but none came. His gaze returned to the note card. "*The Universal Encyclopedia of Christmas* calls our guest today 'the greatest Christmas writer since Dickens.' And the *Reader's Bible of All Things Mystery* says 'no one writes them any twistier' than her. So now it's my, um, pleasure, to introduce or, ah, to welcome to Bookville for the very first time, making her last appearance before Christmas this year—" He looked up and blinked once or twice, "—the loveliest—I mean most beloved author in the whole wide world, Dame Ariadne Carlisle! Let's give a big . . ."

But the audience was already clapping and cheering. Out from behind a curtain that looked a little like a bedsheet strode a woman who smelled lovely, kind of like one of those long boxes with flowers inside at the first moment someone opens it. She glanced at the thin little guy on her way to the podium and in a low voice said, "Dame as in fame not dame as in scram."

The thin little guy turned white, but she didn't notice. Had anyone else heard? Maybe only him and me, him because he was so close and me because, well, I'm me. Meanwhile, I'd left out the most important thing, namely the quality of her voice, kind of like that giant violin humans play between their legs— the name escaping me at the moment—but souped up, so rich and powerful, with a—uh-oh—catlike purr at the core.

Two uh-ohs in one day? That was when I began to worry.

Two

Aside from Bernie, I've heard other speakers, Senator Wray, for example, although maybe not a senator anymore—can you still be a senator when you're wearing an orange jumpsuit and breaking rocks in the hot sun? Right there is the kind of thing I don't know, but we're way off course because what I was getting to was the fact that every single one of those speakers had notes in hand, sometimes cards, sometimes—as in Bernie's case, a bunch of papers, which had gotten away from him, perhaps more than once, but that might have been his sense of humor, and there'd certainly been lots of laughter, especially the first few times it happened—but I'd never seen a speaker with no notes at all, not until now.

Dame Ariadne Carlisle held no notes. All she had was a gold pen, a big fat one, dangling from the fingers of one hand. Here's something crazy. I wanted that big fat gold pen, wanted it bad. Normally, I don't chew on metal, but I was sure that this gold pen would be charmingly springy to chew on, as long as I didn't really chew but just sort of held it in my mouth, not too hard, not too soft, but just right. That, by the way, is the kind of thing I do know.

Dame Ariadne Carlisle stood behind the podium. Things got very quiet in Bookville. Her eyes took in the crowd, green green eyes, with something cat-like about them, beyond doubt. Iggy, curled up in Mrs. Parsons' lap, made a sharp little whine in the back of his throat. Iggy missed a lot, but he wasn't missing the cat problem. That was how obvious it was. Mrs. Parsons gave him a gentle pat or two. Good luck with that. I got ready for just about anything.

"Thank you all for coming," Dame Ariadne said. "If it weren't for you"—she made a slow, sweeping gesture with the gold pen, "—there would be no me." That brought a gasp or two from the audience. Mrs. Parsons put her free hand over her heart, and she wasn't the only one doing that.

A book lay on the podium. Dame Ariadne held it up so everyone could see. On the cover was a picture of a Christmas stocking with the handle of a gun poking out the top, a gun that looked a lot like our .38 Special. I began liking Dame Ariadne, if only just a little.

She opened the book. "*Bad or Good*," she said, "number ninety-nine in the Trudi Tremaine Christmas mystery series. Chapter one. Snow fell softly on the sleeping Cotswold village of Potherington. Soft and steady for a night and a day, which was St. Ambrose Day, and the following night. It rounded all the corners, smoothed what could be smoothed, and smothered any sound in the village, a village known throughout the west country for its quiet in any case. Nevertheless, Miss Eleanor Poddle, the village postmistress who lived in Honeycomb Cottage, the last residence on Lavender Lane, sat up in her bed with the conviction she had heard something."

Here Dame Ariadne paused and raised the fat gold pen. The thin little guy hurried over with a glass of water and laid it on the podium. Dame Ariadne drank. All eyes were on her. Once I'd attended—rather briefly—a Valley PD party featuring a hypnotist for entertainment. I had no idea what a hypnotist does, but this was like that. Everybody—although not Bernie, same as at the Valley PD affair, now that I thought about it—had the same expression on their faces, like they'd gone sleep-walking. I'll get to my experiences—more than one, amazingly enough—with sleepwalking pyromaniacs some other time. But one other thing: The whole time Dame Ariadne was telling us about this snowstorm or whatever it was, she hadn't even glanced at the book. Those green eyes were on us.

"Miss Poddle, of a certain age but still rather sharp, peered at her bedside clock. Half after three, the quietest time of the quiet nights in this quiet village. Perhaps, she said aloud, speaking to herself as was her long habit, I only imagined something, or dreamed it. We are such stuff as dreams, Miss Poddle began, and then had the strangest thought: could it be Santa, just practicing for Christmas, only two weeks away, after all? How bizarre! Miss Poddle had ceased believing in Santa Claus eons ago. She felt oddly dizzy. Then came the sound, clear now and coming from the roof, not the racket that Santa would make, with all those reindeer and the sleigh, but more like some small animal, a cat perhaps, was making its way across the thatch. Coincidentally, Miss Poddle's own cat—named Kittypoo—had disappeared only last week. Miss Poddle sprang to her feet. 'Kittypoo,' she called. 'Here, Kittypoo.'"

What did it? The mention of the cat? The springing to the feet thing? Calling Kittypoo, Kittypoo? Some questions, Bernie says, have no answers, and he's always the smartest human in the room. I knew this was one of those questions, but even if there was an answer, it was only known to one being, and that being was Iggy in his flashing Christmas collar, now charging the podium at full speed, leash flapping behind him, ridiculously short tail wagging at one end and ridiculously long tongue flopping at the other. At that moment I figured out something important about Iggy—that was how he kept his balance. Wow! The longer you stick around the clearer it gets. I made up my mind then and there to stick around forever.

Everyone saw what was happening right away, except for Dame Ariadne who was still going on about this poodle person or whatever she was when Iggy launched himself in a leap I'd never have believed he had in him, the little guy, and snatched that fat gold pen clean out of Dame Ariadne's hand. I was shocked. Everyone was shocked. Dame Ariadne just stood there with her mouth open, all of a sudden looking much older. No one knew what to do.

Well, no one except for me. That pen did not belong to Iggy. It belonged to Dame Ariadne. Or me. But not Iggy. I left my spot in the audience and after an easy bound or two pounced on Iggy, grabbed him by the scruff of the neck, and trotted back to Bernie's side. Bernie handed the end of Iggy's leash to Mr. Parsons, at which point I took possession of the gold pen. Ah! The taste, the feel, the heft, all just as I'd thought or even—

"Ch—et?"

Moments later Bernie was walking up to the podium and offering the gold pen to Dame Ariadne. She did not take it.

"Do you mind?" she said.

"Uh," said Bernie.

"The slobber, if you please."

"Slobber?" Bernie gazed at the pen. "Ah." He wiped the pen on his jeans and handed it over.

"Ta," said Dame Ariadne.

"Any time," said Bernie. "Well, not any time. I just meant . . ." His voice trailed off and he came back to his seat, his face somewhat reddish, possibly from the room being a bit on the warmish side, what with all the humans. Human crowds give off a lot of heat, in case you don't know. It can be close to unpleasant at times.

Dame Ariadne shot Bernie a quick glance—catlike for sure!—and went back from looking old to looking merely no longer young. Then she tucked the pen in the pocket of her jacket, a fancy-looking jacket of thin black and gold stripes, gazed out at us, held up the book, and said, "But there was no response from Kittypoo, and no more sound from up on Miss Poddle's cottage roof. She had never been one to leave stones unturned. Despite the hour and the snowfall, she decided to venture outside for a quick look see."

The crowd, other than me and Bernie, sank back into a— what was the word? Trance? Close enough. Even Iggy was now in a trance, gazing adoringly at Dame Ariadne. As though she, or anyone, would forget! But that was Iggy every time, my best pal.

A little while later, if I was following things right, an elf, whatever that was, or possibly a vicar, whatever that was, dressed up as an elf, seemed to have taken Kittypoo prisoner, and Trudi Tremaine, whoever she was, had noticed a light showing in the loft of an abandoned sheepcote, whatever that was, and Dame Ariadne left things right there. Fine with me. I'd had some experience with sheep, none good. The audience clapped and clapped for the longest time. Because the folks were happy they didn't have to hear about the sheep? That was my takeaway.

After that, everyone lined up to buy copies of *Bad or Good*, and then lined up again to meet Dame Ariadne, sitting at a table and writing something in each and every book. With the gold pen, I should point out. Of course, I'd known the gold pen was important. You get a feel for things like that in this business.

"Well, well," said Dame Ariadne when it was our turn at her table, Mrs. Parsons in front, Iggy, on his leash, in back, Bernie, Mr. Parsons and me in the middle. "The little miscreant—although his collar is superb—and my big and handsome rescuer."

"Um," Bernie began, "it really wasn't—"

"I refer," said Dame Ariadne, "to your quick-thinking companion." She pointed at me, her fingernail bright red.

"Ah," said Bernie.

"What's his name?"

"Chet."

"Chet. Thank goodness it's not something ridiculous." She held out her hand. Bernie gave her the book he'd bought. She opened it and got busy with the gold pen, talking as she wrote. "To Chet, who saved the day. Your new friend, Ariadne Carlisle."

Mr. Parsons, who these days seemed very quiet, not piping up often, piped up now. "You don't write the Dame part?"

"Oh, Daniel, for God sake," said Mrs. Parsons.

"He's not the first," said Dame Ariadne, "not by a long chalk. I could use the honorific at signings, sir, perfectly properly, in fact, but I already feel sufficiently like a relic, thank you very much."

"Oh, that's wonderful," Mrs. Parsons said. "Sufficiently like a relic. I won't forget that ever. And I just love your books. They mean so much to me."

Dame Ariadne bowed a little bow.

"I hope you don't mind signing all these—it's my entire Christmas list for everyone." Mrs. Parsons had a tall stack of *Bad or Good*s in her lap.

"This is the easiest part of the job," said Dame Ariadne.

"What's the hardest part?" Bernie said.

Dame Ariadne gave Bernie a close look. One of her eyebrows—nothing like Bernie's when it came to fullness, but neither was it one of those drawn-on eyebrows you see on women of a certain type—rose slightly. I got the feeling—and it was a first—that Dame Ariadne's eyebrows also had a language of their own, not especially friendly.

"That's quite the question," she said.

Mrs. Parsons laughed. She was having a good time. "That's Bernie, always asking good questions. He's the best private eye in the Valley."

"How interesting," said Dame Ariadne. She held out her hand. Mrs. Parsons gave her the top book on the stack. "Anything in particular you'd like me to write?"

"I don't want to put you to all that trouble. Just your name will be fine."

"Let me at least personalize the first one. What's your name?"

"Edna Parsons. And this is my husband, Daniel."

Dame Ariadne smiled a fleeting smile. Do cats smile? I'd never seen it, but if they smiled their smiles would be like this one. She wrote with the gold pen, talking at the same time. "To Edna and Daniel, Merry Christmas always, Dame Ariadne Carlisle."

Bernie's eyebrows did a little talking of their own. Surprised? Yes, but there was more to it than that. We're dealing with Bernie here, folks.

"But she ended up using the honorific when she signed," Bernie said. "And everybody got a personalized inscription except me."

"And Iggy," said Weatherly.

"True," Bernie said. "But also disconcerting."

"My point," said Weatherly. And then they were both laughing, their eyes joining in on the laughter, one of the best human sights there is. But what was funny? I had no idea. That didn't keep me from enjoying myself, here at the Dry Gulch Steakhouse and Saloon, where we were out on the patio with a perfect view of the giant cowboy riding a giant bucking bronco, a six-gun in one hand and a foaming beer mug in the other. Yes, made of wood, but did that keep the cowboy from knowing a thing or two about having fun? I couldn't think why, and even if I could there wasn't time, because Trixie, dozing under the table and therefore at her best, as far as I was concerned, suddenly opened her eyes and gave me a look I didn't appreciate, a complicated look but it came down to what her looks always come down to: I'm better than you.

"Do you hear growling?" Weatherly said.

"Why would there be growling?"

"No reason. So I must not be hearing it."

And then they were laughing again. I myself heard no growling. Maybe now is a good time to explain about Weatherly Wauneka and Trixie, who like me has no last name. There are those who claim—a never ending annoyance—that Trixie is like me in other ways as well. I have no problem at all with Weatherly, a sergeant on the Valley PD with a big future. Once—and you may not believe this—I'd seen her slap the cuffs on Klaus "King" Konghaus, who'd won the strongest man in the west competition and later got involved in stealing tiny houses from an artists' colony, carrying them off on his back, the last time with some artists still inside, which had led to the scene with Weatherly and the cuffs, extra-special huge ones she always carried in the squad car. But that was Weatherly, a total pro, just like us, meaning me and Bernie. Us always means me and Bernie, by the way, just so you know.

Trixie is not a total pro. We'd rescued her from a cave or abandoned mine, just a normal day at the Little Detective Agency. Then it turned out Trixie had been kidnapped from Weatherly. That brought Weatherly into our life. No problem there. The problem was that Trixie and I—this is from what I've heard, not really seeing it myself—look alike. Why on earth? Just because our coats are the same—shiny black except for one white ear? How come my being so much—or at least somewhat—bigger didn't count for anything? One little irritation was another fact, namely that aside from the she-ness of her scent and he-ness of mine, they were rather similar. But who knew that other than Trixie and me and every single member of the nation within, as Bernie calls me and my kind? Certainly not Bernie or Weatherly. So how had they arrived at the strange idea that Trixie and I must have been puppies together? I can barely even think the thought.

We all had another round, beer for Bernie, red wine for Weatherly, water for me and Trixie, first in a shared bowl but very soon we each had our own.

"I know what I'm getting you for Christmas," Weatherly said.

"Oh? What?"

"You want me to spoil the surprise?"

"Yeah."

"I was brought up better than that."

"I won't be able to sleep a wink, wondering about it."

"Ha. You're the best sleeper I know."

"Is there, um, a long list of sleepers?"

Her foot, which had been resting on his, now stomped down.

"Ouch," said Bernie. He took a big drink, gazing at her over the rim of the glass.

"What do you want for Christmas?"

"Think."

Bernie closed his eyes tight, for a moment looking quite a bit like his kid Charlie, who lived with Leda, Bernie's ex-wife, and her husband Malcolm, who recently—and this was a bit of a surprise—had turned into kind of a pal of ours. The look on Weatherly's face, watching Bernie at that moment, was one I'd never forget, although I probably will. But you get the point.

Weatherly was right about Bernie being a great sleeper. We in the nation within don't sleep the way you do, so we're up and down quite a lot at night, and during one of those up periods I was standing by the open window in our bedroom, Bernie's and mine, just feeling the breeze and listening to some bird with heavy wings flying circles over the canyon out back, when Bernie suddenly sat right up and said, "I know what I'll get her!"

Three

The next morning, we paid a visit to Mr. Singh's American Dream Pawnshop, finding Mr. Singh behind the counter listening to Mrs. Singh. The language was unknown to me, but she was telling him something in no uncertain terms.

"Ah, Bernie," she said, "just the man. Please talk some sense into my husband. He wants to lose all our money."

"Happy to take some of it off your hands, Mrs. Singh, if that'll help."

Mrs. Singh put a hand on her hip. "Always the jokester, Bernie. You'll be rolling on the floor when you hear this. With an arranged marriage, of course, you must be prepared for any sudden insanity, but ours was not arranged, much—" She shot Mr. Singh the kind of look no one wants shot at them, "—to my father's disappointment, which puts it mildly. So imagine my state of mind when Padmaj proposed we mortgage everything to create a business based on drone delivery of marijuana to retail purchasers throughout the state."

Mr. Singh raised his hand. "May I point out that the numbers work?"

Mrs. Singh ignored him completely. "I'm sure you're aware that marijuana consumption is legal now, Bernie?"

Bernie nodded a very slight nod. He's a wonderful nodder, with all kinds of nods for this and that. This particular nod meant he wanted to be somewhere else, and pronto.

"But," Mrs. Singh went on, "is drone marijuana delivery legal? Not yet, is how Padmaj puts it. Not yet, meaning our first step is to hire a big-time lobbyist."

Mr. Singh's face brightened. "Do you know any, Bernie?"

"Um," said Bernie.

"Oh, someone in your line must."

"There's Bibi Wagstaff. But he's . . . out of town at the moment."

"Oh, Bernie!" Mr. Singh said. "Can you set something up when gets back?"

"That may not be for a while."

"No problem. I'll need time to prepare the presentation."

Maybe I should step in here. The part about Bibi Wagstaff being out of town was rock solid. Northern State Correctional, where Bibi was now breaking rocks in the hot sun, was way out in the desert, in the middle of nowhere and near no towns at all.

"Bernie?" said Mrs. Singh. "You're taking his side?"

"Tell her, Bernie. Tell her it's a good idea."

"Uh, I don't want to get in the middle of this."

"Too late," said Mrs. Singh, crossing her arms.

Bernie glanced at the door. I'd seen that glance from many perps in my career, a glance that comes right before they make a break for it. But Bernie—you don't need me to tell you this—is no perp. "Well," he said, "it's very . . . creative."

"Thank you," said Mr. Singh.

"The only problem is that right now we have this parallel situation when it comes to marketing weed. There's the new legal market, all taxed and regulated, and there's the old illegal market, now thriving as never before due to how easily they—untaxed and unregulated—can undercut the legal retailers."

"But there's room for everybody!" said Mr. Singh. "This is America!"

"For sure," Bernie said. "Meaning there's a flesh and blood component."

"I don't understand," Mr. Singh said.

"Well," said Bernie, "imagine you're an operator in the old illegal market—all those operators being well-armed as I'm sure you know—and you happen to spot a Singh Air Drone—"

"Singh Air!" said Mr. Singh. "Yes, imagine! In big red letters!"

"—flying by, what would probably pop into your mind?"

"To right away call the owners of the drone company and ask if they were looking for investors," said Mr. Singh.

Bernie and Mrs. Singh exchanged a quick glance.

"What?" said Mr. Singh. "What?"

"They will shoot down all of your drones, each and every misbegotten single one," Mrs. Singh told him.

Mr. Singh, a round little guy, seemed to lose some of that roundness, reminding me of a basketball I'd once encountered at an actual game at Valley C.C. and—well, never mind that for now.

Mrs. Singh went over to the little and now less round guy and patted his hand. "So now, my darling spouse, let's get back to what you do best. I assume, Bernie, you've brought the watch?"

Mr. Singh's face brightened, and he puffed up to his normal roundness. "Ah, yes, Bernie. How is our beautiful timepiece today? I've missed it."

They were talking about Bernie's grandfather's watch, our most valuable possession? Bernie's grandfather once owned a big ranch where Mesquite Road and our whole neighborhood was now, but lost everything except the watch, possibly because of a drinking problem, although the drinking problem might have come from some other story Bernie had told me, a story about another relative. But not Bernie's father. Bernie had only talked once about his father, who'd been dead for a long time. But that once! Who could forget? Is there time for this now? Probably not, but I'll be quick. They don't call me Chet the Jet for nothing! Once I'd raced an Olympic champion on a real track. How springy it was, just lovely. This was also at Valley C.C. now that I think about it, but it had to be before the basketball incident, on account of we're no longer—well, that's in the past. What is the point of the past? Ask yourself that. Or not. Where I'm going with this is . . . is . . .

"We didn't bring the watch," Bernie was saying.

"You've brought us something else?" Mr. Singh said.

"In fact, we're here to buy. Or at least shop."

"My goodness! That's a first!"

"Padmaj!" said Mrs. Singh. "Where is your discretion?"

"But this is Bernie," Mr. Singh said. "A friend. With friends you don't need discretion, not here in America."

"Claptrap," said Mrs. Singh. "What is it you're looking for, Bernie?"

"Actually, um, I would say a ring."

"What kind of ring?" Mr. Singh said.

"Hmm." Bernie thought about that. "A nice one."

"Of course, of course, nice is always our standard—we are known for our choosiness," said Mr. Singh, "throughout the Valley. But what type of ring?"

"Type?" said Bernie.

"Is it for yourself, for example? Or—"

"Paddy!" said Mrs. Singh. "It's an engagement ring. What could be more obvious?"

"Three carats, Bernie," Mr. Singh said, "for all practical purposes. Nature's beauty in carbon form, my old friend. See for yourself."

He handed Bernie a ring and a sort of binocular for one eye. Bernie put the binocular to his eye and examined the ring. The sight of him doing that was so disturbing—like his eye had turned into . . . oh! I'm not going to go there!—that I wanted to leap up and grab that thing, and after that let whatever was going to happen, happen. But before I could, Bernie lowered the binocular and said, "It looks kind of yellowish."

"Exactly!" said Mr. Singh. "That's why I call it the Desert Star. It—" He turned to Mrs. Singh. "What is the word?"

Mrs. Singh gazed at Mr. Singh. Was she happy with him? I didn't think so. She was silent.

"Oh, you must know," Mr. Singh said. "With your mighty brainpower!"

Mrs. Singh sighed. "Conjures," she said. "But why would you ever suppose your so-called charm stills work on me?"

Mr. Singh clapped his hands. "Conjures! Perfect! This ring conjures up the yellow hues of the desert, Bernie, like wearing a tiny sandstorm on your finger."

A tiny sandstorm on your finger? I was lost. And from the look on Bernie's face, a sort of softening, I could tell that he was lost, too, but somewhere else, if that makes any sense.

"How much?" he said.

I sensed trouble on the way.

We drove down Mesquite Road, the Beast rumbling beneath us, sending a message and that message is *heads up, amigo.* But what was this? Parked right out front of our place was a bright blue, fancy, and brand-new car, the brand-new part obvious even to humans. How often have you heard them say, "Oh, that new car smell!" Mixed into the new car smell was a scent that all our

Porsches had had, and so did every one I'd ever come across, a sort of burned oil smell, hard to describe. What I'm getting at is that this bright blue car was a Porsche, looking much more machinelike than the Beast, which was animallike, for sure. I knew right away it wasn't getting the message.

The driver, a youngish dude of the clean-cut type, was gazing at himself in the rearview and adjusting his hat. A very strange hat with a long and somewhat floppy red and green striped cone on top, a cone that ended in a fat white pom-pom. I'd seen a hat somewhat like this once before, worn by an elf sidekick of a mall Santa where we'd taken Charlie last Christmas, a visit that had started very well. Here's something I admit I have a little trouble understanding—not everything that starts well ends well. Why would that be? I just don't get it. In this case, the mall elf's hat hadn't been topped with a silver bell. Instead, there'd been a little ball that reminded me very much of a ping pong ball, a ball that makes a very interesting cracking sound if you so happen to—well, never mind.

We pulled into the driveway and hopped out of the car, me actually hopping and Bernie not hopping but moving smoothly, meaning we were having a good day with his poor leg, the one that got wounded in the war. Meanwhile, the driver of the brand-new Porsche was walking toward us, stuffing the elf hat into the pocket of his khakis. He smiled a very friendly smile, toned it down a bit, and said, "Hi, my name's Chaz LeWitte. I'm looking for Bernie Little."

"You found him," Bernie said. "Now what?"

"Ha-ha. Then this," said Chaz LeWitte, turning to me, "must be Chet."

"Correct."

He gave me a close look and turned up the smile. "I'm a cat

person myself but even I know an alpha dog when I see one. What would be the cost?"

"Of what?" Bernie said.

"Hiring him for a few days," Chaz LeWitte said, or might have. On account of a couple of distractions, I couldn't be sure. Cat person was the first distraction, as I'm sure you already guessed. The second distraction was the fact that this Chaz character was wearing tassel loafers. Do I have to explain about the mouthfeel of leather tassels? Surely not.

"We charge five hundred a day plus expenses," Bernie said.

"We?" said Chaz LeWitte. "I'm only interested in Chet for this job, no offense, of course."

"No offense taken," Bernie said. "It's out of the question." He made that little *chk-chk* sound that meant we were taking off, which at the moment seemed to mean we were heading into the house.

"I'll double the fee!" Chaz LeWitte called after us. "Triple it!"

We went inside and closed the door. Bernie dumped out the water in my bowl and refilled it with fresh, so nice of him although it actually makes no difference to me. Then he poured himself a beer, sat at the kitchen table, took out the Desert Star and just sort of stared at it. I went into the front hall and gazed out the little round window by the door. Chaz LeWitte was sitting in the bright blue Porsche, talking on his phone. Perhaps you might not have heard him in a situation like this, but I could. "Now you tell me," he said, and then after a pause, "I didn't mean it to sound rude. You know I'd do anything for you." He got out of the car, now not looking happy, tucked his phone in his pocket, and came to the door. I barked my low, rumbly bark, just letting Bernie know. I'm in charge of security at our place on Mesquite Road, and in fact on the whole of Mesquite Road as well as the canyon out back and parts beyond. A big job, perhaps, but are we afraid of hard work, amigo? Hard work is what makes the Little Detective Agency what it is, except for the finances part.

Bernie came ambling into the hall, now barefoot, beer in one hand, the Desert Star on the tip of his pinkie. "Something up, big guy?"

Knock, knock.

"We could drive a hard bargain," Bernie said. "Is octodruple a word?" he added, losing me completely. He opened the door.

Chaz LeWitte got rid of his unhappy look and smiled a shy sort of smile. "My apologies," he said. "I must have misunderstood the situation. I want to hire you as a team after all." He glanced at Bernie's feet, beautiful feet for a human, strong and wide, sure to make a good impression.

"We are a team," Bernie said. "What's your problem?"

Chaz looked up. "It's not mine, except indirectly. It's my boss's. Well, ours really. In fact, the whole team."

"Who's your boss?"

"Dame Ariadne Carlisle—I understand you met her."

Bernie nodded.

"You made a very favorable impression."

Bernie nodded a slight nod, one of his many nods, meaning this or that. This might have been the one that meant cut the sweet talk. I myself like sweet talk, but if Bernie's against it then that's that. "And the problem?" he said.

Chaz gave Bernie a long look, almost like he was trying to peer inside him. "Can I trust you?"

"What does that mean?" Bernie said.

"Can I trust you to keep your word?"

"Maybe you should ask around, check me out."

"Maybe—but I thought I was just hiring Chet."

"A mistake," Bernie said. "You can trust me on that."

Chaz laughed, one of those strange laughs that comes mainly through the nose, like a sniff only backward, if that makes sense. Then he nodded, perhaps saying yes to some thought in his mind. "Okay, Bernie, just promise me that if I tell you Ariadne's problem you won't tell a soul."

"Has she murdered someone?"

"Is that a joke?"

"Or done something else I'd be obligated to report?"

"No, of course not, it's nothing like that."

"Then I promise."

"Shake on it?"

They shook hands.

"Her problem," Chaz said, "is writer's block. No one knows but us, meaning Ariadne, me, and now you."

What about me? Hello? Wasn't I, too, in the know? I was only missing what writer's block actually was, almost certainly a minor issue.

"Writer's block?" Bernie said. We were on the patio out back, Bernie and Chaz sitting by the swan fountain, and me in the little pool surrounding the swan. A dry pool, since we no longer turned on the fountain, due to the aquifer problem, whatever that was, exactly, but even dry it was nice and cool by the fountain, with a very faint but pleasant watery smell, almost like a memory. The swan fountain was all that Leda left behind after the divorce. "Does that make you the swan, Bernie?" said a guest who hadn't been invited back. "What a funny joke!" I hadn't gotten it then and got it even less as time went on.

"She's written—what—ninety some novels," Bernie was saying. "How can she have writer's block?"

Chaz clasped his hands together, inside out style, and did one of those knuckle-cracking things. I hate that. Why? Couldn't tell you. But I liked him anyway. He was likable through and through, a human type that's easy to spot, at least for me.

"*Bad or Good* is number ninety-nine," Chaz said. "She's stuck on one hundred, stuck for the very first time in her life. The deadline has come and gone. Every other book has been on time—in fact, a day early. Ariadne always delivers a day early. She can write a whole book in three weeks when she gets rolling. Naturally the publisher will accommodate her but . . ."

"But not forever," Bernie said.

"Exactly," said Chaz. "It's a business. The problem is it's a business built around artists. Artists are never safe, Bernie, so neither are the businesses."

"Not safe how?"

"They're vulnerable inside, part and parcel of the art that comes out. And if it gets dammed up inside, well then we're looking at a one person ecological disaster. That's according to Ariadne's therapist." Chaz smiled an odd sort of smile, like something funny was going on, and shook his head. "Not the one she fired yesterday," he went on. "This was the one before, or maybe the one before the one before. She actually doesn't believe in therapists. I think it's a kind of sport for her."

I was lost. Sometimes when you're lost it's helpful to take a nice long pee and get your thoughts organized. I can always take some sort of pee, but at the moment I didn't have it in me for one of the nice and long, thought-organizing kind. Here's a bit of a secret. I have lifted my leg against the swan, not often, but more than once. Was this a good time? I went back and forth on that.

"She doesn't seem vulnerable," Bernie said.

"You're referring to her talk?" said Chaz. "That's different. She's done those so many times she goes on autopilot."

Bernie has a look he sometimes sort of flashes on people, quick but deep. I saw it now, probing—would that be the word?—into Chaz LeWitte and then gone. "How long have you known her?"

"I've been Dame Ariadne's personal assistant for almost eleven years."

"What did you do before?"

"This is my first job after college."

"How did you get it?"

Chaz smoothed his hair, thick fair hair, kind of longish. "Short answer, I heard there was an opening, applied, and was accepted."

"What's the long answer?" Bernie said.

Chaz laughed. "I was an English major and loved her writing. I wrote my senior paper on her use of imagery and sent it to her. That's probably what separated me from the more experienced candidates. I could go into the details but right now I'd like to firm up our arrangement."

"We don't have an arrangement," Bernie said. "And I don't see one coming. Writer's block isn't exactly our beat."

Chaz leaned forward. "Maybe a bit of background will help," he said. "Dame Ariadne does her writing in winter, one book before Christmas and one after. She prefers—well, insists on—cold and snowy conditions in a remote place. She has a ranch—Kringle Ranch—near Durango, in an area she's known for a long time. Although she's tried other places—do you know Megève?"

"No."

"Probably wise on your part. But the ranch is perfect. She's done some of her best writing ever there. *Blood and Tinsel* is at one hundred thousand five-star reviews on Amazon, and still counting. In my opinion, she has entered one of those wonderful late periods some artists have. Titian comes to mind."

Chaz paused, possibly for Bernie to say something about Titian, most likely a perp of some sort. Heads up, Mr. Titian. Any chance orange is your favorite color? Bernie, too clever to fall into any trap a Chaz-type could lay, kept his mouth shut.

"Which makes it all the worse," Chaz went on. "Think of what will be lost, culturally speaking."

"You're talking about the writer's block?"

"Exactly."

Bernie sat back, got a faraway look in his eyes. Sometimes, like now, he thinks so hard you can feel it, or at least I can. Finally, he took a deep breath and said, "Maybe she should try just sitting down and writing anything."

"I'm sorry?"

"Well, just see what comes out. Maybe there'll be at least something good in it and then she can start, uh, expanding on that."

Humans have some wonderful looks—when they throw back their heads in laughter, for example—but there's also the not-so-wonderful kind, such as we had going on now from Chaz. He was looking down his nose at Bernie, no doubt about it, suddenly not so likable through and through. Well, who is? Other than Bernie, of course. I can look down my nose, too, by the way, but I only do it when I want to see what my nose is all about. What a nose! I'll leave it at that.

"I'll be sure to pass that along," Chaz said.

Bernie rose. He never looks down his nose at anybody. "Safe trip," he said.

Chaz held up both hands, palms up, like someone was pointing a gun at him. "Whoa, there," he said. "We seem to keep getting off on the wrong foot. Maybe I should have started with the money. We'll pay two thousand a day and if the investigation ends in success there'll be an added bonus of fifty thousand dollars."

"Success meaning we . . . we unblock the writer's block?"

"Yes," said Chaz. "Well, yes and no. I've left out Rudy. Maybe that's actually where to start, better than the money. The writer's block began right after Rudy's disappearance, the day after Thanksgiving. Ariadne hasn't drawn the connection herself, not out loud, but I know she's upset. She talks about Rudy in her sleep."

"Oh," said Bernie.

Chaz's face turned a little pink. "I—I can hear her from down the hall. Our rooms are in the same wing of the cabin."

"This is at the ranch near Durango?"

"Kringle Ranch."

"The cabin has wings?"

Chaz nodded.

I've been confused before—just one of those things in our line of work—but never more than this.

"And Rudy lives there too?" Bernie said.

"Yes, with the others. Outdoors, of course."

"I don't understand."

"Ariadne didn't mention Rudy in the talk?"

"No."

"She usually does. That's a sign, right there."

"A sign of what?"

"That Rudy's at the root of the problem." Now he rose, too. "I did check you out, by the way. Captain Lou Stine at Valley PD says that Chet—um, you and Chet, I now understand—are the best trackers west of the Mississippi. The best is what we want. Please find Rudy for us."

A slight breeze started up, right behind me. In no time at all I realized it was my tail, pleased about something—probably what Captain Stine, an old buddy and perhaps a captain on account of us, although that whole story was now gone from my mind, had said. True, there were parts I didn't get at all, such as west and Mississippi. But if you keep things bottled up inside until you understand each and every last detail, your tail's going to be droopy for the rest of your days. And then what?

Meanwhile, Bernie was saying, "Have you got a picture of Rudy?"

"Comin' right up!" said Chaz. He tapped at his phone again and held it so Bernie could see. "A typical male of the species but on the large size—as you can see."

Bernie stared at the little screen. "Rudy's a deer?"

"A reindeer, as I'm sure you meant. Imported—not without difficulty—from Lapland. And strictly speaking Rudolph is the full legal name. Ariadne keeps him at the ranch. Didn't you know?"

"No."

"That's weird. It's on all our social media."

Four

"Whacha reading?" Esmé said.

We were sitting at a bench on the school playground, Bernie, Charlie, Esmé on the bench and me sort of—not lurking, exactly, let's not put it that way, more like simply standing nearby while the kids got busy with their after school snacks. Have I mentioned that Charlie's Bernie's kid or that Esmé's one of his pals, and that we sometimes pick him up after school, and on this particular day Esmé's mom was late so we were waiting with her? Any of that? Did I mention even any? Keeping track of everything that's ever happened or even a little of it isn't so easy.

Bernie held up the book so Esmé could see.

"*Bad or Good*," Esmé said. "By Ariad—how do you say that?"

"Ariad Nee," said Bernie.

"Hmm," said Esmé.

Charlie said, "What are you guys talking about?" Or something like that, kind of hard to tell, what with how he'd just taken a bite of his peanut butter sandwich, a real big bite, the kind I'd have taken if the peanut butter sandwich was mine. You had to love Charlie, and I did. And just then—would you believe it?—a far from tiny chunk of peanut butter sandwich somehow got loose. Well, well, well. I've been lucky all my life, or at least since I met Bernie. And what came before that is pretty much forgotten, other than flunking out of K-9 school on the very last day, something to do, perhaps, with the involvement of a cat. So there you have it.

Esmé pointed to the book. "We're talking about how come it's not Ariadin."

"Huh?" said Charlie.

Bernie shot Esmé a quick glance. "Uh, had we already gotten to the reason?"

"I don't know about you," said Esmé.

Bernie cleared his throat. Is that the sound of human brains kicking into higher gear? That was as far as I could take it on my own. But Bernie doing it? This was a first. He needed a higher gear for Esmé? True, she was the smartest kid in the class. Charlie had to be right behind her, or at least somewhere behind.

"Ariadne's a Greek name. She was a goddess, had something to do with the minotaur and the maze, if I remember right. But that's off topic. The point is you pronounce that *e* on Greek names—like Chloe. Isn't there a Chloe in your class?"

"Her tooth fell out in gym," Charlie said.

Bernie and Esmé both glanced at Charlie, their mouths slightly open. Then Esmé turned to Bernie. "Can I look at it?"

Bernie smiled and handed her the book. She examined the cover, with that .38 Special poking out of the Christmas stocking.

"It's about Christmas?" she said.

"I think so," said Bernie.

She pointed to the gun. "And murder?"

"Well, I don't know about—" Bernie began, but he stopped when Esmé started singing.

"He knows when you've been bad or good so be good for goodness sake."

Bernie smiled. "Esmé! You can sing!"

"Can't everyone?" said Esmé.

"Yes and no," Bernie said.

Charlie, biting off some more of his PBJ, somehow managed

to pick his nose at the same. Can everyone do that? Not even close, amigo. Charlie was going places, no doubt about it.

Esmé opened the book. "What's dedicated?" She pointed out something with her skinny little finger.

Bernie leaned over, read over her shoulder. "'This book is dedicated to T.L., in memory.' It means the book is a sort of offering to someone whose initials were *TL*—like yours are—what's your last name again?"

"Spearman," said Esmé.

"*E S*, then. And Charlie is *C L*."

"Yeah?" said Charlie, chewing away, but with a look I'm sure was thoughtful on his face.

"Offering is . . ." Esmé said.

"Like a gift."

"She's giving the book to T.L.?"

"Well, not exactly in this case. That's what the 'in memory' part is all about. T.L. is no longer with us."

"You mean dead?"

"Yes."

Esmé closed the book and handed it back. She turned to her lunch box, open on the bench. And—and found it empty. She seemed a bit . . . puzzled, I guess you could say, and slowly raised her gaze in my direction. I felt a sudden need for a bit of exercise and wandered off.

We were all packed and ready to go when Weatherly pulled into the driveway in her cruiser and hopped out, yes actually hopping. Sometimes the PD uniform makes the cop inside seem smaller and sometimes bigger. With Weatherly she made the uniform bigger, if that makes any sense, even though she herself, while kind of sturdy, is not particularly big. So maybe it doesn't make sense, and besides it's not my thought, but Bernie's, just something he told me late one night over a glass or more of bourbon. He tells me things, in case I haven't made that clear by now.

Weatherly reached into the truck bed, pulled out a clump of chains, and came over to the car where Bernie was trying to stuff one more thing under his seat.

"What you got there?" he said.

"What's it look like?"

"Chains."

"Bingo. Checked the weather up where you're headed?"

"Um."

"Lows stacked up over the Pacific. That means blizzards and more blizzards in the mountains. Ever driven with chains?"

"Not yet."

"Know how to put them on?"

"Sure."

"How about I demonstrate?"

"Well, um."

"First," said Weatherly, removing a small clump of chains from the big clump, "you need to know your tire size in order to get the right fit."

Bernie bent down toward one of the wheels.

"What are you doing?"

"Checking the size. I don't know the numbers by heart."

"We're past that, Bernie. I've already done the homework. Now you lay the chain out flat like so, and—"

And after not too long, Weatherly had one of the front wheels all chained up. She rose, separated out another clump, and tossed it—more like a heave, in fact—to Bernie. He caught it in that easy way he catches everything, his big strong hands sometimes surprisingly soft and foldable.

"Now you," she said.

"Really?"

"I want to see you do it."

But Bernie did not do it, at least not right away. Instead, he walked over and took her in his arms, the chains dangling from his hand. They looked into each other's eyes.

"Gonna make it back for Christmas?" she said.

"Take it to the bank," Bernie told her.

Did he mean our bank, where there'd been some problems recently with Ms. Mendez, the manager? I got a bit confused.

"That desperate to see what's under the tree?" Weatherly said.

Bernie said something in a low voice, his lips close to her ear. No other human could possibly have heard. But I, as you know if you've been following this at all, am not another human. This is what Bernie said: "In every way, for as long as you want."

Then some kissing started up, which I broke up as quickly as possible.

Two dudes, open road, top down, and lots of country, wide and endless. It can't get any better than that. Whenever things can't get any better, Bernie starts singing. "Death Don't Have No Mercy," "If You Were Mine," "God Walks the Dark Hills," "Eighteen Yellow Roses," "Oh! Susanna"—there's nothing Bernie can't sing. He's the best singer in the world, a secret between the two of us, since he never sings when anyone else is around.

Meanwhile, we were going up and up into a land that got

greener and greener. When things get greener you know you've left the Valley.

"Notice something, big guy? No snow and it's December."

No snow? I'd missed that completely. No problemo. I counted on Bernie to fill in my blanks. And . . . and he counts on me to fill in his! Wow! I'd never realized that before. I was on fire. But then came a little glitch. How could I fill in his blanks when he didn't have any? So in the end I'd only come close to an important thought. But coming close had to be pretty good.

Not long after that we stopped for gas and a quick snack, a Slim Jim for me and I'm not sure what for Bernie, on account of how a Slim Jim can really grab your entire attention, as you may or may not know.

"No snow yet," Bernie said to the nice old lady behind the counter.

"Meaning no skiers," she said. "Costing me an arm and a leg."

This was confusing. The nice old lady, as I could plainly see, had both arms and both legs. That was the moment that I realized this case—if it was a case—might be a big problem. So therefore—hey! So-therefores were Bernie's department but here was me, Chet the Jet, having one on my own. But the so-therefore was . . . was . . . oh no! I'd forgotten. But at that moment I did think of something I was trying to remember a while back, namely about Bernie's dad. Bernie has only talked once about his father, who died when Bernie was a kid, but before he died, he gave Bernie a single piece of advice: "Always piss downwind and downhill and you won't go wrong." So in case you've been wondering where Bernie's brilliance comes from, now you know. As for what I'd just been trying to remember: no cigar, which was fine with me, and if you've ever chewed on a cigar stub found in some gutter you don't need me to explain.

Meanwhile, we were back in the Beast, climbing twisty roads higher and higher in green mountains, and all of a sudden it was one of those times when it was just the two of us in the whole wide world.

"Feel that mountain air, big guy?"

Oh, I did, I did.

"A bit thinner up here but you'll get used to it in a day or two."

I had no idea what Bernie was talking about. As for this lovely crisp air I was used to it already. This particular air made me very energetic, in fact, amazingly so. For example, I got a brand-new and fresh idea: how about racing the Beast? An obvious idea, you might say, but I didn't beat myself up about why I hadn't thought of it before. Where does beating yourself up get you? I didn't even bother trying to figure that out. Instead, I was turning my brand-new and fresh idea over in my mind. True, it would mean hopping out of a moving car, but we weren't really moving all that fast, so it seemed entirely reasonable to—

"Ch—et?"

Not long after that, we turned onto a single lane road, a very unusual road paved with red and green bricks. Soon we rolled up to a gatehouse and came to a stop. A very tall dude with a tiny strip of tinsel caught in his beard stepped out.

"Merry Christmas!" he said. "Welcome to Kringle Ranch! Mr. Little, I presume?"

"Bernie," said Bernie.

"And this must be Chet. My goodness!" He pressed a button and the gate swung open. "Second left, third right'll take you straight to Cratchit House. Key and welcome note are under the mat. Enjoy your stay! Merry Christmas!"

"Same to you," Bernie said.

"That's what I like to hear! They don't call me Santa's gate-keeper for nothin'." He gave the Beast a little tap.

We drove on, around a bend and up a little rise. "I had this crazy desire to pluck that tinsel right out . . ." Bernie began. But whatever that was—and it sounded promising—never got said, most likely on account of the view from the top of the rise, a view of a beautiful little valley tucked into a sort of pocket between mountain tops. A beautiful little valley with a stream, a small lake, and some buildings, all log cabin style, even the huge one, which stood by the lake. There was snow on the roofs of the buildings, snow on the ground, snow all over the valley. But none on the mountain tops or anywhere else. Kind of strange, and also strange were these white eruptions going on here and there, like little white storms.

"She's blowing snow," Bernie said. "Blowing snow over her whole valley." He took a long look and pointed to something hanging in the sky, huge, round, and green. I'd never seen anything like it.

"It's a blimp, Chet. A blimp shaped like a wreath. See that glint? It's sunlight on the cable anchoring it to the ground."

Glint? Blimp? Wreath? I was lost.

"You know what this reminds me of?" Bernie said.

I couldn't wait to hear.

"Opening a picture book when I was a kid. It was like you landed in another world."

I was sure that made perfect sense—Bernie's always the smartest person in the room—but not to me.

Five

We drove down into the snowy valley, the road icy, narrow, and winding. I could sense the grip of the Beast, like it was grasping the earth with giant paws. Bernie laughed softly to himself, a laugh I love, meaning he was pleased about something. Pleased about me? That was my take, although I wasn't doing much at the moment, just sitting tall in the shotgun seat, my mind pleasantly blank. I sat a little taller, tried to make my mind a little blanker, hoping for another of those soft laughs, which I'm sure was on the way but before it could arrive we had a sudden distraction up ahead, namely a small sedan coming around the corner perhaps a bit too fast. The driver saw us and his mouth and eyes opened wide.

"Uh-oh," Bernie said. "He's going to slam on the—"

And the next thing we knew, the small sedan was spinning round and round and skidding right toward us. There are moments, like now, when Bernie's hands take over. Without tightening their hold on the wheel or even moving much at all, they steered us through the tiny gap between the spinning car and the big trees lining the road, and then we came to a nice easy stop. The sedan had also come to a stop, although not nice and easy. Instead, it was in a sort of ditch off the other side of the road, perhaps more of a little stream than a ditch, the rear wheels in the water, the front ones high and dry. The driver's side window slid down a bit and ground to a stop, making an actual grinding sound, like a hunk of glass getting crunched. Through the little opening came some grunting, some struggling sounds, and then the kind of language children weren't supposed to hear. Of course, there were no children on the scene, but still.

Bernie turned the car around and we rolled slowly over to this road . . . what would you call it? Mishap? Something of the sort. It was a little mishap for sure compared to many we've come across, or even been in. We parked by the side of the road, quite close to the driver's door of the sedan.

"A rental," Bernie said.

How did he know that? The way he knows so many things—by . . . what's the word? Magic? What you need to remember about Bernie is that just when you think he's done amazing you, he amazes you again.

Meanwhile, the dude in the rental was trying squeeze his head through the partly open window, but there was only space for his nose. Not a particularly interesting-looking nose, certainly nothing like Bernie's, and beneath it a scruffy mustache, also uninteresting. Plus, he was bald on top although somewhat bushy on the sides. In short, a look you saw all over the place. "Not everyone," as Bernie's mom, a piece of work—she calls him Bernard!—likes to say, usually after someone she's just met has left the room, "is on earth for their looks." Let's leave it at that.

"Hey!" he called. "Help."

"Are you hurt?" Bernie said.

"What do you mean?"

We got out of the car. "Physically hurt," Bernie said. "In pain. Dizzy. Short of breath."

"You mean so I can sue Hertz?"

"For what?"

"Huh? You missed what just happened? Car's a piece of crap."

Bernie said nothing. He reached for the door handle on the rental.

"Don't bother," said the dude. "It's jammed."

Bernie opened the door with no visible effort, untangled the seatbelt, helped the dude out. Just a little guy, it turned out. He looked up at Bernie.

"You a writer?" he said.

"No," said Bernie. "Why would I be a writer?"

"Touché."

"You're losing me."

"It's just that I've asked myself that very question way too often." He checked his watch. "How much to drive me to Durango? My flight's at two."

"Well, Mr., ah . . ."

"Wordsworth. Woody Wordsworth."

"Well, Mr. Wordsworth—"

"Woody."

"Well, Woody, how about first we see if we can get your car back on the road?"

"Huh? You mean climb down in that stream and what? Push it out? Like this is the world's strongest man contest? And the water must be freezing."

Bernie laughed.

"What's funny?"

"The world's strongest man thing—it's a funny line."

"I do funny lines. I do sad lines. I do bittersweet. I do 'em all."

"I don't understand," Bernie said.

Woody took a card from his pocket and handed it to Bernie. Bernie read it aloud.

"Woody Wordsworth, Ghost Writer in the Sky. If your problem is in black and white I can fix it. Discretion is my middle name."

"That's actually true," Woody said. "I went before a judge."

"What about the rest of your name?"

"Also true, although not my birth name, if you're the type who gets sidetracked by irrelevant technicalities."

Bernie's eyes brightened, the way they do when he's having fun. And when Bernie's having fun, I'm having fun. Just then, I spotted a fish swimming by in the stream. What a sight! It made me think fun things—and that was the mood I was in already. What a life!

"We are that type," Bernie said.

Woody blinked twice, then blinked twice again, making a total of . . . well, I'll leave that to you.

"Who's we?" he said.

"Chet and I."

"He's a dog."

"Correct. We're partners."

"Partners? In what?"

Now Bernie took out our card—the one with flowers on it, designed by Suzie. Maybe we can get to her a little later but how come the flowers, instead of the .38 Special or if not that at least the single shot 410, both of them locked in the safe at home?

Woody examined the card. "A private eye? Are you here professionally or just passing through?"

"You first," Bernie said.

"Discreetly speaking, it's none of your business," Woody said. "But I can tell you that there are a number—a big number—of best-selling writers who aren't especially good at writing. That's where I come in, although not this time."

"I don't quite follow," Bernie said.

"I myself am good at writing," said Woody. "Very, very good. Now do you get it?"

"You're a bestselling writer?" Bernie said.

"For crissake, no," said Woody. "That's the whole point. I'm too good."

Bernie thought about that. I watched him think, always one of my favorite sights. "Are you saying you actually do write best-sellers," he said, "only for someone else?"

"Bingo."

"Including Ariadne Carlisle?"

Woody shook his head. "She seems to have written all her books by herself, kind of refreshing, I suppose. They called me in, although her problem is writer's block, not lack of ability. Which she wouldn't admit to, by the way. Can't hide things like that from me."

"Then why did she call you?"

"She didn't. I was hired by Cole Samuels, but evidently without her knowledge. She threw me out."

"Who's Cole Samuels?"

"Her manager. He's in L.A. He was under the impression there was a plotting issue, and I can plot like there's no tomorrow. He may have gotten the idea from her agent in New York or her other agent in London. She's a business."

"That must be hard," Bernie said.

"Spare me. She's raking it in."

"What about family?"

"Huh?"

"Does she have any family?"

"Who knows? Who cares?"

"Well, it is Christmas," Bernie said.

"You're not making much sense," said Woody. "Meanwhile how about that ride to Durango? Name your price."

Bernie smiled. Was he enjoying himself? That was my take, but as for the why of it I had no clue. "Just sit tight," Bernie said.

We have a tool or two in the Beast, but all we needed was the coil of rope under the shotgun seat. Bernie got one end tied to something under Woody's car and the other to the hitch at the back of the Beast. I helped out the whole time, mostly by staying real, real close to Bernie in my most encouraging way, although I took a break or two to slurp up some of the icy and very tasty water from the stream. Then there was a bit of something else on my part—"For God's sake, Chet!"—which we'll skip over for now. After that the Beast hauled up Woody's car.

"What do I owe you?" Woody said.

"Advice on writer's block," said Bernie.

"Huh?"

"What's a good way to get past it?"

"Why would you want to know that?"

"Call it curiosity."

"You know what they say about curiosity."

I did! I did know that! I'd heard it many times. Curiosity—whatever it was—had this amazing power to—well, let's just leave it like that. But what was curiosity? That was the question. Oh, what I'd give to know the answer! Not that I'd actually use the knowledge, of course, unless . . . and all at once my mind was wandering through possible situations where the curiosity power might come into play, and it was on account of that mental wandering that I missed Woody telling Bernie his writer's block solution, although I did catch Bernie's reaction.

"That's it?" Bernie said. "Kill somebody off in the next paragraph?"

"In the next sentence, if you can manage it," Woody said. "The next phrase, if you've really got talent."

"Who should you kill off?"

"It doesn't matter—like life in that way, if you see what I'm getting at."

"I don't," Bernie said.

"Then stick to your day job," said Woody. "You're no writer."

Bernie laughed. Then he patted Woody on the shoulder. Bernie likes most of the humans he comes across, even the perps and gangbangers. "Safe trip," he said.

We drove down into the snowy valley. "Don't you think those bestselling writers must be doing something right?" Bernie said.

I had no idea, didn't understand the question. Was it important? I was about to take a swing at figuring it out when I got distracted by the taste of something fishy in my mouth. Something fishy? Wasn't that a human expression? I understood it at last!

Meanwhile, Bernie was making a call. "Hi, Nixon. Bernie here. Just checking on our little project."

Nixon Panero—owner of Nixon's Championship Autobody, best autobody shop on the whole autobody strip, which goes on and on to the edge of the desert in both directions—is our car guy, as I may have mentioned. As for a little project, I knew nothing.

"Should be okay," Nixon said. "Just waiting for Rui to come up with the finishing touches. Waiting and hoping."

Rui was the paint guy, responsible for the Beast's wonderful rippling black and white coat, and lots of other cool details on

Porsches we'd had, now all gone in different and exciting ways, none easy to forget.

"Hoping?" said Bernie.

"He's—how did he put it? Blocked. Rui's blocked at the moment."

Bernie was quiet for what seemed a longish time. Finally, he spoke. "Tell him to kill somebody."

"Did you say kill somebody?"

"In the next paragraph," Bernie said, clicking off.

"Second left," Bernie said, turning onto a gravel lane that led down toward the lake. In the distance I could see the huge log house. Snow was piled high all around it and on the roof. A column of bluish smoke rose straight up from the chimney, a very nice sight, but there was also something odd about that roof that—

"Third right," Bernie said.

—that I couldn't sort out before we took another turn and entered a little forest of Christmas-type trees with snowy branches. In the middle of the forest stood a log cabin all decorated with Christmas lights. A sign hung over the front door. Bernie read it aloud. "Cratchit House." We got out of the car and stretched, both of us with somewhat different styles, me more of the butt up head down type and Bernie standing straight with his arms up high. He took a deep breath. "Ah, that air. Nothing Dickensian about it. The Cratchits would have been amazed."

Were the Cratchits in the cabin? Was this their place? I looked forward to meeting them, but when we got inside there was no one. I knew just from the smell—when people are around, they're smellable, take my word for it—but I explored the whole cabin immediately, security being part of my job at the Little Detective Agency. The cabin was small with not a whole lot of rooms—kitchen and living room downstairs, a loft bedroom upstairs, the bed nice and big so there'd be plenty of room for Bernie, too, and I should also mention the fireplace in the living room, where a fire was burning, hot and crackling, and a Christmas tree stood in one corner. It was hung with all the usual lights and decorations, plus one rather unusual decoration, at least in my experience. This unusual decoration, hanging on the very highest branch, where no human could possibly reach without a ladder, was a Slim Jim. Well, well! What a Christmas this was going to be! The trick in this situation—as I'm sure you've already guessed—was to take possession of the Slim Jim without toppling the tree, or even disturbing it in any way. A rather easy trick, as it turned out in the end.

By the time I went into the kitchen, Bernie had already filled my water bowl and was reading a letter that had been left on the table.

"A note from Chaz LeWitte—we can help ourselves to—" he began, but then came a knock on the door, a rather odd knock, as though the knocker was very strong but clumsy. We went to the door, Bernie briefly in the lead.

"A little space, big guy."

I gave him as much as I could spare. He opened the door, and then backed up a step, not like he was afraid—that wouldn't have been Bernie. It was more like he was amazed. I was less amazed, but only because my nose already knew something was up.

"Oh my God," Bernie said. "It's Rudy."

Six

If what we had standing at the door of Cratchit House was Rudy—and since Bernie said so, that was that—then Rudy turned out to be a sort of deer. A very large deer, yes, and with antlers so huge I kind of felt sorry for the neck of this creature, but a deer for sure. First, we had the smell, a mixture of old pee, a dash of something that would remind you—or maybe not you, no offense—of the cleaner Bernie sprays on windows when he finally decides they need cleaning, plus an underlying funkiness, particularly strong in Rudy's case. Then there were the deer-type eyes—gentle, on the timid side, and just a bit crazy. For a moment or two none of us moved and things got very quiet. Then Rudy shifted sideways for no apparent reason, his knees making a surprisingly loud cracking sound.

"That's a caribou thing," Bernie said quietly. "Reindeer is just European for caribou. There's some kind of weird tendon snap in the knee. The louder the sound the bigger they are. It sends a signal."

I had no idea what he was talking about but at the same time knew it was brilliant. If you're ever wondering why the Little Detective Agency is so successful—except for the finances part—there you have it in a nutshell, whatever that means, exactly. Eating nutshells is kind of pointless, as I'm sure you know, so why do I scarf up every nutshell I come across, say behind the bleachers at Chisholm High, where we'd worked a recent case, all the details forgotten except for a few rather exciting moments involving a monsoon and a slot canyon? But monsoon season was over, and we didn't seem to be in slot canyon country. We catch a lot of breaks, me and Bernie. I was suddenly in the mood to chomp on nutshells. Not everything makes sense in this life.

Meanwhile, Bernie had taken out his phone. "Hi Chaz, Bernie Little here."

"Arrive all right?" Chaz LeWitte said. Bernie's phone wasn't on speaker, but it doesn't have to be for me.

"No problem. But we won't be staying. We have Rudy, at least for the moment. "What do you want us to do with him?"

"Wow. You found him already?"

"He found us."

"Where are you?"

"At Cratchit House. I think he wants to come in."

"Inside? He'll get panicky."

At that moment, Rudy made a sudden attempt to enter Cratchit House, but his antlers were way too high and thumped against the door frame hard enough to shake the whole cabin. Bernie reached out and grabbed Rudy's collar. Did I mention that he was wearing a green-and-red-striped collar? I'm mentioning it now. And please feel free to rearrange this whole story any way you want. I'm not fussy about things like that.

With his free hand, Bernie reached up and patted Rudy's shoulder. "Easy there, fella." He glanced at me. "Aren't reindeer domesticated? Rudy probably responds to—"

Before Bernie could get to whatever it was, Rudy appeared to respond to some sort of thought of his own. He made a grunt deep in his throat and shook his head, like he was trying to shake himself free. Which he did, although briefly. I barked at Rudy in no uncertain terms and nipped at the back of one of his legs.

Not an actual nip—I hardly ever start out that way—more like letting him know that nipping was in the cards. Rudy went still, except for those big, dark eyes, which did some rolling around. Bernie took hold of the red and green striped collar.

"Is there a problem?" Chaz said.

"We're just . . . getting to know Rudy," Bernie told him.

"I hear you," Chaz said. "He loves sugar cubes—that's probably why he came. And congratulations. I'm on the way."

Rudy shifted a little bit, making that knee-cracking sound again. I was coming close to not being a fan. Then Bernie said, "The quickest fifty grand we've ever made." And I started looking on Rudy less harshly.

Rudy began to make some hoofing motions in the snow, strange snow by the way, kind of hard and icy, although I'm no expert on snow, having seen it only a few times. I know a little bit about hooves, horse hooves particularly, and Rudy's seemed a little hairier than the horse kind.

"Keep an eye on him, big guy," Bernie said, and he went into the house, leaving the door open, and headed toward the kitchen cupboards. Rudy did a bit more hoofing. I growled this sort of confidential growl I have, low and soft, a just you and me buddy kind of sound. Rudy went on hoofing, but not so much. Bernie returned with sugar cubes in his hand. He offered one to Rudy. Rudy turned his head away, like he was too good for sugar cubes. I myself don't have a lot of sugar cube experience, but I'm not too good for them. I'm not too good for any food product. That's one of my core beliefs. Not that any of this matters, because the sugar cube wasn't offered to me, possibly because Bernie got distracted by a sort of car on skis that came speeding up the lane. There was a name for cars on skis, a name I knew well from all the times Bernie and I spent watching a TV show about gold prospectors in Alaska. Whoa! Were we in Alaska now? I was going back and forth on that when suddenly it came to me: snowmobiles! That was the name of those cars on skis. Wow! I was on fire. That doesn't happen every day. But on lots of them, it's true. Who's got it luckier than me?

The snowmobile pulled up and came to a stop. Chaz LeWitte, now wearing a red snowsuit, got off and hurried toward us, his eyes on Rudy and a big smile on his face. It began to fade.

"He doesn't seem to be interested in sugar cubes today," Bernie said.

Chaz sighed and turned to us. "No," he said, "Prancer hates them. It's just one of his many weirdnesses."

"Prancer?" Bernie said.

"This is Prancer, not Rudy." Chaz motioned to the reindeer— Prancer, not Rudy, if I was following things right—with one of those buzz off gestures. Prancer walked away, a quick walk that came close to running but didn't quite get there, in a way I found annoying. Also annoying was that clicking sound from Prancer's knees, which I could still hear long after he'd vanished in the woods.

"There's more than one reindeer?" Bernie said.

Chaz looked surprised. "Nine, of course—Dasher, Dancer, Prancer, Comet, Cupid, Donner, Vixen and Blitzen, plus Rudolph."

"I meant here at this . . . place."

"Kringle Ranch, the name," said Chaz, "chosen by Dame Ariadne herself. When it comes to naming things there's nobody better. Just another one of those wonderful . . ." He paused and turned away, almost like he was about to cry. But maybe I was wrong because he turned back real quick, maybe wiping his eyes on his sleeve even quicker, and said, "Yes, we have all nine reindeer, painstakingly imported, as I mentioned, from Lapland, along with a genuine Lapp herdsman who unfortunately moved on to less bucolic things."

"Such as?"

"He's a dealer out in Reno."

Bernie turned toward the woods where Prancer had disappeared. Disappeared to my eyes, but not my ears, still hearing those bothersome knees. "Where are they all?"

"Who?"

"Blitzen, Comet, all the rest of them. Have they gone missing, too?"

"Oh, no. They pretty much roam around in the day—playing reindeer games, if you will."

Bernie laughed. That meant something about reindeer playing games was funny. What kind of games? Fetch? Crazy running back and forth until your tongue hangs out? Digging deep holes for no reason? Those are games, my friends, and I was having a hard time picturing Prancer playing any of them. Was that the funny part? Ah, I got it. Of course it was! Bernie and I are a lot alike in some ways, a little fact that might help you follow this story from here on in. You could even go back and start over. I won't think less of you. The truth is I won't think less of you no matter what you do. Almost.

Meanwhile, it was pretty clear to me that Bernie was enjoying himself. Some cases are more enjoyable than others. For example, the porta potty pyramid scheme case—which I hadn't understood from beginning to end but will never forget—was not enjoyable. A huge pyramid, by the way, but not stable. This case—about a missing reindeer, was it?—was enjoyable so far, although the cold, crisp air was making me very hungry, perhaps long before the next scheduled meal. I made what Bernie calls a mental note to . . . to be on the alert, let's leave it at that.

Meanwhile, Bernie was gazing into the woods, now silent, meaning Prancer was no longer moving or he'd gone farther away. "What's to stop the reindeer from wandering off for good?"

"Nothing, really, but they don't. Our Lapland buddy trained them to stay on the spread, about ten thousand acres, give or take."

"How did he do that?" Bernie said.

"He reasoned with them," said Chaz.

"How?"

"In Sami."

"What's that?"

"The Lapland language."

"But what did he say?"

"He wouldn't tell me," said Chaz. "Evidently it doesn't translate in English."

Bernie nodded, like things were making sense. And here I'd been thinking the opposite! I changed course at once.

"Where do they go at night?" Bernie said.

"The old barn," Chaz said. "I can show you, if you want."

"Sounds good."

"We could hop on the snowmobile and zip over."

Bernie glanced at the snowmobile, rather small when it came to seating, and then at me.

"Or," said Chaz, "if you have any snowshoeing experience we could try that. It's less than a mile."

Bernie's eyes brightened. What was this? He had snowshoeing experience—whatever that was—and I was just finding out now? I went over to a nearby tree and lifted my leg. Marking every tree in the forest was my true desire, but I just didn't have it in me. You've got to face reality in this life. At times.

I wear no shoes of any kind, but Chaz had snowshoes in a compartment under the snowmobile seat for himself and there was another pair in Cratchit House for Bernie. Soon we were walking through this strange, icy snow toward the woods, first Chaz, then Bernie, then me, after that Bernie first, followed briefly by me with Chaz last, and finally we found the best way with me out front, and them trailing, perhaps trailing by quite a bit. Snowshoes made a very nice crunching sound in the snow. Other than that, I wasn't impressed. The subject of human feet is huge, and in the end kind of depressing—a very good reason to move onto something else immediately.

We entered the woods and things got very quiet, except for the crunch, crunch, crunch of the snowshoes. These trees— evergreens, if I remember right from a ride home from school when Esmé was explaining trees to Charlie—seemed very alive to me, especially when clumps of snow thumped down from their branches, like the trees were getting ready to ramble. I really paid no attention to where I was going, simply followed Prancer's scent without effort. That smell—old pee, window cleaner, funk—was like a long straight road in open country. After a while it grew stronger and stronger, as though other old pee, window cleaner, and funk streams, all slightly different, were flowing into a whole big river. Meanwhile, we also had the smell of these trees, so Christmasy, mixed in with some smokiness from a nearby fire.

I soon reached a small clearing with a log cabin in the center, not big but beautiful, like a picture in one of Charlie's books.

Bernie sometimes reads to him, and lately so does Esmé. I believe Charlie likes it better when Esmé reads but I couldn't tell you why, and also we don't have the time.

This strange snow seemed thicker here than anywhere else on the ranch, reaching high up the walls and blanketing the roof. Daylight was fading now, but light glowed in the cabin windows, soft and warm. Smoke rose straight up from the chimney, carrying a spark or two, up up and gone, vanishing in a sky turning very fast to night. Prancer and a bunch of other reindeer were standing around the cabin, facing different directions, pretty much doing nothing, and not exactly looking with it. The cabin windows were very big, especially the front one, facing me. Sitting at the desk in that window, a laptop before her, was a white-haired woman wearing what I believe is called a housecoat. She was slumped forward on the desk, her head in her hands. It took me a moment or two to realize it was Dame Ariadne Carlisle.

Bernie and Chaz came up behind me and saw what I saw.

"Poor thing," Chaz said. "She's stuck."

High above, the wreath blimp thing hung motionless and bright above the growing darkness below.

Seven

We stood there out in the snow and watched Ariadne. She didn't move, just sat at her desk, head in her hands. Outside it got darker, making the inside brighter and bringing Ariadne closer to us.

"This is the Dickens Cabin, where all the magic happens," Chaz said.

"It doesn't look like fun," said Bernie.

"Not these days," Chaz said. "She's cudgeling her brain, cudgeling and cudgeling."

Whatever that was sounded horrible. A reindeer knee made the cracking sound, somehow fitting right in. I felt a tiny pain in my own head, there and gone, but still. Once—this was in a safe down Mexico way, a safe where the door had suddenly swung shut, locking all of us inside with the detonator ticking down and no way of stopping it—a safecracker name of Lupe who was part of a safecracking family that included three brothers, a sister, and two tias, all of whom were also inside, said, "We're all in this together." Here outside the Dickens Cabin in these snowy woods, that got me thinking.

"Can we talk to her?" Bernie said.

"This may not be the time," said Chaz.

"But she knows we're at the ranch."

"She knows you're coming." Chaz glanced at the sky. "We'd better get going if you want to see the barn."

At that moment the reindeer turned as one and headed back into the forest. Bernie, about to say something, changed his mind, and we followed the reindeer—me first, then Bernie crunch crunch crunching, and Chaz crunch crunch crunching after him, Chaz's crunch crunch crunching not as smooth as Bernie's and not nearly as powerful. But that would be Bernie, every time. He's good at doing all sorts of things. For example, he got us all out of that safe in the nick of time. Then kaboom! And all those stacks and stacks of C-notes turned into confetti, raining softly down on all of us, some of them getting wedged down the front of Lupe's sister's dress, which led to problems with one of her boyfriends later that night.

I was trying to remember just how Bernie had gotten us out of the safe, but the knee cracking of the reindeer shut down that part of my mind. The reindeer led us through the woods and into another clearing, this one bigger and with a pond, a barn, and a big propane tank. There's no missing the smell of propane. It took my mind straight back to that night in Mexico, who knows why.

Meanwhile, the barn door swung open.

"It's on a timer," said Chaz, coming up behind us and huffing and puffing a bit. Those huffs and puffs rose from his mouth like tiny clouds, an interesting sight. I was enjoying myself, no doubt about that.

The biggest of the reindeer stepped forward.

"That's Blitzen," Chaz said. "He thinks he's the alpha now that Rudy's gone."

A sort of branch near the top of one of Blitzen's antlers had broken off, leaving a stub with what looked like a sharp edge. I barked a low rumbly bark, just letting him know that I was . . . well, me. Blitzen rolled his eyes in a way I found quite pleasant and hurried into the barn. The others followed and we followed them, Bernie and Chaz first unstrapping their snowshoes.

It was very dark inside the barn. I felt a sudden desire to herd all the reindeer into a very small circle. Their scents changed immediately. Did I make them nervous or what? This was turning out to be a fun trip. Several amusing reindeer ideas came to mind, and I was still trying to choose when Chaz switched on a light, and in the brightness everything changed with the reindeer, their nervousness vanishing. They started to graze on the straw that covered the floor, and then came a beep, followed by all sorts of green leafy stuff and pellets flowing from a pipe and into a trough. The reindeer got to the trough in a hurry.

"Also on a timer," Chaz said. "It's just a small supplement in wintertime. They turn out to be pretty good at finding lichen under the snow."

Whatever this supplement was didn't smell like food to me. I began to wander around the barn. There was a row of horse stalls along one side but no horses had been here.

"Do they sleep in the stalls?" Bernie said.

"They don't even sleep in the barn, not unless it gets really cold. With the exception of Rudy. He's an outlier in so many ways."

"You're saying he sleeps in the barn?"

"Sometimes. When he doesn't show up in the mornings Ariadne sends me down here to rouse him. He's always lying in his stall with his eyes open, but very still, like he's in a reverie."

"Show up where?" Bernie says.

"Why, to Dickens House, of course—the writing cabin. She likes the sensation of knowing he's above her while she works."

"I don't understand."

"Literally above her, up on the roof top of the cabin. There's usually so much snow in winter—ours or nature's or both—that he can easily jump up. He stays there for hours, hardly moving. She says he's feeling the connection."

"What connection?"

"Between the two of them. Like—don't laugh—he's her muse."

"I'm not laughing," Bernie said.

"So you accept the idea?"

"Why not?"

Chaz gave Bernie a sizing-up look that reminded me of a poker player we once knew. Well, we still know him but he's not getting around much these days. That—and wow! I was just realizing this now for the very first time—is the whole point of Northern State Correctional! It keeps you from getting around. My goodness. The things humans dream up. There's really nothing like that human touch.

"Can't argue with success, huh?" Chaz said.

The expression on Bernie's face changed, just a little, or maybe not at all. It might have actually been the expression behind his face, if that makes any sense. But right away I knew he wasn't liking Chaz quite so much at the moment.

"That's not why I accept the muse possibility," he said. "And you can argue with success—and maybe you should. It's just hard to win, that's all."

"Hmm," said Chaz. "What's your background?"

"My background?"

"Your CV. Where you went to college, that kind of thing."

Chaz waited for an answer. He was about the same height as Bernie—a fairly big guy, in fact—but as he waited, he seemed to get shorter.

Finally, Bernie said, "We'd like to see Rudy's stall."

"Sure thing," said Chaz, kind of enthusiastically, like he was stoked to be moving on to something else. He led us deeper into the barn, passing all the stalls, and stopping in front of the last one.

A typical stall with rough wooden planked walls and straw on the floor, the big difference being what couldn't be seen, namely the smell, which was all about reindeer instead of horses. Right away, I knew we had two separate smells going on in here, the general reindeer smell and the specific smell of one particular reindeer named Rudy, if I was following things right. Rudy's smell was a lot like Blitzen's—who seemed to have followed us to the stall, which I knew without having to look—but even stronger, especially in the funk department. And one more thing. Rudy's scent also had some nuttiness in it, the almond kind of nuttiness. Here's one of those amazing things that can happen in life. Do you remember that story about the safecrackers down Mexico way? It turned out we weren't done with them! After they got out of jail, they opened a tequila bar in one of those fun little border towns and invited us down. The special that night was an almond tequila fling, I believe it was called—and Bernie tried it and tried it again a number of times. He himself ended up smelling of almonds for days, so I knew I couldn't be wrong about Rudy. The almond smell is in my wheelhouse, a very big wheelhouse when it comes to smells.

"We weren't too concerned at first," Chaz was saying.

"The morning after Thanksgiving?"

Chaz nodded. "That kind of thing has happened with all of them at one time or another. But after a couple of days, she— we—started getting anxious. We searched the whole ranch, on foot, with ATVs, snowshoes, skis, everyone on the payroll and Ariadne, too, but . . ." He shrugged his shoulders.

Bernie nodded. He has many nods for this and that, as I

may have mentioned already. This particular nod, one of my favorites, meant we'll take it from here. "Want to go in and nose around, big guy?" he said.

I couldn't think why not. Thinking why not might not be one of my strengths. But . . . but could it be that turned out to be one of the reasons for the success of the Little Detective Agency, except for the finances part? What an idea! I hurried into Rudy's stall and nosed around like you wouldn't believe.

When you're nosing around you lead with your nose, or at least that's how we do it in the nation within the nation, which is what Bernie calls me and my kind. Humans—and you have to feel bad for them sometimes—really don't have much to lead with when it comes to nosing around. And yet they sometimes come up with things. Take Fritzie Bortz, for example, at one time a motorcycle cop who got into too many wrecks and is now sheriff of the county next to ours back home. Once he stubbed his toe on a lawn flamingo—how often have I lifted my leg against lawn flamingos, gazing into their eyes, which, despite being painted had a way of letting me know their opinion about me, but back to Fritzie's lawn flamingo, which turned out to be the murder weapon everyone was looking for. So my point is . . . is . . . yes, this! You can't count humans out when it comes to nosing around. And now there's talk of Fritzie being governor one day, which I believe is a step up from sheriff, although don't bet on that.

Meanwhile, I found myself at the back of Rudy's stall, pawing at the straw but not in an energetic way, my mind on Fritzie, motorcycles, and flamingos, and my nose on almonds, tequila, and various aromas of Mexico, a very rich place in the aroma department. Take just the subject of . . . hmm. What was this? Something hard down there under straw?

"Chet?"

I swept some straw to the side and there on the rough old floor of the stall, I found something, a gold little something with a green stone in the middle. A ring? I got it between my teeth and trotted over to Bernie.

"Did he find something?" Chaz said.

Bernie held out his hand. I dropped the ring in it.

"Good boy," Bernie said.

I felt great, and I'd been feeling great already. What a day!

"What is it?" Chaz said.

Bernie showed him.

"A class ring?" Chaz said.

"A Dartmouth class ring," Bernie told him. "Do you recognize it?"

Chaz shook his head.

"You mentioned that you started work for Ariadne right out of college," Bernie said.

Chaz gave Bernie an unfriendly look.

"What college was that?" Bernie went on.

"UConn," said Chaz. "That should be easy for you to confirm."

"No need," said Bernie, sticking the ring in his pocket.

What was going on? Was Chaz a perp of some sort? If so, I'd never met one like him, and I've gotten to know many, many perps in my career. I was still going back and forth on Chaz when Blitzen turned and trotted out of the barn. When we got outside the reindeer were gone.

Eight

Chaz's phone beeped. He checked it and looked up. "Busy for dinner tonight?" he said. "You're invited to the North Pole at seven."

"Excuse me?" Bernie said.

"Oh, that's just the name of the big house, the one by the lake."

Bernie nodded. "Invited by who?" he said.

"Ariadne, of course. And Chet's included. Dress is holiday casual."

Dinner, and Chet included. Life can make total sense.

"Thanks," Bernie said. "We'll be there."

"One small thing," Chaz said. "This is the annual team Ariadne dinner—they've flown in from all over the place—so of course everyone's on her side, one hundred percent, but to avoid misunderstandings please don't mention why you're here."

"No one knows Rudy's gone missing?" Bernie said.

"Oh, not that. You can talk about Rudy all you want. But not the underlying reason."

"Your theory about the writer's block?"

"Not the theory—the fact of the writer's block itself. That's a state secret."

"In what state?"

Chaz laughed, one of those strange human laughs where whatever's funny isn't happy at the same time. "More like a village. Specifically, the Cotswold village of Potherington—which is where the Trudi Tremaine stories are set."

Bernie nodded. "That was in the reading. Is Potherington a real place?"

"In the minds of millions of readers, yes. On the map, no."

Bernie thought about that. I could feel his thoughts, like slow, heavy-winged birds. "How would Trudi Tremaine find Rudy?" he said.

Chaz blinked. "Trudi Tremaine is like Potherington—made up."

"But," Bernie said, "the person who makes her up is on the premises."

Chaz frowned, one of those human frowns you see a little too much of, mixing annoyance and puzzlement. "What are you saying? That you think this is trivial? You're not interested in the case?"

"We're interested in the case, Chaz. If we weren't you'd know in plain English."

"Sorry," Chaz said. He glanced around, the darkness now almost complete, snow machines blowing in a sort of whispery roar all over the valley. "Why can't it just snow? Like out of the goddam sky?"

Dinner at the North Pole? That's going to be a big problem for me. Not the eating part. How can eating ever be the problem? But getting it all arranged in my mind so I can pass it on to you? So much went on! And so many people! Plus a bird named Scroogy! And a Christmas tree in every room, at least every room I was in, which was maybe not all of them. I do try to check out all the rooms in any new place but the North Pole—a cabin in the woods, yes, but huge—had so many. I'm not sure I even visited all the wings. So what to leave out? What to include? What do I even remember?

How about starting with the drinks before dinner, which we had in the enormous living room, with a roaring fire in a fireplace bigger than some living rooms I've been in, for example, our own on Mesquite Road, which I actually liked better than the living room at the North Pole. Why was that? No time to figure that out. Once—this was in his sleep—Bernie said, "There are more questions than answers." This was during a terrible time for us, when we were working on the broom closet case, the only case we didn't solve. Well, not quite right. We did solve the broom closet case, although too late. The little girl's name was Gail Blandino. Later that night we'd taken care of justice on our own, just me and Bernie. Bernie said we had to forget that part, and I can forget like nobody's business, but my memories of that night are still with me, way too clear.

Never mind all that, and now I'm even farther off course than when I'd started! Back to the drinks. Water for me, of course, in a big silver bowl that a waiter refilled every time I took a sip, and each time he refilled he added an ice cube. I love ice cubes so I did what I'm sure you'd have done in my place, namely taken many, many sips.

Everyone else—except for Bernie—was drinking champagne. Bernie stuck to bourbon. We'd had problems with champagne in the past, not the drink itself, which, from the scent must be a kind of wine, but with those skinny glasses. Bernie has the surest hands in the world—I once saw him catch a roaring chain saw thrown at him by—well, let's skip the rest of that story for now. The point is that despite the sureness of his hands he has trouble holding onto those skinny champagne glasses. Why them and only them, out of all the objects in the world? You tell me. Meanwhile he saw me looking at him and maybe got the idea that I was having thoughts about all that—meaning the champagne and the bourbon—which I was, but mainly I was simply looking at him, always a nice use of my time. But not realizing that he raised his glass and said, "There'll be champagne at the wedding, of course."

Wedding? What wedding was this? But before I could even get started on any of that, a woman of perhaps Bernie's age or a little younger stepped out from behind an enormous gingerbread house, so big I could perhaps have squeezed myself inside—although I doubt there'll be time to go into what happened to it later in the evening—and said, "Were you just talking to this gorgeous dog?"

"Well, yes," Bernie said.

"That's so sweet. Is it a he or a she?"

That was a stunner. Had I ever heard such a thing? Maybe I'd imagined it. Maybe I was actually asleep and dreaming. What an amazing thought! I considered nipping at the heels of this woman as a sort of test to find out if this was all a dream, but before I could get going on that I got distracted by the big smile on Bernie's face, like he was enjoying himself. How could he enjoy himself after what he'd just heard? That was the moment I got—what would you call it? The inspiration? Yes, close enough. My inspiration concerning the gingerbread house.

Meanwhile Bernie was saying, "His name is Chet."

"Ah," said the woman. "The famous tracking dog from Arizona? I heard he was coming up to help us. You're his trainer? Bobby, was it?"

Bernie's smile got even bigger. "Actually Bernie. And I'm more of a partner than a trainer."

The woman, who hadn't really looked at Bernie, looked at him now. Then she took off her glasses—she'd been wearing these big, black-framed glasses—and stuck them in her purse. Weren't glasses to help humans see better? I'd have to rethink that one, so forget it, rethinking, which I've heard mentioned from time to time, being a complete mystery.

"That's so interesting!" the woman said. She kind of batted her naked eyes. A very strange idea, naked eyes, but that was how hers seemed without the glasses. "My name's Georgette, by the way, Georgette Eliot. I'm Ariadne's publicist. Not one of any of her publishers' publicists, but her own personal full time publicist. I always have to say that, just to avoid confusion."

"What kind of confusion?" Bernie said.

"Crossed wires," said Georgette. "There's a push pull between writers and publishers. I'm on Ariadne's side, one hundred and ten percent, no matter what. She really misses Rudy. Of course, nothing can stop her work—she writes every single day of the year, rain or shine—but that's all the more reason she deserves to be happy. Plus I was planning a photo shoot with just the two of them standing by the tree—not this one—" She pointed to the decorated tree in the middle of the room, the top branches almost touching the ceiling several floors above, certainly more than two. "—but the really big outdoor one that goes up tomorrow—for posting on all our social media on Christmas morning. A from-us-to-you moment to the entire readership all around the world. What do you think of that?"

"Um, posting on social media?" Bernie said.

"Ha-ha. A sense of humor, no less! I meant the photo, Bernie—just the two of them together, enjoying a quiet moment on a day that—as Trudi Tremaine herself once said—can be a bit over the toppish at times."

"Is that how Trudi talks?" Bernie said.

"Oh my God, don't tell me you're not familiar with the series!"

"Well, uh, I know about it."

"But you haven't read any of the books?"

"Not yet."

"Wonderful! You're a publicist's dream come true. I'll send you a few of my favorites, ASAP."

"Thanks but I don't expect I'll have much time for—"

"Where are you staying? Cratchit House?" Georgette tapped at the huge watch on her wrist. "Done! How else can I help?"

"That's very nice already," Bernie said. "We really don't—"

"How about I introduce the dramatis personae?"

"I'm not quite sure—"

"It's no bother," Georgette said. "I know what it's like to wash up at a party full of strangers. It's my life!" A waiter came by bearing a tray of those skinny glasses filled with champagne. "Thanks, Dombey. And what are you drinking, Bernie?" She sniffed. "Scotch?"

She sniffed? Kind of adorable. She'd gotten it wrong, of course, and the difference between scotch and bourbon aromas was unmissable, at least to me—I mean really! Fresh bread versus corn on the cob! Come on!—but at least she'd tried.

"Bourbon, but I'm fine right—"

"Dombey? Another bourbon for Bernie, if you please." She raised her glass. "Here's to you and Chet, Bernie. Merry Christmas, happy holidays, happy new year."

"And to you."

They clinked glasses. Bernie had plenty left in his glass but after the clink he seemed to have downed most of it. Then came a moment when Georgette was looking at Bernie in a thorough sort of way, thorough but very brief. Oh no. Was she a woman of a certain type? I hadn't thought so, but now I wasn't so sure. Bernie's helpless with women of a certain type.

"Over there by the hearth," Georgette said, pointing with her chin, "is—no, there—" she gave Bernie's shoulder a little push, turning him slightly, her hand perhaps not disengaging any too quickly "—that's Cole Samuels, Ariadne's manager."

"The white-bearded guy with the red pants and suspenders?" Bernie said.

"No, that's Hal Pelgotty. He's a manager, too, now that I think of it—the property manager of the ranch. His family's been in this valley for generations. The man he's talking to is Cole. He's the business manager, flew in for dinner from L.A."

"What about Thanksgiving?" Bernie said.

Georgette looked confused. "Thanksgiving?"

"Were you all here for Thanksgiving, too?"

"Oh no—tonight's a once a year special. Chaz is the only one on the book side of things who actually lives on the ranch." Georgette sipped her drink. "Over on Cole's right is Missy Havisham, his numbers gal."

"The one wearing the antler hat?"

"Missy's a hoot."

Hoot was a new one on me. Owls hooted, of course, but Missy, busy with her phone, looked nothing like an owl. Her eyes weren't very big, for one thing, although, to be fair, there was something a bit talon-like about her long glistening nails.

"Isn't that a little surprising in a numbers person?" Bernie said.

"Not on our team!" Georgette said. "Someone—I think it was in Vanity Fair—said Ariadne's team is reminiscent of Potherington village, delightfully eccentric." She did that little wiggling two fingers on both hands thing that you see from time to time, possibly sending some message, the way my tail, for example, sends messages. Little finger wiggle. Mighty tail wag. You be the judge. "Potherington," Georgette went on, "is the village where—"

"So I've heard," Bernie said. "But are all these people on the team?"

Georgette glanced around. At that moment, a bell clanged, deep and booming, somewhere high above. A man wearing a tall white hat and holding a spatula appeared. That would be the chef. I knew chefs from several cases we'd worked, all involving showers of sparks and flying frying pans. I got ready for anything.

"Dinner is served."

Georgette gave Bernie's arm a little squeeze. "To be continued."

The chef's voice, high and thin, was quite unlike the booming of the bell, which continued for a while in my head, actually quite a pleasant feeling. But knowing that dinner is just around the corner makes everything nicer. You can say the same about breakfast, of course, and also snacks.

The dining room had floor to ceiling windows along both sides, a crackling fireplace at both ends, and in between the longest table I'd ever seen, a table made from some glowing yellowed wood that smelled irresistible. Through the windows I could see Christmas lights shining in a waving sort of way in the trees, the branches blowing in the wind. We sat at a corner, Bernie in the last chair along the side, me on the floor, and at the end, Cole Samuels. Very soon there was someone in every chair, except the one at the other end. Across the table from me the numbers gal—a hoot but not owlish, and how could anyone be owlish while wearing an antler hat?—Missy something or other, possibly Havisham, spoke under her breath, possibly so no one could hear. I'd seen that before—a not even particularly unusual thing—but what was the point of speaking if you didn't want anybody to hear? And then, for the very first time, I got it. Missy Havisham, the numbers gal, was speaking to me. All those people in the past had been speaking to just to me and only me! You really had to be fond of people sometimes, and I was, in fact almost all the time.

What Missy said under her breath so only I could hear was, "Three, two, one." Three? That rang a faint bell. Something to do with numbers. Wow! I was on fire, felt I was on the verge of a marvelous advance of some sort. The only thing standing in my way was the business of two and then one. Shouldn't it have been the other way around? Otherwise, three would be coming before two, and all this time I'd been happily going along in life with one coming before two. I tried to think my way out of this trap, and was getting nowhere, my fire flickering and going out, when Ariadne swept into the dining room.

She wore a red dress with no sleeves, possibly the type of dress called low cut. Around her neck hung a big green jewel, most likely an emerald. I knew emeralds from a difficult case involving an emerald—also big but not as big as Ariadne's—and a septic system. Chaz, halfway down the other side of the table, rose, and then so did others, Missy Havisham the last, and again speaking under her breath, "Oh, for God's sake." I began to think we were becoming buddies, me and Missy Havisham. But that wasn't the most important thing, which was the change in Ariadne. The last time I'd seen her, through the window of the Dickens Cabin, she'd been an old white-haired and frail lady with her head in hands. Now she was back to looking the way she had at the bookstore—not so old, the white hair now not white but silver and shining, the bare skin revealed by her dress the skin of someone younger, her bearing erect, her head held high. What had Chaz said? Something about magic happening in the Dickens Cabin? That had blown right by me but now I began to get it. The magic was all about getting younger. I told myself I was never going in there, being plenty young already.

Ariadne came to her place at the head of the table and paused, looking around. Was she just realizing that everyone was on their feet? Except for me, curiously enough.

"Oh, please. Sit, for the love of god. You're making me nervous."

Everyone laughed—so Ariadne must have said something funny—and sat down, Missy Havisham the last to stop laughing and the last to sit down. Bernie noticed her and his face went still for just a tiny moment, a sign that thoughts were happening.

A woman—older than Missy and Georgette but younger than Ariadne—stood up and clinked her glass. "Hi, everybody," she said. "For those who don't know me, I'm Maddy Defarge and I have the honor to be Ariadne's U.S. publisher. First, Ariadne, if you were delayed tonight by your muse, I'm sure all of us would have been happy to wait till dawn."

"Hear, hear," said Cole Samuels, and there was lots of nodding yes around the table. Ariadne's face showed no reaction at all. She reached for her wine glass and seemed to be holding it tight.

"Second," Maddy Defarge went on, taking out her phone, "I've just received a text from the New York office." She checked the screen. "*Bad or Good* will be number one on the New York Times fiction bestseller list for the fourth straight week on Sunday! Here's to our brilliant and beloved author!"

"Ka-ching!" said someone down the table.

Everyone drank, including Ariadne, who emptied her glass in one long, long gulp, like she was starving for red wine.

"And if I may," Maddy Defarge went on, "the text came from our wonderful head of marketing, who added this: 'If you happen to get a chance, please tell her we're all super exited to see the next one, number one hundred. Wow! Is there a title yet? Her titles are genius!'" Maddy Defarge, eyebrows raised, looked down the table at Ariadne.

"Drum roll, please," someone called out. That was followed by lots of laughter, and then silence.

All eyes were on Ariadne. The silence seemed to go on for quite a long time. Finally, Ariadne smiled—a very big but also strange smile, her eyes not taking part.

"It's still in the oven," she said.

That brought more laughter. Then Maddy Defarge said, "Here's to whatever you've got cooking."

And again, very softly, so only I could hear—yes, we were buddies for sure—Missy Havisham said, "And turn up the frickin' heat."

Everyone drank again, including Ariadne, who tipped her glass to her lips and showed no sign of realizing it was empty, just sort of drinking a mouthful of nothing. As for the whole cooking part of this, there were plenty of food smells in the dining room, but I smelled nothing in an oven. Things cooking in an oven—even if the kitchen is some distance away—don't happen without my nose getting the message.

Nine

After dinner there were drinks in various rooms of the house—
the swimming pool room, where I possibly gave in to a sudden im-
pulse, the other swimming pool room—where, would you believe
it? well, no time for that now—the billiard room, the theater, the
library, the art museum, and others I never got to or forgot—but
first I should just mention the bowl brought out to me by one
of the waiters when we were still at the table, a nice size bowl
filled to the rim with steak tips and bacon bits. Steak tips and
bacon bits together! Can you imagine? That was a first in my life,
and one of the best firsts ever. I glanced up at Bernie—helpfully
crushing a huge lobster claw with one bare hand for Georgette,
Ariadne's publicist if I was remembering right, which probably
doesn't matter since I have no idea what a publicist does—in the
hope he might say something about this job, whatever it was, last-
ing for a good long time, but he did not. Instead he handed the
claw, now in two pieces, back to Georgette, who said, "My, my,
now I've seen everything." And stuck a teeny weeny fork inside
one of the halves, plucked out a chunk of lobster, dipped it deep
in a silver pot of melted butter, and popped it in her mouth, a
teeny weeny buttery trickle leaking out from between her lips.
An interesting sight for sure, although perhaps Bernie's eyes were
on it a little too long. Georgette certainly noticed his gaze, because she said, "Oh, sloppy me," and dabbed at the corner of her

mouth with a napkin, all the napkins thick and white, and decorated with candy cane images.

"No, um, of course not," Bernie said. "Melted butter isn't easy to . . ."

His voice trailed off. He reached for his bourbon glass—half full, but it wasn't his first or second, in fact somewhere beyond that—and then paused and laid his hand flat on the table. Georgette's gaze went to his hand.

"You don't wear any rings," she said.

"Not, ah, no," said Bernie.

"I'm a very tolerant person but I hate jewelry on a man," she said.

Bernie tried to think of something to say, but let's leave it there since I've gone on too long already. I only wanted to mention the steak tips and bacon and then get back to the after dinner drinks, which we had in the library, a book lined room that smelled like the bookstore but even more foresty, maybe because of the fire in the stone fireplace—me, Bernie, and some folks who I'd seen at the dinner table, including Hal Pelgotty in his red pants. At the same time, I was feeling that lovely feeling when the warmth of a fire is drying off your coat, which may have somehow gotten a bit dampish. So I was already in a good mood when Ariadne came over and gave me a scratch between the ears. A quick one but very, very good. Meanwhile, she was looking me right in the eye. I looked at her back the same way. Her eyes turned out to be less cat-like than I'd thought, which was nice to see, but so unhappy, which was not. She turned to Bernie.

"Thank you for coming," she said. "I hope this isn't too tedious."

"Not even a little bit," Bernie said.

Ariadne smiled one of those here and gone smiles meaning the smiler's not in a smiling mood but can't help it. "If there's anything you want or need just tell me," she said. "I—I want Rudy back. I've racked my brain, but I can't think where he might be. It's not like him. He's a funny fellow, different from the others. Rudy's a real homebody. This will sound stupid, but he's like family."

"It doesn't sound stupid to me," Bernie said. "In what way is he funny?"

"For example," Ariadne said, taking out her phone, "he doesn't like having his picture taken." She tapped at the phone and showed us what was on the screen—showed us, me and Bernie. She was turning out to be that kind of human.

What I saw was a reindeer. Mostly the butt end of the reindeer, although his head was half-turned to the camera, his eyes wide open and alarmed. Ariadne's own eyes were filling with tears, and the phone got a bit unsteady in her hand. In fact, she was shaking slightly all over.

"Can you send that to me?" Bernie said, his voice businesslike.

Ariadne nodded. Then came a few moments when they were sitting side by side on the hearth and working with their phones, their heads quite close together in a way that was quite pleasant to see, although I couldn't tell you why. Ariadne's eyes dried up and her body stilled itself.

"Got it?" she said.

"Yup."

Bernie started to rise, but before he could, Ariadne pointed to the screen on his phone and said, "Who's that?"

"Weatherly Wauneka. She's a sergeant at Valley PD."

"She sits a horse very nicely."

Bernie gazed at the screen. "She can rope and ride."

Ariadne glanced at him. Bernie, eyes on the screen, didn't notice. The look in Ariadne's eyes went from being right with us and close to happy to faraway and even sadder than before. She rose and started moving away, perhaps a little heavily, like she was carrying something. Bernie looked up, kind of surprised, but by that time Ariadne's back was toward us and she was on her way out of the room.

Hal Pelgotty came over and started poking at the fire.

"This here's Chet, the tracker I been hearing about?" he said.

"Yes," said Bernie.

"My, my," Hal said. "Always been a dog lover myself but I don't have one now and won't again."

"Oh?" said Bernie.

"Their life spans don't match up with ours. I couldn't take it after a while."

Bernie nodded, but a very slight nod. Perhaps he didn't get what Hal was talking about. I sure didn't.

The fire flared up. Hal stuck the poker in the rack. "I hope you find Rudy," he said. "For the boss's sake. Personally, I'm not a big fan."

"Of her or Rudy?"

It was a bit hard to see the expressions on Hal's face on account of his bushy white beard, but I was pretty sure he looked shocked.

"Hell," he said. "Rudy, of course—too big for his damn britches. Ariadne's almost family to me."

"How so?" Bernie said.

I may have lost track right around here. Wasn't Rudy a kind of deer and weren't britches a kind of pants? But not only did Rudy wear them but they were too small? Then it hit me. I knew how this case was going to end—with me grabbing Rudy by the pant leg! At that moment I felt pretty good about myself, so actually it was like many moments.

"We spent summers together when we were kids," Hal was saying, "and some Christmases, too."

"You grew up in the UK?" Bernie said.

"Huh? Do I sound like a Brit?"

"You sound like you're from right around here."

"I am from right around here—what's your name again?"

"Bernie."

"I am from here, Bernie, going way back. My great, great, greats came to these mountains in 1856 with two mules and a buckboard wagon."

"Prospecting?"

"Sure. Hit it big, lost it all, hit it big, lost it all again, and then a few more times."

"Ending on the down swing?"

"Of course. Family went to work for some folks from Denver who started a sheep ranch up here, converted it to a dude ranch, and then after the war just used it as a second home. My folks took care of things for them up here. Follow me so far?"

"Yes, sir."

Hal tilted his head slightly, maybe seeing Bernie from a new angle. "You're a private eye?"

Bernie nodded.

"Came out of law enforcement?"

"I had some law enforcement experience, but my background is mainly military."

"Thought so."

"How come?"

Hal didn't say anything, just tapped the side of his nose. What with that big bushy beard I hadn't given this nose the attention it deserved, and, my goodness, it deserved a bunch. That was the moment I became a fan of Hal Pelgotty.

Meanwhile, Bernie was gazing into the fire, like he'd forgotten what we were doing, which had to be working the Rudy case, meaning this conversation was actually an interview. Bernie's great at making interviews seem like normal back and forth—it's one of our best things at the Little Detective Agency—but maybe now he was taking it a little too far.

"The truth is law enforcement's probably in my blood," he said.

"Your dad was a cop?"

Bernie smiled. "That wouldn't have been a good fit. But my own great, great, great was an Arizona ranger."

"Ah," said Hal, and he held out his fist, kind of massive and lumpy, like it had been in a dust up or two. They fist bumped, Bernie's hand just as massive, or close, or pretty close, but not lumpy. Somehow, even though he'd been in dust ups, many more than two, his hands are still the most beautiful you'll ever see on a man. In case you don't know by now, Bernie is very special.

"So how," Bernie said, "did this valley pass from the Denver folks to Ariadne?"

"When did I say that happened?"

"You didn't. I assumed that's where you were going."

"Know what they say about assumed?" Hal said. "Makes an ass out of you and me. Ass meaning donkey, Bernie."

Bernie smiled, like he was enjoying himself. Enjoying himself when donkeys were in the picture? How was that possible?

"What I'm getting to," Hal went on, "is that the valley never passed from the Denver folks to Ariadne. Ariadne is the Denver folks."

"I thought she's a Brit."

"She's a Brit, all right. But back before the war—World War Two, I'm talking about—Nancy Blake, Denver family's name being Blake—went to off to Oxford University where she met this Carlisle gentleman, who had some kind of title, not a big one like prince or duke, and they got married. Ariadne's the daughter—like Winston Churchill, if you follow."

"American mother, English father," Bernie said.

Hal laughed. "No flies on you," he said, which was completely true. There were no flies anywhere in the house. They've got a toilet-type smell that can't be missed and there wasn't a trace in the air. Still, an odd thing to say. Had Hal had one too many? His glass, almost empty, stood on the hearth, tiny reflections of the fire flickering in the ice cubes. Was his nose—really quite magnificent—a bit on the red side? I thought so and decided to cut him some slack.

"Point being," he went on, "Ariadne and her mom came here for summers when she was a kid, maybe till she was ten or so. Then the Carlisle gentleman hit a rough patch, not the unlucky kind but the screwed-up kind, and they stopped coming." He waved his hand. "The whole spread—not close to the size it is now—went to seed, the buildings boarded up, land gone to ruin, and me and my folks ended up at Vail, doing resort work. Over in England, Nancy and the Carlisle gentleman got divorced—no alimony on account of by then he'd pissed away all her money and had zip to give—and later Nancy got cancer and died, that part happening real quick. Ariadne was in college herself by then but she had to drop out."

Pissing away money? I'd seen quite a bit of pissing in my career, often in surprising places by surprising people—and let's not forget other creatures, including horses, an elephant name of Peanut, creator of yellow lakes, and once a bear. Our eyes met and that bear sent me a message: when this is done so are you, amigo. But the doing took the bear a long time—stopping in the middle not being the easiest thing in the world, as you may or may not know—and by the time he was ready for me I was over the hill and gone. All that by way of making it clear that I'd never seen anyone piss money, or even piss on money. So: something to look forward to. You keep learning things in this business if you keep your ears open and I do. How would you even close them, exactly? Eyes are a different story.

"She came back here first—this was in late summer. She lived in a tent, all by herself, just on the other side of the pond, back of where you're staying now. Cratchit House, I'm talkin' about 'cept there was no Cratchit House then. Stop me if I'm repeating myself. Seems to be happening more these days."

"To everyone," Bernie said.

"Yeah? Why do you think that is?"

"No idea," Bernie said. And then quietly, more to himself than anyone else. "Maybe because no one listens anymore."

Hal's head went back a bit, and he gave Bernie a careful look. "Anyways, Ariadne was livin' all by herself up here, and doing a lot of reading which I know because when I drove over from Vail—just makin' sure she had firewood, things like that—she had me bring a whole bunch of books."

"What kind of books?"

"There was a big, long list." Hal squeezed his eyes shut, which is how humans remember better. "Mostly crime, I'd say. Mysteries. Don't get me wrong. She wasn't a hermit or anything like that. There were people around. This was just before the Silver Mountain development got going—the resort, skiing, all that—but these mountain towns were growing for the first time in years, so she did some socializing. There was even a boyfriend." Hal shook his head, like he was getting rid of a bad thought. "But sometime after Christmas, January or February, I'd say, she went back to England, moved from Oxford to London. Waitressing in a pub, tour guiding, anything she could do to support herself. But in her time off, she was writing. She'd absorbed all those mysteries and was ready to go, is my theory. The story she tells is all about false starts and wastebaskets piled high with crumpled paper." He sipped his drink, swirled those fiery little ice cubes around. "But—just my opinion now, don't go asking for proof— she's just saying that to make us normal folks feel good about our- selves. This highfalutin Dame Ariadne that the world sees—well, I knew her way back so I can tell you there was no wastebaskets and crumpled paper."

"She's a natural?" Bernie said.

"Like the kind of ball player who comes along once in a while."

"Willie Mays?"

"You could say that. She's the Willie Mays of cozy mysteries, which is the category she's in. Stop me if I'm telling you stuff you already know."

"We're not even close to that," Bernie said.

"Long story short, the first book caught on, right from the get-go, and she was launched. Ten or fifteen books in she was set for life—hell, for a buncha lives—and she got the idea of . . . well, this—Kringle Ranch. She flew over and sounded me out. We tramped around this valley half of one summer. Most beautiful summer I can remember up here." He swirled his drink, started up a little whirlpool.

"The two of you must be about the same age," Bernie said.

Hal looked up quickly. "What's that?"

Bernie repeated the age thing.

"I expect so." Hal took a big swig of his drink, wiped his mouth on the back of his hand. "'Course she's much better preserved. But what I'm getting at is that by then she was doing most of her writing in wintertime. The wintrier the better. She'll crack open the window by her desk in Dickens House on a ten below morning—and when we had that huge Valentine's Day blizzard a few years back she reeled off a hundred and fifty pages in three days." Hal shook his head and downed the rest of his drink. "So now she spends winters and most of the summers here, the rest back in London."

"How come she still does it?" Bernie said.

"Does what?" said Hal.

"Write."

Hal narrowed his eyes. "How come you still breathe?"

Bernie said nothing. He has many ways of saying nothing. This one—like his own eyes would never blink again—meant *I'm not buying it.*

"All right, then," Bernie said. "But how come Christmas?"

"How come Christmas? What kind of a question is that?" Hal reached into a pocket of his red pants and pulled out a red hat lined with white fur and put it on. And suddenly he was Santa! I knew Santa from last Christmas when we'd taken Charlie to the mall. That Santa had been drinking, too. I made what Bernie calls a mental note.

Bernie said nothing more about Christmas. He just looked down for a moment. You didn't see that every day.

Hal patted Bernie's knee, reached into his pocket again and this time took out a bottle, one of those flat bottles, smaller than the round ones but easy to carry around. Bourbon—which I could smell even though the bottle was capped. Also it was the kind

Bernie likes, with the roses, so maybe you could say my eyes were helping out my nose, a kind of cheating. I was okay with it.

"Freshen your drink?" Hal said.

"Thanks."

They clinked glasses, sipped their drinks. Beads of sweat rose on Hal's wrinkled forehead but he didn't take off the Santa hat.

"We saw her writing today," Bernie said. "Through the window. But it wasn't open."

Hal shrugged.

"Book number one hundred, right?" Bernie said.

"Correct."

Bernie gazed into his drink. "How do you think it's going?"

"Same as the others, I expect," said Hal. "Ariadne never talks about her work when she's writing. Don't talk about it at any time, really, except when she's on tour."

"To nobody?"

"Not to my knowledge."

"Is there a husband?"

"Never married."

"Boyfriend?"

"Nope."

Bernie gave Hal a direct look. "How about you?"

"You're kind of a nosy bastard down deep, huh?" Hal said.

"No denying it," said Bernie.

Whoa! Hal said that? Nosy bastard? With a nose like his? Where did he get off? Look, as humans say, who's talking.

But Bernie didn't seem at all upset, the opposite if anything. Hal smiled at him. "Ariadne and I are more like brother and sister. None of your business but also it's no secret. I don't go that way. Clear enough?"

Bernie nodded. I myself had no clue. But right there is one

of the strengths of the Little Detective Agency. Only one of us has to get it! The other can be fast asleep! We're a team, me and Bernie. There's no taking that away.

"Anything else you need to know?" Hal said. "Big day tomorrow. The sleigh's arriving."

"Sleigh?"

"For the reindeer to pull on Christmas Eve. The old one's seen better days, so I had a new one run up by some boys in Alaska who do these things right. We'll be fitting new harnesses, plus we'll be wanting extra rehearsal time."

"So you'll be needing Rudy?"

"Ho ho ho," Hal said, downing his drink and rising.

"One more thing."

Bernie reached into his pocket and took out the gold ring with the green stone. I remembered finding it in the barn. Wow! Was I sharp today or what? And then came an odd thought: We had two rings going on right now—the Desert Star and this green one. Did that mean anything? Not that I could figure out.

"Have you ever seen this before?" Bernie was saying.

Hal peered at the ring and shook his head. "It's a class ring?" he said.

"From Dartmouth. Where did you go to college, Hal?"

"I didn't," Hal said. "Didn't even finish high school—went to work at sixteen." He touched the ring. "Why are you asking? Is it important?"

"We're working on that," Bernie said. "Do you know anyone who went to Dartmouth?"

"Nope," Hal said. "My kind's not that kind."

Whatever that meant seemed to please Bernie. I could see that in his eyes. A smile was on its way, but before it came Hal said something that seemed to take Bernie by surprise.

"What kind are you, Bernie?"

Bernie's eyebrows rose. He thought for a bit. "A hybrid, I guess," he said. "Or more like a mutt."

Had I ever heard anything more amazing? But maybe I should have expected it. Maybe I'd even known it all along. We're a lot alike in some ways, don't forget, me and Bernie.

Bernie picked up the poker and stoked the fire, a thoughtful kind of stoking, not resulting too much in the way of sparks. "Santa and Rudolph," he said. "How far back in Christmas history does that story even go? Did Santa and Rudolph have problems? We might have to do some research, big guy, maybe starting with—"

A bunch of folks came streaming into the library, every single one of them with a drink in hand, and Bernie went silent. One of those folks was Georgette. She spotted us and changed course, veering our way.

"Bernie!" She took off her glasses. "We meet again!"

"Uh—"

She plunked herself down on the hearth beside him. "Don't you just love this library? It's my favorite room in the house. As you'd expect, I'm a book lover myself." She waved her glasses in the air. "Are you a book lover, Bernie?"

"I wouldn't say so."

"But you're obviously an educated man."

"Never heard that one before."

She laughed. "And a sense of humor to boot! What's your all-time favorite book?"

Bernie thought. Georgette watched him thinking. I understood that, watching Bernie think being a favorite pastime of mine, but through the doorway I caught a glimpse of Chaz standing by himself and peering into the room. Then he took a deep breath, turned, and walked away, the tassels on his tassel loafers reflecting for a moment the firelight's glow. I followed.

I had no intention of following Chaz for a long time, had no intentions of any kind. My mind was empty of intention, in fact, empty period. I was on the move and the smell of shoe leather was in the air. That was pretty much it.

We went down a long wide hall lined with paintings and flowerpots, turned into a much narrower corridor with photos on the walls, all of them showing snowstorms. I wasn't far behind Chaz and was making no attempt to be quiet, but he didn't notice me. This corridor wasn't well lit and got darker as it went along. Darkness is no biggie for me, of course, and Chaz seemed to know his way around. He came to a staircase off to one side and started up. And wouldn't you know it? Moonlight coming through a window shone on the tassels! So who wouldn't have kept following? Not I.

At the top of the stairs Chaz turned down a long broad hallway lined with Christmas wreaths that made the whole hallway smell like a forest, and stopped at a closed door with a silver bell hanging on it. He knocked. Through the door came Ariadne's voice. "Who is it?"

"Me," said Chaz.

"It's open."

Chaz opened the door. I caught a glimpse of Ariadne, no longer in her fancy dress, but now wearing what I believe Bernie's mom calls a ratty old robe. Just to clear up any confusion, she didn't mean her own robe, which, as I remembered from her last visit—quite some time ago with no new visit scheduled, as far as I knew, not always very far—was made of the finest Japanese silk. "So buzz off, pooch," she'd said when I came near. None of that was important, the important thing being the rattiness of Bernie's robe, which by the way doesn't give off the tiniest aroma of rat. Neither did Ariadne's robe, which wasn't as ratty as Bernie's, but still it was a surprise to see her like this, slumped in a chair in front of a desk, hair sort of wild, make-up only partly washed off her face, fingers, now ringless, on the keyboard of her laptop, curved, ready, motionless. Beyond her I glimpsed a bedroom that seemed to go on and on. Then the door closed with me on the outside. I stayed there, waiting for an idea.

Meanwhile I could hear perfectly well what was happening on the inside.

"What are you doing?" Chaz said.

"What does it look like?" said Ariadne.

"You left so early."

"It felt late to me."

"People noticed, that's all."

"What do they want from me?"

"No one wants anything from you, Ariadne. Just to be happy."

"I'm sorry."

"Nothing to be sorry about. I just hate to see you like this. Maybe it shouldn't be a secret."

"What are you saying?"

"The . . . the writer's block business. Maybe if people knew it would take the pressure off."

"Chaz. Please. You don't know what you're talking about."

"Or why not just stop?"

"Stop?"

"Retire. You don't need to keep doing this."

"Are you telling me my needs?"

"No." Then there was a silence. Finally, Chaz said, "I just wish I was one of them. Your needs."

"Of course I need you."

"You know I don't mean that way."

"Chaz, don't start."

"People can't help their feelings. I love you."

"That's fantasy, not feelings. You know how old I am. You know how old you are."

"I don't care. You're the most amazing woman I'll ever meet. I can't help the timing. But what if we simply give it a try?"

"Give what a try?"

"You know." Chaz laughed. Sometimes—you see this with a lot of perps—people pick the wrong moment for laughing. "Maybe it will unblock you."

There was another silence. Then Ariadne burst into tears, sobbing and sobbing.

"Oh, Ariadne, I didn't mean—"

She screamed at him. "Get out!"

Her voice turned out to be one of those human voices that could be scary. I backed away. Chaz's footsteps approached the door. I can just sort of melt away if necessary. I melted away.

And that was that, except it looks like I forgot to tell you about Scroogy the bird, who croaked and croaked "Humbug!" over and over until . . . until an opportunity suddenly arose, an opportunity involving a series of incidents, of which only the last is clear in my mind, namely the opening of a window that was partly open to begin with. The Scroogy story will have to wait for another time.

Ten

The next morning Bernie was up before me. When had that ever happened? And it was very early. The light coming through the windows of our room at Cratchit House was dim and milky, but bright enough to see the bed was empty. I myself had slept by the window across from the bed, a window that was cracked open a bit so I could enjoy the feeling of the cool night breeze. Perhaps in human terms a cold breeze, but I don't seem to get cold so I couldn't tell you. A nice bonus that comes with sleeping under a cracked-open window—especially if you're in charge of security—is that the nose can keep track of what's going on outside while the rest of you is roaming in dreamland.

I rose, had a nice long stretch, stretching the last little jumbles of dreamland clear out of me, and padded out of the bedroom. Bernie, wearing sweats with the hoodie up over his head, was sitting at the kitchen table, pencil and a sheet of paper before him. I barked.

He looked up and smiled. "Hey, there, sleepyhead. Hungry?"

I barked.

"Thought so."

I barked again, somewhat louder—you might have even said on the fierce side—sending a message.

Bernie lowered the hoodie.

That was the message. Bernie with the hoodie up is not the right look. I went over and sat beside him. He scratched between

my ears. Ah. He was the best scratcher in the world, not counting Tulip and Autumn, two friendly young women who work at
Livia Moon's Coffee and More in Pottsdale back in the Valley,
specifically in the More part which turns out to be a house of ill-
repute, the meaning of that still unclear to me, perhaps because
all Bernie and I did there was buy fresh coffee beans.

He gestured with his chin, one of the best human moves
there is—I'd like to see more of it—at the blank sheet of paper
on the table.

"Thought I'd take a swing at writing, big guy. Writing a story.
Made up. You know. Fiction."

I did not know but whatever this was had that nonstarter feeling about it. For some reason I thought right away about Hawaiian pants and tin futures. Hawaiian pants and tin futures are the
worst things that ever happened to our finances, perhaps wiping
them out or something even worse that that—lifelong debt, was
it? Although I had no clear picture of what that was—or, for that
matter, what tin futures were either. All I knew about tin futures
was that an earthquake in Bolivia, happening or possibly not happening, had been the end of them. But I have a very clear picture
of Hawaiian pants since we have a self-storage in South Pedroia—
also part of the Valley but very different from Pottsdale—packed
with Hawaiian pants from floor to ceiling. We sometimes go there
just to look at them. Bernie's great at quitting cigarettes but he
always has a smoke when we're at the self-storage. "Everybody
loves Hawaiian shirts," he'll say. "I just don't get it."

Now he picked up the pencil, held it over the paper, almost
touching. "Come on," he said. "I know lots of words, maybe not
lots but enough, right? And I know cursive, meaning I know how
to get them on a page. So what's the problem?"

I had no idea, in fact, saw no problem. Well, it was breakfast time and the actual fixing of breakfast hadn't started. That was a problem.

Bernie bit his lip. That was a first. He was not a lip biter. Hoodie? Lip biting? What was going on? Whatever it was had to be stopped, as I'm sure you'd have agreed. Seizing the sheet of paper and possibly the pencil in the same fell swoop was not out of the question. I shifted slightly closer to the table.

"Ah!" Bernie snapped his fingers. "How about a cowboy?"

And now cowboys? We'd run across cowboys, of course, comes with the territory, and cowgirls, too, so was Bernie planning to write about Hoss Winkler, for example, a cowboy who couldn't ride horses as it turned out, bad luck for him during the getaway, although he did have some rope, which was what we used to tie him up with when we brought him in? Hoss means horse out in these parts, although Hoss in no way resembled a horse. For one thing, he was tiny and for another he had a short face, real horses, as I'm sure I don't have to tell you, being known for their long faces, and also prima donna personalities.

"A cowboy." Bernie bent his head closer to the sheet of paper. "A cowboy what? A cowboy what, Chet?" The pencil tip made tiny motions in the air but failed to come down on the page. "What does the cowboy do? He has to do something. You can't have a story where nothing happens. But what? A cowboy what?"

Poor Bernie. Our situation was clear. He hadn't gotten enough sleep, had no business getting up when he did. Otherwise, he'd be making sense. Bernie knew perfectly well what cowboys did. They roped. They rode. That was it. I rose up, ready to do what had to be done.

But at that moment there was a knock at the door. Well, not a knock, exactly, more like a bump with some sort of scratching at the same time. I was there in a flash, and Bernie soon after, the sheet of paper caught in his back draft and wafting off the table to settle in the shadows beneath it, maybe forever.

Bernie opened the door. Standing on the threshold, eyes big and at the same time rather dull, was a reindeer, specifically the one missing an antler branch, the stub sharp-edged and a bit on the menacing side.

"Blitzen?" Bernie said. "Something up?"

Blitzen rolled his eyes. Yes, I'd seen him do that before, possibly—or even likely—his only move. Human eye rolling is a big subject. It's mainly a woman thing but you see it sometimes from a man, although not Bernie. Bernie's mom is an eye-rolling champ and Leda—his ex-wife and the mother of Charlie—is also pretty good at it. I've never seen any eye-rolling from Weatherly. For a moment I felt like I was real close to a big understanding, but the next moment it was far, far away. As for reindeer eye rolling, I had no clue.

Blitzen backed up a step or two, so now on top of the eye rolling we had the knee cracking. I knew one thing for sure: I'd had more than enough of reindeer already. So now it was time for Bernie to say, "Shoo, Blitzen. Vanish. Vamoose." But Bernie did not say that. Instead, he said, "I think he wants us to go somewhere with him, Chet."

Why would Bernie think that? Wasn't it obvious that Blitzen had absolutely zip going on upstairs—I mean, come on, there was a tuft of yellowish lichen dangling from his lower lip!—and had shown up on our doorstep for no good reason, probably no reason at all.

But perhaps not obvious to Bernie. That's where lack of sleep will get you. He'd gotten up way too soon, and the next moment came the proof, big time.

"It's like he read my mind," Bernie said. "I've been thinking that the key to finding Rudy is all about embedding ourselves in the herd."

Embedding meaning getting in bed? Herd meaning the reindeer? We were getting in bed with the reindeer? I was stunned. First of all, where would we find a big enough bed? To say nothing about the whole idea making me want to—

"Chet? Mind staying here with our friend Blitzen while I get dressed? Don't let him wander off."

Bernie went inside Cratchit House, closing the door behind him. That left me and Blitzen all by ourselves. Our friend Blitzen? That had to be Bernie's sense of humor, sometimes popping up when you might think humor wasn't a good fit. I closed in on Blitzen, just to make sure he knew what was what. He backed up and then twisted around in a weird way, taking a glance behind him, like he was making plans. Blitzen couldn't possibly have any plans that were going to cut it with me. I growled. There are many growls at my command, way too many to go into now, but this one, soft and quiet up front but with a low buzzing rumble at the back, was one of my faves. Blitzen didn't like it, not one little bit. A new smell rose from him—from the tail end, specifically—a smell perhaps unappealing in one way but very appealing in another, namely the smell of fear, in this case a deerish version, but not too different from the cattle version. Was this a good moment to show ol' Blitzen my teeth? I couldn't think why not.

That was when the door opened and Bernie came out wearing his cold weather clothes, smelling of mothballs, one of those smells that clears your head but good. My head was already totally clear so the mothball hit was a bit much. Was taking momentary unpleasantness out on ol' Blitzen in the cards? A making him pay kind of thing? I couldn't think why—

"Ch—et?"

We tramped and tramped through snowy woods, on and on, Bernie the only tramper, tramping along on his snowshoes, me in my light go-to trot which I can keep up forever, an easy-peasy kind of gliding, and Blitzen . . . Well, Blitzen turned out to be rather surprising when it came to getting around on snow. Not that there was anything smooth or pretty about his movements, but he was quite . . . I wouldn't want to call it fast, or effortless, or certainly not graceful. But. But. Let's leave it at that.

"Chet?" Bernie said, as we climbed a rocky and snowy trail up a steep slope, "maybe let Blitzen lead the way? Just this once, since he seems to have some sort of destination in mind?"

Oh, Bernie! Wasn't it clear that Blitzen's mind was a complete blank? With Blitzen in the lead—yes, I'd let him lead from time to time, being a very good boy, but only because it was Bernie doing the asking—we'd been up and down, back and forth, even crossing our own path more than once. Crossing our own path! How shameful!

"Chet?"

Okay, fine. I moved slightly aside to let Blitzen go by. But only slightly. I felt Blitzen nosing in close behind, but not passing me because he wanted more room. Forget it, bud, take what you're given and wag your tail. And by the way you call that a tail? How about I—

"Chet?"

Okay, fine. I shifted right off the trail, moving around an

enormous tree stump, and—what was this? I barked my low, rumbly bark.

Bernie clomped over in his snowshoes. Blitzen came, too. He spotted lichen growing on the side of the tree stump and lowered his head. But Bernie's attention was on what I'd found. Me, by the way. The finder was me. Not Blitzen.

Bernie squatted down and examined the object lying in the snow. "A hat," he said. "An elf hat."

Ah, yes, the elf part. I'd forgotten that. This strange sort of hat, red with a very long and floppy top, ending in a pom-pom that looked like a small snowball, was called an elf hat, although, looking more closely, I saw that the white pom-pom was missing. Still, I had a pretty strong memory of seeing it before, but of course from the smell I already knew whose hat it was.

"Just like the one Chaz had when he drove up to the house," Bernie said.

We're a team, me and Bernie. Maybe you can see why.

Bernie reached down to pick up the elf hat, but paused, his hand motionless over the hat. "How did it get here? I don't see any tracks. Unless . . ."

And he spotted what I'd already noticed—more from the scent rising off the snow than the sight—namely that there were tracks after all, although not human. Bernie got down on his hands and knees—and right then anyone could tell how alike we really are—for a real good view.

"Canid for sure," Bernie said, losing me right from the get-go. He crawled—what a charming sight!—to another print, this one perhaps a little clearer. "Could be someone from the nation within, a medium size someone," he said. "But isn't the shape a bit too narrow? And what about these—" He pointed to some tiny marks. "Pointing in. On one of your guys they'd be pointing out." Bernie rose. "So what we've got here is a fox."

Do tell, as humans might say in this situation. But wasn't that a bit mean? Oh, no. I'd had a mean thought about Bernie! What a disgrace! I went over and gave his hand a quick lick. There!

"Something on your mind?" Bernie said.

Nope, not a thing. We were good.

He looked around. "Over here we have fox tracks leading away from the hat and disappearing between those two pines. And thataway are the incoming tracks. Unless the hat fell from the sky the fox carried it with him. To find out where from all we have to do is backtrack." Bernie glanced up at the sky. Was he checking for more hats raining down? What a strange day this was, and it had barely started! Had we even had breakfast yet? For heaven's sake! We had not. I knew that as well as I'd ever known anything in my life. We were out in this Christmasy place where the snow didn't come from the sky—if I was understanding things right—but hats did! And all this on no breakfast. Everyone knows breakfast is the most important meal of the day, even . . . even Blitzen, chewing steadily on a mouthful of lichen. I barked at him in no uncertain terms and my mind cleared at once.

Bernie smiled at me. "Are you wondering what I'm wondering? Did Blitzen lead us here deliberately or does this spot just happen to be on his grazing circuit?"

I was not wondering that, didn't understand it from beginning to end.

"Let's give him the benefit of the doubt. Nice job, Blitzen."

But Blitzen had disappeared, leaving behind fresh tracks in the snow and the scent of lichen in the air, a bit like mushrooms. Still, nice job, Blitzen? I had to listen to that on no breakfast? I was close to being beside myself. When beside yourself, as I'm sure you already know, the only thing you can do is race around wildly, cutting sharply across the lawn, back and forth zip zip zip and tongue hanging out until you catch up with yourself and slip back inside. I was just about to get started on all that—not an easy prospect in these steep and slippery conditions, nothing at all like a lawn—when Bernie turned and winked at me. Winked at me? What did he mean by that? Surely nothing bad. So therefore—hey! Had I come up with a so-therefore, normally Bernie's department, me bringing other things to the table?—so therefore . . . so therefore . . . something good! That wink meant something good. Right away I went back to feeling tip top, my usual state, after all.

Bernie picked up the elf hat—not putting on surgical gloves, maybe because he was already wearing winter gloves—slid it in a baggie and stuck the baggie in his jacket pocket. Then he took out his phone. "Should be a map in here somewhere." He peered at the screen. "My guess is we're at the southeast corner of the ranch, on the west side of Mount Murdstone, meaning Silver Mountain's thataway." He pointed with his elbow, a human move they really should use more often. "All set for some back tracking?"

I was on my way.

Bernie laughed. "Wait for me, wild Bill."

Which didn't make any sense at all, but Bernie hadn't had breakfast either. You give a pass to someone in that situation, and I always give Bernie a pass in any case. Two passes then, for Bernie. Whoa! Had . . . had I just done something with numbers? I was on fire.

What happened next seemed to go by fast, but that's often the way when you're on fire. Not that I was really on fire. Never have been, not once in my whole career. True, down in Mexico we'd once been blown clear out of a window, and the whole flea-bag hotel—not a flea in it, by the way, and I'd know—went up in flames, but they didn't quite reach us. But forget all that. All you need to know is that out here in this steep, snowy, and rocky forest I went bounding along the trail left by the fox, a trail that had something to do with the elf hat. First, I zigzagged up and up between snow-covered trees crowded close together, sometimes so close I had to creep along under the lowest branches—just as the fox had done, although maybe not, foxes never the hundred plus pounder types—and then I zigzagged back down the other side of the ridge, then up and up on a second ridge, even higher, the air getting colder on my nose, and then at the top—Whoa. I hit the brakes.

There was no back side to this second ridge. Well, not quite true. There was a back side, but it was more like a cliff than a slope, even the steep kind of slope I'd just climbed. A slope, no matter how steep, you—or maybe not you, but me—can deal with, up or down. Cliffs were different.

I stood at the very edge, peering down. It was a long, long way to the bottom. On the other side rose another cliff face, rocky and sheer like this one, with only a few gnarly bushes sticking out here and there. This second cliff face was kind of curved at the ends, those ends maybe joining up with the cliff I stood on. What we seemed to have here was a sort of box canyon squeezed into a smaller space than usual, making what was almost a notch or hole in the earth. Not a wide hole, but very deep. And way down there at the bottom was a twisted-up body, lying still.

I barked.

There was no movement from the twisted-up body.

I barked again, louder this time. The mountains sent back my bark, the way they sometimes did. Then a snowflake came wafting down from the sky. And another, and another, more. Not hats, but snow.

Real snow. I felt and smelled the difference at once. I barked once more.

Silence.

Eleven

Fat, feathery snowflakes were melting on my nose, snow falling heavier now as Bernie came up beside me, his breath cloud arriving slightly ahead of him. Have I mentioned the smell of Bernie's breath, not always the same every day or even at different times during the day, but the best smelling human breath out there, no matter what?

"Hey, big guy." He huffed and puffed a bit, then put his hands on his hips and the huffing and puffing amped right down. That's just one of his many, many tricks. You had to be in awe of someone who could make huffing and puffing go away, and I was.

He glanced around. "What a spot! Never seen anything quite like it." He looked down. "Kind of like—"

And then he went still, seeing what I had seen down at the bottom. He leaned over the edge and cupped his hands to his mouth. "Hello! Can you hear me?"

Silence from down in the hole.

"Hello down there! Can you speak? If not, can you make a sound? Can you move at all?"

There were no sounds down there, no movements. Bernie checked the ground around us, there at the top of this cliff. I'd followed the fox tracks to this spot but now the snow was covering them up fast. Also getting covered up were—well, it was hard to know what to call these, not footprints or anything like that, more in the way of disturbances in the snow, where it had gotten packed down a bit, meaning packed down on the old hard and icy snow we had going on in this valley, somewhat strange snow made by Ariadne, if I was in the picture. Meanwhile the new snow, coming from the sky, was burying all this . . . didn't we have a word for it in our business? It wouldn't come to me.

Bernie peered down, squinting a bit, not a good look on most humans—although not so bad on him. But with that unpleasant downside, humans must have a strong reason for doing it. Maybe I'd find out one day. Something to look forward to, if not in a huge way.

Bernie went still. "Was that his breath? I thought I saw his breath."

I gazed down. What I saw were snowflakes, falling in little streams and swirls. Wow. Seeing them from above instead of below—going down, not coming down, if you're with me, and I won't blame you if you're not—was so different! What a strange place this valley was! Why were we here, again?

"He—I think it's a he, but I'm not sure—may be alive," Bernie said.

Got it! We'd come to this strange valley to help this guy or maybe gal. Bernie has a way of answering my questions almost as fast as they arise. And then the word I'd been searching for came to me. Evidence! That was it. Evidence was big in the law enforcement business. You heard about it all the time. Bottom line: ol' Chet was still in the picture.

We started walking along the cliff top, close to the edge. The edge, rocky and mostly snowless, was like a path. It led us part way around the deep hole, until we came to a tree with a long, long trunk, not standing very straight, in fact leaning somewhat over into space, like a tree that had had one too many. Whoa!

What an odd thought! Not me at all, but more like it had leaked in from some other mind. Yikes! And now I was scaring myself. I gave myself a quick shake—mostly just my head, with a slight ear flap, although my ears aren't really made for flapping, like Iggy's, for example, but . . . but Chet! Stop. Get back in gear.

Sorry. The only important point was that this big, tall tree was not the Christmas tree type of tree but the other kind, the kind with no leaves in winter. Winter up here, is what I mean. Back home is different. I'd heard Esmé explain the whole thing to Charlie, so now you know what I know.

We moved around the tree, me first, which is how we move best. The ground here was uneven and not so bare, with rocks poking out of the snow. In short, easy for me but maybe not so easy for Bernie in his snowshoes. I glanced back and he shot me a quick grin, at the same time reaching out to steady himself on the tree.

Then came a big and rather noisy surprise. *CRACK!* And that cracking sound wasn't even the loudest sound we had by the end of this . . . interlude, would you call it? This noisy and rather scary interlude. First came the crack, then a nasty splitting sound that seemed to come from under our feet, and all at once this big, tall tree was on the move. It leaned and leaned, leaning farther into space, and there was a sort of whooshing rip and the part of trees you never see, the roots and all that, came exploding out of the ground, the tree now on its way to being upside down, and it was just at that moment that a tangle of roots grabbed Bernie.

Oh no! My Bernie. He was going to get whisked away! He reached out to get hold of something but there was nothing to get hold of. And now the tree was starting to fall, with Bernie caught—caught and struggling in the bottom, which was now the top—and getting nowhere. I caught a glimpse of his face, saw no fear whatsoever. But that was Bernie. Was and is, I told myself, and I sprang forward, dug my paws way down deep, right into solid ground, and in the same motion grabbed him by the pant leg. The tree didn't like that, not one little bit, and tried to tear Bernie away from me. Good luck with that. I hung and hung on, every muscle in my body digging way down deep. The tree pulled and pulled, and then a huge clump of roots and a great ball of frozen dirt tore free and the rest of the tree went diving head first off the cliff. What was left—clump of roots, ball of dirt, my Bernie—I dragged back to safety.

Then, from down below, came an enormous *CRASH* and the earth shook under my paws. After that: the most silent silence I'd ever heard.

Bernie wriggled free from all the tangle and crawled over to me.

"You all right?" he said.

Tip top, actually. He gave me a careful look and felt gently along my sides and back. Then he kissed my head.

I moved up to tip-topper level. But then I realized something important. I'd grabbed Bernie by the pant leg. That was a first. Normally when a pant leg gets grabbed the case is over and we head for home. The heading home idea seemed like a good one right now but was the case solved, whatever it happened to be? I didn't think so. Also Bernie was not the perp, could never be a perp of any kind. I felt confused and pressed against him, perhaps pressing him a bit too close to the edge.

"Easy on the instant replays," Bernie said, with a soft laugh, so something funny must have been going on. He gave me a little pat on the head. Pat pat. One two. I love those one twos, wish they could go on forever. But Bernie was studying the fallen tree in a way that told me the next thing was already on his mind, and more patting wasn't part of it.

"A bridge," Bernie said.

A bridge was the next thing? I didn't get it.

"A bridge," he said, "and not too far. What we're going to do . . ."

He moved back to the cliff edge, his voice trailing away, and had a careful recon, as we say in the business. The tree, torn loose, had caused a bit of a landslide up here at the top of the cliff wall, making it not so steep for a little way down. There, just where the wall started going back to being steep, the roots of the fallen tree had gotten themselves wedged into the rocks. The rest of the tree—meaning the trunk and a few big branches that hadn't been snapped off in the fall—stretched out down and down, but not straight down, instead at an angle, the top coming to rest on the gentle slope near the bottom which was how the cliff face rounded out, if you can see what I'm trying—and it's not easy—to make clear. Namely the floor was kind of flat, then sloped up to-ward the cliffs on all sides, which rose pretty much straight up from there. At the very bottom lay this person, most likely a he, according to Bernie. At the top was us. In between was the fallen tree, now in the position of . . . of a bridge! Wow! I got it.

Bernie took off his snowshoes. "I'd better take the lead on this one," he said, and started crawling down our tree bridge, in the beginning head first, then feet first, then head first again. I didn't keep up with all the changes because part way down, even though I'd very nicely let him take the lead, I just couldn't bear it anymore and vaulted right over him and kind of trotted the rest of the way down the tree trunk, leaping off it for the last little bit and landing on the slope. Whoops! Somewhat slippery. I skidded slightly over the snow—which turned out to be quite enjoyable—then got a grip—hey! In more ways than one! And walked over to the person, lying between two rocks—possibly jammed between them—and both of them the pointy type of rocks.

Yes, a he. This he was turned sideways so I couldn't see his face, but the human male scent in the air was unmissable. The man, wearing a ski suit but no hat, lay twisted in a way I didn't like to see. Beneath one of his legs was part of a broken snowshoe. The foot on that leg was pointed pretty much backward.

Bernie walked up, looking fine except for a scratch or two on his forehead. He walked around the man to get a look at his face.

"Chaz," he said. Which I already knew.

Bernie knelt. I sat beside him. Chaz's eyes were open, but motionless and dull, and there was a bruise, maybe sunken a bit, over one eyebrow. Bernie took off his gloves and placed a finger on the side of Chaz's neck.

"He's got a pulse." Bernie's eyes took on an inward look, like he was trying to hear from far away. "But feathery, Chet. Weak and feathery." He touched the side of Chaz's face, very gently. "Chaz? Can you hear me?"

No answer from Chaz. No reaction of any kind.

"We've got to get him to the hospital," Bernie said. He glanced around—at the floor of this small and strange box canyon, at the fallen tree, at the cliff tops high above. "But it has to be done right."

Maybe Bernie could take Chaz on his back, and I could help him crawl up the tree, pushing from behind if needed? That was as far as I could take it on my own.

Meanwhile Bernie had taken out his phone. "No way there'll be service here, but . . ." He checked the screen. "But of course there is."

Bernie made a call. Snow was falling harder now. A flake landed on one of Chaz's open eyes. Blink it away, Chaz. Blink it away. But he did not. The flake melted and turned into a tear. It overflowed Chaz's lower eyelid onto his cheek and froze.

Twelve

After Bernie got off the phone, he removed his jacket and covered as much of Chaz with it as he could. Up above the wind was growing stronger, making whistling sounds and blowing the falling snow sideways. But it wasn't blowing down here, and the snow had almost stopped, even though it was snowing harder on the cliff tops. Bernie looked up.

"It's like we're in the opposite of a snow globe," he said.

I didn't get that at all although I was familiar with snow globes, had even had odd mishaps with more than one. But before I could figure out what Bernie was talking about, or just take the very first step, I heard a *whap-whap-whap*, not too distant.

"They're sending a helo—shouldn't be too long before we hear it," Bernie said. He really is the best. "But I'm not so sure they'll be able to bring it down in here." He felt Chaz's neck again. "And how long can he—"

WHAP-WHAP-WHAP. A helo with a big red cross on the side went zooming by up above, then slowed and came around in a big wide turn and hovered, not very high over the top of the hole.

Bernie rose and waved. An arm appeared out of the cockpit window and waved back, cockpit being helo lingo. I'd flown in helos more than once. The best part is when they land and open the doors and you race out.

"Very tight fit, big guy," Bernie said. "Maybe they'll just lower an EMT with the gear, so we'll need to—"

But nothing got lowered. Instead, the helo came down and down, slow and without the slightest wobble, the blade tips close to the cliff face once or twice but never touching. The helo wind blew down on us, the WHAP-WHAP-WHAP rising to somewhat unpleasant levels, and we got on our bellies, Bernie covering me with one arm. The helo touched down just a few steps away, seeming to take up all the space there was. Then came shutdown—the blades making one last fluttery turn— and quiet.

We rose. The side door of the helo opened and two young EMTs, a man and a woman, both in white uniforms with red crosses on the chests, came running over, unslinging backpacks on the way.

"What we got?" the woman said.

Bernie started to explain.

"Huh?" the man said. "You and the dog got down here without any equipment? How the hell did you manage that?"

"Can we get to that later?" Bernie said.

The man frowned. His mouth opened like he was about to say something possibly unfriendly but at that moment the pilot, a big dude with a salt-and-pepper mustache came walking up.

"What's the situation?" he said.

"That's what we're trying to find out from this guy," said the male EMT. "But we're not making much—"

The pilot shot Bernie a look. His eyes opened wide. "Captain?" he said.

Bernie smiled. "You're looking good, Albie. And it's just Bernie now."

"Not to me," said the pilot, Albie by name if I was getting

the facts right. He wrapped his big arms around Bernie and pounded his back. Bernie did the same to him. The pounding seemed quite hard to me, thudding like drums, and must have hurt, but there was no sign of pain on their faces, far from it.

"Um, sir?" said the female EMT.

Albie turned to the EMTs. "Kids?" he said. "Patty and Matty? Meet Captain Little. You can blame him for how come you're stuck with me."

Patty and Matty's eyes were open wide.

"No him, no me," Albie said. "The captain here saved my goddam life. And not only mine."

"It's just Bernie," Bernie told Patty and Matty. "More important—" He pointed. "This is Chaz. We don't know how long he's been here, but his pulse is weak and getting weaker."

Patty and Matty got to work, fast and silent, all of a sudden looking quite a bit older.

Albie put his arm over Bernie's shoulder. "So, captain, fill in the blanks."

"You first," said Bernie.

Bernie and Albie filled in their blanks, meaning what, I couldn't tell you. Sometime during the filling in of the blanks Albie gestured at me with his elbow. Whoa! That made two elbow pointings in the past not very much time at all. This was going to be a special day. "Who's this amazing lookin' character?" Albie said.

Bernie talked about me. I learned stuff I hadn't known! And wish I remembered now, but I was distracted by Patty and Matty, putting a breathing mask on Chaz's face, sticking tubes into his arm, bracing his neck and his back and his legs, and finally and very gently getting the stretcher beneath him. We all helped carry Chaz to the helo, me mostly supervising, sometimes from in front, sometimes from in back, sometimes from the side, supervising more complicated than you might think.

We squeezed inside with Patty and Matty. As the helo slowly rose, Matty took a few sidelong glances at Bernie and then said, "Amazing, huh, how he can get in and out of spots like this."

Bernie's eyes got a faraway look. "Under fire he's just the same."

There was silence after that until we were landing on the roof of a hospital.

"Chet allowed treats?" Patty said.

What a question!

We sat in the waiting room of a small hospital, me and Bernie, a dude with a full length cast on one leg across from us. Soon another dude with a cast on one leg came crutching in. He took a seat near the first dude. They eyed each other, both of them long-haired, strong-looking, smelling of weed, their faces weathered except for around the eyes, giving them a squirrely appearance, which was maybe what sparked a sudden desire in me to chase them around. But what kind of sport would that be, chasing two dudes with casts on their legs around a waiting room? I said to myself, Ch—et, just the way Bernie does and what do you know? It did the trick. I sat motionless, the most motionless kind of motionless, where anyone around says, "What a good boy!" Although no one was saying it now. Meanwhile, my mind was busy with plans for chasing these dudes the moment they got outside. You've got to be true to yourself eventually!

A man in scrubs who looked a lot like the two squirrely dudes except for the leg casts came through a doorway at the back and went over to them.

"You early birds!" he said. "Howja manage to do this already? We ain't had a lick of snow till today."

"Baldy Chutes," said one.

"Corbett's," said the other.

"Lucky guys!" said the man in scrubs. "C'mon down to ortho."

The two dudes crutched after him, through the doorway and out of sight. Have you ever noticed that things can happen right before your eyes and you still don't have a clue? This was one of those times.

Bernie reached into his pocket and took out the pom-pom-less elf hat. He looked it over, turned it inside out, looked it over that way, then did maybe the most amazing thing I'd ever seen. Bernie held that elf hat close to his face and sniffed it, not one big, long sniff but several real quick sniff sniff sniffs, like he was an expert sniffer. Bernie! An expert sniffer? Of course not, but he's still—even more so!—the most interesting human in the world.

A beefy old man in uniform came in, not a hospital uniform but the law enforcement kind, meaning there was a star on his chest and a holstered gun on his hip. Because his beefiness was the apple-shaped variety, the gun—not recently fired, by the way—hung lower than usual, somewhat dangling in space in a way that made me want to—I don't know—give it a nudge, for example. Something to look forward to perhaps.

He checked the room, empty except for us, and came over.

"Lookin' for . . ."

He took a scrap of paper from his pocket and squinted at it. Again, the human squint, again not showing them at their best, especially when, as in this case, the eyes are small and squinty to begin with. Although this guy was big, most of his features were small, excepting the nose, large and reddish, especially the bulby end. I came close to having a thought about that nose.

He looked up. ". . . fella called Bernie Little."

"That's me," Bernie said. "And this is Chet."

Most law enforcement guys and gals have a soft spot for members of the nation within. This one didn't give me the slightest glance.

"You the one found the injured party?"

"Chet and I, yes."

Now he did look at me.

"The dog?"

"Exactly."

Sometimes two men don't like each other from the get-go. I can smell when that happens, and I was smelling it now.

The man gazed down at Bernie. "I'm sheriff of this county. Name's Monk."

Bernie nodded.

Then came a silence, maybe the awkward kind. Sheriff Monk held out his hand. That seemed awkward as well. Bernie rose, making the sheriff not look quite so big anymore, just a lot rounder. They shook hands, Bernie looking the sheriff in the eye, the sheriff looking Bernie in the forehead. In short, that was awkward, too.

"Been sheriff a long time," the sheriff said. "So, I feel responsible—like the county's family. You get me?"

"I'd be the same," Bernie said.

"'Kay," said the sheriff. "Okay then. Back to the injured party, Chaz LeWitte. Works for our local celebrity, Mizz Carlisle. You know her?"

"Slightly."

"Slightly," said the sheriff. "How about LeWitte? Know him, too?"

"Again, slightly."

"Slightly," the sheriff repeated. A lot of slightlies, all of a sudden. Whatever it meant, I liked how Bernie said it better.

The sheriff tugged his holster up a little higher. "Familiar with these parts?"

"No."

"Devil's Purse," the sheriff said.

"Not following you," said Bernie.

"That's the name we got for that notch, back of Mount Murdstone. It's what they call a rare geological site. Something about continental drift. I don't pretend to understand it. But the point is, it's hard to find, even for someone who knows the terrain." He waited, maybe expecting Bernie to say something. When Bernie did not, the sheriff said, "Albie Rudge, the pilot, claims he knows you."

"That's true."

"Speaks highly of you."

"I think the same about him."

"Also says you're a private operator from out of state."

"True."

"Arizona?"

"Correct."

Ah, yes. We were from Arizona. That sometimes slips my mind, so it was nice to hear it now. Was this conversation going well? I went back and forth on that.

"Private operators from Arizona need a license to work in this state," Sheriff Monk said.

Bernie said nothing.

The sheriff reddened a bit, except for the bulby end of his nose, already red. It seemed to whiten, if anything. He held out his hand. Bernie ignored it. "Hey, bud," the sheriff said. "Show and tell."

"What are you talking about?" Bernie said.

"Your license to work in this state."

"Who said we were working?"

The sheriff reddened some more, the bulby nose now even whiter. I was hit by the craziest thought, not me at all. Maybe I should keep it to myself, but here goes. But first you have to know that kids' song, the one Charlie sings in front of the Christmas tree, Bernie playing the ukulele alongside. It's called "Rudolph the Red Nosed Reindeer." Okay, now here goes. The sheriff—or at least his bulby nose—was the opposite of Rudolph—or at least his red nose. Crazy, as I mentioned, so forget all—whoa! At that moment I got hit by another crazy thought, maybe linking to the thought I couldn't quite get to just a little while back. Was Rudy—our Rudy, the one we were searching for—actually Rudolph the Red Nosed Reindeer? All at once I knew this case was very important.

Meanwhile, the sheriff did a foolish thing, namely reaching out with that empty hand of his and placing it on Bernie's shoulder. Bernie didn't shrug it off or twist away. He just said, "Take your hand off me."

"Who's gonna make me?" said the sheriff.

I got ready for anything, but before any kind of anything could get started, the door to the hallway opened and Ariadne hurried in, wearing a white fur coat that smelled a bit weaselly. We have weasels out in the desert—not so easy to catch on account of how quickly they can slip into very small holes you never notice till it's too late—but they're brown and orange, not white. So this coat of Ariadne's was a bit of a mystery, plus we had the mystery of why anyone would want to go around smelling like a weasel, somewhat skunky, in case you didn't know, if a little more . . .

what was the word? Leda often used it about Bernie. Subtle? Was that it? As in: *you're not exactly subtle, Bernie.*

But back to Ariadne's coat, a beautiful-looking coat for sure, although buttoned up wrong, so one side hung lower than the other. Also, her hair was windswept and dotted with snowflakes, and her long scarf had mostly slipped off and trailed on the floor.

"Sheriff Monk? Bernie? What's going on?"

The sheriff took his hand off Bernie's shoulder and turned to her real quick.

"Hello, ma'am. Excuse us, ma'am. Just sorting out a little problem with this here private investigator from out of state. Seems that—"

"Problem? What possible problem could there be? Bernie and Chet are here at my invitation."

"Huh?"

"To do me the great service of finding Rudy."

"Who's Rudy?"

"Really, sheriff? I'm sure your department was notified about Rudy's disappearance, although if we ever heard back I wasn't told. But don't we have more important things to deal with? Bernie, is it true you found Chaz?"

"Yes."

She crossed the floor and took Bernie's hand. "How is he?"

"I don't know."

"Please! Is he badly hurt? Is he conscious?" She grabbed the collar of Bernie's vest.

At that moment the door at the back opened and a woman with a stethoscope around her neck came in. Ariadne wheeled around to her.

"Dr. Woodcourt? How is he? How is Chaz?"

"Not good, I'm very sorry to say. We've got him in a medically induced coma and are still determining the state of his injuries. It's amazing he's still alive. That's a long, long fall."

"Fall? It wasn't a snowmobile accident?" Ariadne said.

Dr. Woodcourt turned to Bernie. "You're the one who found him?"

"Yes," said Bernie. "And there was no sign of a snowmobile. I believe he was on snowshoes."

"How could he have hurt himself so badly on snowshoes?" Ariadne said.

"Well, a long, long fall, as I mentioned," said the doctor.

"Where?" Ariadne clasped her hands to her chest. "Where did he fall?"

"At Devil's Purse, wasn't it?" Dr. Woodcourt said.

"I didn't know the name at the time," Bernie said, "but yes."

Ariadne's eyes rolled up and she slumped down. Bernie caught her before she hit the floor.

Thirteen

Now comes what you might call a confusion of events, not so easy to get in order. In fact, what does get in order even mean? It's probably one of those human things that it's best to stay clear of. How about I just go with my memories as they pop up? Here's one: As Ariadne fell, a little notebook slid from the pocket of her weaselly coat and spun down to the floor, reminding me for some reason of Albie's chopper. Funny how the mind works.

Then there's the memory of us: me and Bernie all by ourselves, somewhere else in the hospital, maybe another waiting room, and Bernie glancing at me and saying, "What have you got there?"

Nothing much. Just the little notebook. I'd pretty much forgotten it completely! How can anyone forget something they've got in their mouth? Don't ask me.

I went closer to Bernie so he could take the notebook, but as he reached out, I pulled back, just couldn't help myself. I had no actual plan but it's always fun to play with Bernie. For example, what if I could get him on his feet, chasing me around and around this waiting room? Or back and forth across it? Or both! Around and around and back and forth at the same time! Did life just keep getting better and better? I swerved in close to Bernie—kind of buzzing him!—and threw in some bobbing and weaving. Why not? I can bob and weave like nobody's business, hadn't done nearly enough bobbing and weaving in oh, way too long, so now there was plenty to get out of my system. I bobbed and weaved and weaved and bobbed and weaved, weaved, weaved and bobbed, bobbed—

"Ch—et?"

I dropped the notebook at Bernie's feet and sat down, nice and peaceable. That part, nice and peaceable, is for sure. It's one of my very strongest memories ever. What a good, good boy! Bernie didn't actually say that but I'm sure he was thinking it as he examined the notebook.

"No name on it," he said, "but it's obvious whose it is. There's her handwriting, so distinctive, the letters so plump and—could you say generous?"

I had no clue, didn't have the slightest notion of what he was talking about.

"And at the same time," Bernie went on, "all the words lean slightly backward." He glanced at me. "Would we know all our writers better if their books had to be in their own handwriting?"

I was lost. Wouldn't it be better use of our time to be chasing around the room? I gave some thought to snatching the thing back.

Bernie turned a page. "I've heard of writer's diaries," he said. "This looks like one." Humans have different voices when they read aloud, don't quite sound like themselves anymore. Bernie now spoke in his reading voice, still a lovely voice but not quite connected to him, if that makes sense, which I'm pretty sure it does not.

"'I just feel so . . . so dim. Not even that. More like the bull after the banderilleros and the picador are through with him and his head is hanging just how the matador likes it. God-awful, that afternoon in Madrid. And then everyone wanted to go out for paella! I wanted to be sick.' Then comes a little sketch of a mounted picador." Bernie gazed at the page. "It's good. It gets the whole . . ." He paused, maybe searching for a word. The word he found was new to me. I had no idea what it meant, but just from how he said it, I knew it was bad.

". . . loathsomeness. The whole loathsomeness of the picador idea."

He turned the page. "'But of course I'm not just the bull. I'm the picador, the banderilleros, the matador, the whole shooting match, all inside this stupid old head. What's next? What's next? Trudi Tremaine opens a door. Trudi Tremaine lifts the corner of the rug. Trudi Tremaine answers the phone. Hello? Trudi speaking. And then? Does she ask a question she knows the answer to? That's part of her modus. But what is it? And then? And then? I've done and thens thousands of times, tens of thousands. But is there a limited supply? Have I come to the end? Brain dead?' Then comes a smeared part, where it looks like the bottom of the page got wet." He turned the page—"a spilled drink or . . ." then another, and another. "Okay, legible again. 'Chaz—oh, what a lovely man, the temptation is so . . . but stop stop. Seeing me with no clothes, no make-up, undone? Nonstarter of all nonstarters. The poor boy's blind to reality. And he's so sweet and determined about Rudy. I do miss Rudy but is he the cause of this . . . this lid clamped down on my mind? I NEED TO WRITE ABOUT CHRISTMAS!'"

Bernie glanced at me. "That's in caps, by the way." So nice of Bernie to loop me in. I knew caps, of course. Was an elf hat a kind of cap? For a moment I had the wonderful feeling I knew where this was going.

Bernie turned back to the little book. "'But Rudy's missing, and missing is something I know all too . . . Oh, dear, the dinner bell. How I dread it. Although seeing that beautiful dog will be nice.'"

Bernie looked up. Our eyes met. Who was this supposedly beautiful dog? I looked forward to meeting him, and possibly letting him know what was what.

"So that part, at least, was written last night," Bernie said. "I wonder what she meant by—"

Before Bernie could finish that thought, Dr. Woodcourt entered the waiting room.

Bernie rose.

"How is she, doc?"

"Better," Dr. Woodcourt said. "I hate exhaustion as a diagnosis—it's such a grab bag—but in this case I think it fits. She's also severely dehydrated, so we've put her on an IV solution and will keep her overnight."

"And Chaz?" Bernie said.

"No change."

"I hate to press you for a prediction about him."

Dr. Woodcourt smiled a smile of the unwarm kind. "Then don't."

That's it for my memories inside the hospital. Outside the hospital we stood in the parking lot for a while, me because Bernie was doing it and Bernie for reasons of his own. Snow was still falling but lighter now and straight down, kind of like a bead curtain in a bar we'd once visited briefly down Mexico way, the dudes on the other side of the bead curtain turning out to be cartel fellows in not their best moods. At the end of the parking lot the woods began, the trees tall and shadowy, some the kind that had lost their leaves, the others the Christmas types, the whole sight a bit unusual, what with that bead curtain and all. And then, stepping out from between the trees came a reindeer. Well, not stepping out. I didn't actually see that. What I saw was the reindeer not there and then suddenly there, a breath cloud rising above its head.

Bernie laid a hand on my back, not to stop me from doing who knows what, just because we come together in big moments. That was how I knew this was a big moment. But why? What was big about it?

Then softly Bernie called, "Rudy? Is that you?"

Oh dear. Perhaps not a big moment after all. I'm sure Bernie must have remembered Blitzen's smell, but it was asking too much to expect him to pick it up at this distance. He's only human as humans say. I've thought about that a lot—humans being only humans—but I don't do it anymore, on account of never having gotten anywhere. Forget that part. The point is that just to help him out, I advanced slowly toward the woods, as slowly as I could under the circumstances. These circumstances were like most circumstances in my experience: they begged for speed.

"Easy there, big guy, don't want to spook him."

Spook? How odd! Spooks were all about Halloween, the worst of all holidays, while Christmas was the best. Of course I didn't want to do anything to hurt Christmas. I came to a complete stop and sat down, mostly on Bernie's foot to help him not spook. Meanwhile, he was squinting at the reindeer.

"I'm not sure . . . no Chet, it's not Rudy. Easy mistake to make, but that broken-off antler is a dead giveaway. It's Blitzen, you can take it to the bank. But he's wandered off the ranch for sure. Why?"

I had no clue. As for the bank suggestion, well, perhaps not

Bernie's best. Our last conversation with Ms. Mendez, the manager, hadn't gone well, as I may have mentioned already. But you can't be too careful, as humans often say, and I don't get every time. I realized Bernie must have meant some other bank—and what a great idea, moving to another bank and starting over! The problem with Ms. Mendez's bank had something to do with the draft. I believe it was simply too drafty and no one would back off on the AC. They liked it—how did they put it? Overly drafty? Over drafty? Something like that. So we're outta there, Ms. Mendez, and we're taking the Little Detective Agency to a bank where the air is still. No matter what happened now today was a great success already. Except for the dead giveaway part. Whatever that meant, I didn't like the sound of it.

And possibly Blitzen didn't either. He suddenly awoke from the sort of trance or whatever it was that he'd fallen into and backed away.

"Is he trying to lead us to Rudy?" Bernie said. "They're herd animals. We've got to take advantage of that."

No problem! I could herd with the best of them, or even better. How many herders do you know with elephant experience? Ask yourself that. But not now. There's no time.

The next thing I knew Bernie and I were moving quickly across the parking lot. Blitzen saw that, rolled his big and rather dumb-looking eyes, and sprang away, actually glancing off a low-hanging, snow-covered branch in his haste. All that snow exploded into a white cloud, and by the time the cloud cleared, me and Bernie now at the edge of the woods, Blitzen had vanished.

"Where'd he go?" Bernie peered into the distance, although there was no distance, the trees closing in all around us. Of course there were tracks to follow, plus a scent, but here's a strange thing. The tracks quickly grew fainter and fainter, and so did the scent, until almost in no time both were gone. Possibly the snowfall was covering the tracks. Possibly the wind was rising at our backs. Yes, for sure, I could feel it. What we had to do now was circle around a bit, pick up the trace. But instead, Bernie had come to a standstill, his face tilted up, his eyes on the little patches of dark cloudy sky, like . . . like he was searching for Blitzen up there.

He shook his head. "It's a wild goose chase, big guy." He made the little *chk chk* sound, turned, and headed back toward the parking lot.

Whoa! A wild goose chase? A wild goose chase at last? I'd heard about them so many times and now when the opportunity arose, we were letting it blow right by? I barked this special bark I have that means business in no uncertain terms.

Bernie looked back at me. "Chet? You okay? Don't tell me your paws are freezing."

He hurried back to me, knelt in the snow, took off his gloves, gently raised one of my paws and felt it. "Feels okay." He rubbed it the way human hands rub when they're trying to warm something up. "Don't worry. You'll get used to the snow."

Worry? About my paws? They were used to the snow already, had been used to it from step one, in fact enjoyed that snowy feel. A lot better than the hot asphalt, almost melting, at some strip mall back in the Valley in summer. Still, if Bernie wanted to keep rubbing my paw—or even better, give each of them a rub, one after the other, and then start over, round and round again, round and round and—

He rose. "Let's get a move on. We've got a lot to do before dark."

How exciting! I beat him back to the hospital parking lot, and by plenty, all set to get started. But when Bernie arrived, he glanced around and said, "I'm an idiot. How did I expect to get back to the ranch? In the helo?"

A fine idea! Bernie was no idiot, and that proved it. I waited for him to shout for the helo, or . . . or call for it on his phone! Wow! One of my best thoughts ever, but Bernie didn't do either of those things. I'm sure he would have—or even come up with something more amazing—but before he could a red pickup with a wreath on the grille came speeding into the parking lot, fishtailed once or twice and slanted to a stop in front of the hospital entrance.

Georgette, wearing high heels, jumped out of the passenger side, the heels snapping off at once, although she didn't seem to notice. Hal Pelgotty got out of the driver's side, not jumping, but going as fast as a heavy old guy can go. They hurried into the hospital.

We went over to the pickup but didn't follow them into the hospital, just kind of stood around. Was there a reason? While I was thinking about that and getting nowhere—although there's always hope, one of those little things that's nice to know—I picked up an interesting smell coming from inside the cab. I went over to the driver's side door and did what we in this business call pointing, a kind of standing very still, head up, tail up, alert. The truth is I'm a natural pointer, point any old time just for the hell of it, say, at something meaningless, like . . . like . . .

While I was trying to think of something meaningless, Bernie came over.

"Something up?"

I gave him a low rumble bark. I have more than one low rumbly bark. This one has very little rumble, comes close to being a whisper.

"Oh, yeah?" Bernie said.

He peered through the window of the driver's side door.

"Don't see anything."

Bernie reached for the handle. There was none of that glancing-around-to-check-if-anyone's-watching move you get from perps. We're not perps, me and Bernie. If we have to do something sneaky we do it for all to see. Bernie opened the door.

He looked inside. We both did, our heads pretty much touching. I stuck my muzzle under the driver's seat, giving Bernie a clue. He reached in and pulled out a shotgun, not like our single shot .410 back in the safe at home. This was the double-barreled kind, old and scuffed, and also not fired recently. Bernie opened it up. There were shells in both chambers.

"Purdey side by side, a collector's item if it was in better shape." Bernie snapped the shotgun shut, stuck it back under the seat, and closed the door.

After that we stood in the hospital parking lot, the air growing colder, the snowflakes still falling, but hardening and losing their fluff. Bernie thought, a faraway look in his eyes. I watched him think. Also I could feel him think, like he was moving heavy boxes around in his mind. I didn't know what was in the boxes, but that was okay. You can't know everything in this life. If you did you'd be a know-it-all, and no one likes a know-it-all. The kind of person everyone likes is . . . is the Bernie type! Yes, that's it. But there's only one and he's mine.

Bernie took a deep breath, let it out slow, and turned my way, the faraway look fading from his eyes.

"Are we approaching this all wrong?" he said. "In terms of the big picture, is what I mean. Put it like this, Chet—reindeer don't have red noses."

Ah ha! I made plans to hang onto that one. It sounded easy to remember so I felt pretty confident. The next moment I felt hungry. So that was how I was feeling, hungry and confident, when Hal Pelgotty came out the hospital door.

He took a step or two, then came to a standstill, like he didn't know where he was going. He unzipped his puffy red jacket and patted the inside pockets, finally producing a pack of cigarettes and matches. But when he tried lighting up his hands were too shaky. Bernie walked over to him. I followed, at first from in back but after no time at all in front. That's how we roll at the Little Detective Agency, just one of the reasons for our success, minus . . . minus what again? Wasn't there a minus? How important could it be if I couldn't remember?

Bernie didn't say anything, just took the match from Hal, flicked it with his thumbnail and held the flame out in his cupped hand. Hal leaned in and got his cigarette lit. He took a deep inhale that seemed to take away some of the worrying he had going on inside him. Don't get me wrong. He had plenty left. We in the nation within are pretty good at sensing these things. In humans, is what I mean. Other creatures can be a big problem in this area. For example, what's going on inside cats? I'd thought and thought about that, and all I've come up with is this: No cat has ever spent one single moment thinking about what's going on in me. In me, Chet the Jet! Can you imagine?

Meanwhile, Hal was offering the pack to Bernie and Bernie was saying he was trying to quit and taking one and lighting up. Then they were smoking together, each holding a tiny fire. You could like humans an awful lot and also feel a bit sorry for them at the same time.

"Any news from inside?" Bernie said.

Hal shook his head. "Doc says Ariadne's resting, wouldn't let us see her. Georgie's gonna stick around. As for Chaz . . ." He shrugged, took another hit off his cigarette, and as he breathed out took a close look at Bernie. "Word is you did a helluva job up at that goddam death trap."

"It was mostly Chet," Bernie said.

Hal looked my way. "Chaz was—is—a big believer in Chet's abilities. For finding Rudy, and all that. How would you rate your chances?"

"We'll give it our best shot," Bernie said.

"Sorry, not a fair question." Hal glanced up at the sky. "Snow at last. Skiers are gonna be happy. So everyone up in these mountains'll be happy, too. 'Ceptin' us."

"Who's us?"

"The team. Everyone around Ariadne. She's big smoke in these parts, in case you haven't realized by now. But not the biggest smoke, that bein' the ski business." He shook his head. "Poor Chaz. He's just a kid."

"Has anyone notified his family?"

"I don't know. They're from back east. His mom died when he was young and his dad remarried, started a new family, the usual story. But someone on the team must be on it."

"Who runs the team, Hal?"

"Good question."

"You?"

"Ha! A glorified janitor is what I am. And happy for it, don't get me wrong."

Bernie smiled. "But in the other world you're at the top."

"What other world?"

"Ariadne's world. The one she made in her imagination."

"Not quite sure where you're goin' with this," Hal said.

"The Christmas world. I thought you were her handpicked Santa up here in the valley."

Hal laughed. "Don't know about handpicked. I more or less grew into it." He patted his big round belly. "Forget the less part."

Bernie laughed, too. For a nice moment or two they were smoking together with smiles slowly fading on their faces, two big guys, one young, or at least pretty young, and the other pretty old, old enough, at least, to be Bernie's dad. Kind of a weird thought, coming from who knows where. Bernie's dad died when Bernie was a kid, which I may have mentioned already. Maybe you remember the pissing advice—always downwind and downhill.

"Anyways," Hal said, dropping what was left of his cigarette and crushing it under his boot, a boot of what I believe is called the shit-kicking type, "thanks for what you did, you and Chet. But damn it to hell, why did it have to be that godforsaken place?"

"Devil's Purse?" Bernie said.

Hal nodded. "The name fits, although funny thing, the name came first and all the bad came later."

"All the bad?" Bernie said.

"Excuse me," Hal said. "Course you wouldn't know. But this ain't the first accident that's happened there, not the first one affecting, touching—don't know the right word—Ariadne."

Bernie seemed to forget the cigarette, held between his fingers and now burning down real close to his skin. "What are you talking about?"

"Don't mean to confuse you," Hal said. "And the first one wasn't an accident—nobody disputes that. But it was a heavy, heavy blow for Ariadne."

"What happened, Hal?" Bernie's voice was quiet but there was a little buzz in it, way at the back. At the same time, the fire now did reach his skin. He let go of the cigarette. It fell on the snowy surface of the parking lot, sizzled for a moment and then went silent.

"Fella got murdered at Devil's Purse—at least that's where they found the body. Long time ago, this was. Ariadne was young. Me, too."

"Who got killed, Hal? Who was the killer?"

"Well, the first I can answer, but not the second."

"Why not?"

"The killer, whoever it was, never got found."

"Meaning it's an unsolved crime?"

Hal nodded. "I guess you could say that." He zipped his jacket up to the very top. "Need a lift?"

Fourteen

"Does Chet like riding in the bed?" Hal said, making one of those thumb-jab gestures at the back of his red pickup.

"Sometimes," Bernie said.

Hal tapped the step-up at the back. "Up you go, big fella."

I stayed put. First, I don't need a step up, leaping being my very best thing. For example, I could leap right over this whole truck if I had a mind to. And all at once I did have a mind to! How about that? With no run-up or any other time waster I sprang over the truck, sticking the landing on the other side. The earth stood still. How nice!

"God in heaven," Hal said.

I ended up riding back to the ranch in my usual riding position, up front. Hal's pickup had a bench seat so it was cozy and comfy between him and Bernie. I sat up nice and tall, on high alert, ready to bark at any creatures appearing by the roadside, or even a bird. But there were no creatures, no birds, only the snow falling and falling, as we climbed up and down a mountain or two.

Meanwhile, there was a lot of back and forth between Bernie and Hal, some of which I missed on account of reliving in my mind that recent bit of fun, namely when I soared over the pickup. Reliving fun in your mind is also fun, as I'm sure you know, although not nearly as much, which is why you need to get out there and have fun, stocking up, if you see what I mean, for the reliving part. Actually, that made no sense to me. I shut the whole thing down and tuned in to what was going on.

". . . this was back in her hard time, her mom dying, dad losing all his money, all that."

"When Ariadne came back here and lived in a tent," Bernie said.

"Exactly. You've got a good memory. Did I mention she had a boyfriend while she was here?"

"You did."

"A very nice young man from over at Silver Mountain. Good enough for her? I don't know about that."

Hal gazed at the road ahead, snow covered except for exposed paved patches here and there. We rounded a long curve, and I felt the back end of the pickup kind of having ideas of its own. Bernie's eyes shifted toward Hal. Hal wasn't looking at him, but he eased off the gas pedal. He wasn't the first to feel one of Bernie's eye shifts.

"Fellow's name was Teddy Leeford," Hal said. "That's who got killed—Teddy Leeford, Ariadne's boyfriend."

"Killed how?" Bernie said.

"He got shot, not sure if they ever established exactly when, but they found the body on Christmas morning, down at the bottom of Devil's Purse."

"Who conducted the investigation?" Bernie said.

"Musta been the sheriff's office over at Silver Mountain," said Hal. "The sheriff back then—long before Monk got the job— was Mitch Cuffy, if I remember right. Been retired for some time."

"Is he still alive?"

"Believe so. I'd have heard if he passed."

"Where do I find him?"

Hal glanced over at Bernie. "Why would you want to do that?"

"There's no statute of limitations when it comes to murder," Bernie said.

The pickup's back end started acting up again. Hal eased off the pedal.

"Wasn't aware of that," he said.

"Meaning that case is still open. So if you know where he lives that would be a big help."

"Couldn't tell ya," Hal said. "You, uh, looking to make some extra cash outta this?"

"We're looking for Rudy," Bernie said.

Hal opened his mouth. He had that yeah but expression on his face but it didn't get said.

Hal dropped us off at Cratchit House. We peed, me outside and Bernie inside, our usual approach, although not always. Then we hopped in the Beast and took off, again on mountain roads, but almost right from the start they were all new to me. Snow drifted down, the windshield wipers swept it away, the trees stood tall, always very close, like they were thinking of taking a step or two and getting in the way. But they never did, so when my eyelids started to get heavy I didn't fight them. In the end there's no use fighting heavy eyelids, as I'm sure you know.

In my dream I followed the aroma of steak tips out of the court-room where I'd been Exhibit B and right into our kitchen at home. The steak tips were waiting for me in a bowl by the fridge. But just at that moment Peanut, the elephant I may have mentioned earlier, came storming in from a snowy storm. No way that could happen in real life, Peanut being way too big to fit through the doorway or get inside the house at all without first knocking it down, which she was perfectly capable of—I'd seen her knock down a whole warehouse south of the border—but in dreams these things can happen. The problem is when you're dreaming, especially an intense sort of dream, involving steak tips, for example, you don't know what's a dream and what's not. In short, Peanut pounded right by me and hosed up all the steak tips—plus the bowl—with her trunk.

I opened my eyes.

Bernie, at the wheel, looked over. "Bad dream, big guy?"

I gazed straight ahead.

"Bit of whimpering there, buddy."

Oh no, how disgraceful!

Bernie smiled. "Let me guess. You were running away from a bear."

What a strange suggestion! I run from nobody, end of story. Although, thinking back, I did once run from a bear, specifically a mama bear on a mountain trail where we'd come between her and her cubs. The look on her face! That was something I'll never forget, and also unforgettable was the way Bernie had run, too. In fact, poor wounded leg or no, he'd blown right by me, maybe the most amazing sight I'd ever seen. I put my paw on his knee. We sped up dramatically. Bernie tapped the brakes.

"We good?" he said.

Quite. Perfectly. The best.

Meanwhile, we were rolling into an old-fashioned, western-type town, of which we've got some back where I come from. Bernie says there are two kinds—falling down and spruced up. This was the second kind, all clean, freshly painted—no missing that smell if you've got even just a smidgen of nose—and all storefronts decorated for Christmas, although some also had displays of fancy candleholders made for holding more candles than two, which I'd encountered before at this same time of year involving a fellow PI, sort of, named Victor Klovsky, and may have nothing to do with Christmas, in fact coming from another holiday completely, the name escaping me at the moment.

We parked in front of the plainest building on the street, a brick building with no decorations of any kind, not Christmas and not . . . Hanukkah! That was it, coming to me by itself! Sometimes—but not always—not trying works better than trying. How come that's so sweet? I'll leave that one up to you.

"Sheriff's office," Bernie said.

We hopped out—me actually hopping and Bernie not, our usual method. But why? Why must I always hop? Uh-oh. What a strange question! I hoped it would never come around again.

We went inside and walked up to the desk. A solidly built woman in a beige uniform sat behind it, gazing at a newspaper, a pencil in her hand and a frown on her face, one of those deep frowns that go along with hard thinking. She didn't seem to hear our footsteps, mine on the silent side, true, but not Bernie's.

"Uh, excuse me," he said.

She looked up, the frown disappearing, and turned out to be younger than I'd thought.

"A tough one?" Bernie said, making one of his chin gestures—so fabulous, but you really have to see them in person—at the newspaper.

"'Hemingway's polydactyls,'" she said. "Four letters."

"Cats," said Bernie.

The woman started writing. "Hey! It fits! Cats is the answer! Thanks, mister."

Cats? Cats was the answer? To what? I glanced at Bernie. He seemed kind of pleased with himself. And she was pleased, too. Both of them finding something pleasing with cats. What about me, the farthest thing from a cat? Nothing pleasing about me? I look around for something to chew on, preferably something valuable, like a silk pillow of Leda's of which I still had fond memories. But there was no silk pillow in the sheriff's office, and nothing at all to chew on, valuable or not. That was the moment I felt this case—if there was a case—slipping away.

The woman, a friendly smile on her face—friendly but somewhat annoying to me—put the newspaper aside. "And what can I do for you?" She gave Bernie one of those second looks and her smile got even friendlier. "I'm deputy Summersby. Estella Summersby, actually. Everyone calls me Stell."

"Bernie Little," Bernie said. "And this is Chet. We're looking for former sheriff Cuffy."

"I haven't seen him in ages, Bernie," said Stell. "You could try Cuffy's Hardware. I think he lives in one of those apartments over the store." She pointed. "A block and a half thataway."

"Thanks," said Bernie. As we headed out, a door opened behind Stell and an apple-shaped man with a bulbous red nose and a silver star on his chest came out. That would be Sheriff Monk, no way to get that kind of detail past the Chetster. He saw us and I saw him, but only because I'm good at seeing what's behind me. Bernie's not so good at that, so he probably missed it, and we were already back on the street, the door closing behind us, when Sheriff Monk said, "What did that guy want?" So Bernie, with his hearing situation, probably missed that, too. Not my problem. Cats were my problem, although no one else seemed to have an inkling.

We walked down the street, not fast, Bernie examining the

window displays—not usually an interest of his—and even stopping in front of a jewelry store. "Hmm," he said. "Check out the size of that one." He pointed to a ring mounted on a sort of velvet finger in the window. "Way bigger than the Desert Star. I'd hate to disappoint her. On the other hand, where does it end?"

Poor guy. He was confused about something. That was as far as I could take it on my own. I pressed against him, mostly from behind, pretty much moving him along, but in the nicest way. We look out for each other, me and Bernie, and the fact that although he did lose his balance the teeniest bit he didn't come close to falling proved it, if you see what I mean.

Soon we came to a store with barbecue grills and portable fire pits in the window. We had a portable fire pit ourselves, its remains now in the garage following an incident where some of our buddies from Valley FD had swooped in at a convenient moment.

"'Cuffy's Hardware, Established 1896'," said Bernie, reading the sign. We went inside. Oh, what a wonderful floor, the wood old, worn, soft, solid! My paws love old wood. Two guys in plaid shirts were shifting a decorated Christmas tree closer to the window while a woman in a plaid shirt was saying things like "a little more this way," "back a few inches," and "not like that." The tree swayed a bit and a gold ball fell off one of its branches. Bernie caught it—the way he catches everything, his hand folding smoothly around it—and hooked the ball back on the branch, all of that in one motion.

"Hey, thanks," said the woman.

"No problem," Bernie said.

"Help you with anything?"

"I hope so," Bernie said. "We're looking for Mitch Cuffy."

The woman glanced at me. "Are you with the folks who visit seniors on the holidays?"

"That kind of thing," Bernie said.

"Two A," said the woman. "Around the back and up the stairs. He loves dogs."

We went outside, down an alley, and around to the back of Cuffy's Hardware. The back—like the backs of all the buildings I could see—was not spruced up. Rickety stairs led up to a landing with a door on either side, one with a wreath hanging on it and the other not. We went to the wreathless door. Bernie knocked.

No answer. That was surprising because I could hear someone breathing on the other side, in fact, right by the door. And not just any someone, but someone with a human male breathing sound, and a human male scent, and not only that but an old human male scent. Phew. Sometimes it's hard to keep up, but in this business keeping up is what we do.

Bernie knocked again. "Anyone home?"

Still no answer.

Bernie knocked harder. "Hello? Mitch Cuffy? Hello?"

Nothing.

Bernie shrugged, then made the *chk chk* sound, meaning we were out of there. He turned to go. I did not turn, did not go. Instead, I barked, far from my loudest or fiercest, but a rather interesting bark in my repertoire, hard to describe, except to point out it has a certain sharpness, kind of metallic, that I believe gets your attention.

"Who's there?" said the man on the other side of the door.

Fifteen

"Mr. Cuffy?" Bernie said. "My name's Bernie Little. I'm with Chet."

"Chet's a dog?"

"Definitely."

"Nobody mentioned dogs."

"No?"

"When you guys called. Holidays with a Senior, whatever the hell it was. I told them no. But nobody mentioned dogs. I woulda said yes."

"Well," said Bernie. "Here we are."

The door opened. On the other side stood an old guy wearing a robe with a hole or two in it, and a watch cap on his head. He was one of those real old guys who'd been big and strong, but mostly what was left now were his real big hands, the knuckles on his fingers all swollen, and his real big feet, one bare, one wearing a slipper. He was pretty much bald, but his eyebrows were wild and bushy. The eyes themselves were watery and colorless. They barely glanced at Bernie before fastening on me.

"A sight for sore eyes," he said.

Ah. His eyes were sore? That explained the wateriness. I was on top of my game.

Meanwhile, he was holding out his big old hand. I sniffed it. There'd been baloney in that hand and not long ago. The man—Mr. Cuffy, if I was following things right—gave me a scratch or two between the ears. Not an expert scratch but a nice try, and plenty good enough for me.

"C'mon in," said Mr. Cuffy, turning to Bernie and adding, "You, too."

At that moment a blast of cold air blew up from the alley, driving a tiny storm of snowflakes inside.

"Don't dillydally, fella," Mr. Cuffy said.

We went in, Bernie closing the door behind us.

"Sit," said Mr. Cuffy, gesturing at a couch and a chair, both lumpy and sagging, and facing a small fireplace heaped with ashes.

I know sit, of course. That's basic. We all did—Mr. Cuffy sitting on the chair, Bernie on the couch, me on the floor between them. I get between Bernie and whoever else is around unless I know them real well, just basic security.

"What'd you say his name was?" said Mr. Cuffy.

"Chet."

"Nice name. I had me a Chuckie once, had a bunch of dogs over the years. Know the problem? Their life spans don't match up with ours, leads to a good amount of grief piling up. Ever think about that?"

Bernie nodded.

"So what's the answer?"

"Couldn't tell you," Bernie said.

"C'mon, you look like a smart guy. Think."

"You overestimate me," Bernie said. "I really have no answer. I've just gone along pretending this particular problem doesn't exist."

Mr. Cuffy gazed down at his feet. There was a big bump on the side of the bare one, at the base of the big toe, and the toes were all squeezed together so tight that one was shoved up above the others in a way that looked uncomfortable. That wasn't all that was wrong with him. I could smell plenty more, going on inside.

"I never thought of that, not in all these years." Mr. Cuffy looked up. "Care for a drink?"

"If you're having one," Bernie said.

"Had to give it up," said Mr. Cuffy. "When I'm alone. But right now I'm not." He rose, or tried to, but couldn't quite do it, the chair sagging low the way it did, and he settled back down.

"Can I help?" Bernie said.

"Cupboard over the sink," said Mr. Cuffy. "Two fingers, two rocks."

Two fingers, two rocks? That sounded alarming. Bernie rose and I half-rose, ready for anything. He crossed the room to the kitchen part—maybe I should have already mentioned that Mr. Cuffy's apartment seemed to be one of those all-in-one room places—and opened the cupboard over the sink. Then came a side trip to the fridge, some banging around with ice trays, and soon he and Mr. Cuffy were clinking glasses and saying cheers. There was no sign yet of fingers or rocks so I relaxed on that score, although not completely.

"How about a fire?" Bernie said.

"That'd be nice. I'm a lazy bastard these days. That's one of those things they don't tell you about old age. You become a lazy bastard."

"Don't be too hard on yourself," Bernie said.

He got busy by the fireplace and poof! Soon we had a nice roaring fire, which is the only kind Bernie makes. Mr. Cuffy kept an eye on Bernie the whole time, and as Bernie rose he said, "You're not from around here, are you?"

"No," said Bernie, sticking the poker back on its stand.

"Where you from?"

"Arizona."

"You a cop?"

"No."

"Sure about that? Chet's got that K-nine look."

Bernie sat back down on the couch. "I'm a private investigator. We're a team, Chet and I."

"So the holiday for seniors thing is total bullshit."

"I wouldn't say that. We're just not officially part of it, that's all."

"Cut the smart talk. That don't work on me." Mr. Cuffy made a cutting gesture, maybe forgetting about the glass in his hand. Bourbon—the aroma very familiar to me—slopped over the side. Mr. Cuffy frowned and drank what was left in one swig. "So you're here under a . . . what's the word?"

"Pretext," Bernie said.

Mr. Cuffy nodded, then held out his glass. "I'll have another."

Bernie went to the cupboard and returned with the bottle.

"Two fingers?" he said.

I stood up.

Bernie poured some bourbon into Mr. Cuffy's glass and sat back down. So did I. The fingers on his hands looked unharmed, and so did Mr. Cuffy's, allowing for the swollen knuckles. No one understands Bernie more than me, but that doesn't mean I understand every little thing he does. Like why he married Leda in the first place, for example. He doesn't understand that one either, by the way: I've heard him ask that very question more than once, but never when anyone else was around, excepting me, of course. Also he sometimes says: "Why the hell did she marry me?" Bernie hardly ever makes no sense at all, but there you go.

Mr. Cuffy sipped his drink and sighed. "The second glass is always the best. That's how come it's hard to stop. One is good, two is better, so who wouldn't think he was on a roll?"

Bernie smiled and took a sip himself, but very small, more like a taste.

"So what is it you want from me?" Mr. Cuffy said.

"Information," Bernie said. "Specifically about the Teddy Leeford case."

Mr. Cuffy's old head came up fast, like he'd been hit. The skin on his face seemed to tighten, showing what was beneath. I'd seen that look before, but only on perps. Was Mr. Cuffy a perp? Would I soon be grabbing him by the pant leg? That was going to be a problem. For one thing, Mr. Cuffy wasn't wearing pants. For another—maybe because of his feet, one bare, one in a worn old slipper—I just didn't want to.

Mr. Cuffy started to lower his glass on the arm of the chair, then changed his mind and took another big swallow instead.

"Who's your client?" he said. "Who's paying you?"

Bernie shook his head. "We keep that confidential."

"Course you do. But you expect me to spill my guts. Everybody wants it both ways. That's what's gone wrong with this country."

"You'd do exactly the same thing in our place," Bernie said.

Mr. Cuffy glanced at me. He set his glass on the arm of the chair. I'd seen guts spilled before, not a pleasant sight but it's that kind of career. I checked Mr. Cuffy's belly and then Bernie's. We were good, at least for now.

"Why, then?" Mr. Cuffy said. "How come you're asking?"

"Another man turned up at the bottom of Devil's Purse," Bernie said.

Mr. Cuffy went still. "Dead?"

"No," Bernie said. "He's in a coma at the hospital."

Mr. Cuffy licked his lips. His tongue looked cracked and dry. "Was he shot?"

"No."

Mr. Cuffy's thick eyebrows rose. "So he fell?"

"Maybe."

"A tourist?"

"No. His name's Chaz LeWitte."

"Never heard of him. But there's so many new folks around these days."

"His employer's not new," Bernie said. "Chaz works for Ariadne Carlisle."

Mr. Cuffy reached for his glass. Then he had second thoughts, or maybe it was because his hand had gotten shaky.

"You know her?" Bernie said.

"Knew her, yes," said Mr. Cuffy. "Way, way back. Haven't laid eyes on her in years. More like decades." His eyes, which had a somewhat faraway look in them anyway, got more so. "That who you're working for? Ariadne?"

"I've already told you our answer to that," Bernie said.

Mr. Cuffy turned to him, the look in his eyes coming closer to the here and now. "A tough son of a bitch? Think you can bully me? Dime a dozen."

Had the conversation taken a turn for the worse? I knew dimes, of course, had seen Bernie shooting spinning ones right out of the air with the .38 Special. But we'd left it in the safe at home because . . . well, because this case was about a reindeer, wasn't it? And we don't shoot reindeers, me and Bernie. That's the kind of thing I know for a fact.

"What would I be bullying you into?" Bernie said.

Mr. Cuffy opened his mouth, closed it, looked down.

"Something on your mind?" Bernie said.

Mr. Cuffy shook his head, kind of overdoing it, like he was trying to shake something right out of it. He reached for his glass, hand steadier now, and downed what was left of it. Then he wiped his mouth with the back of his hand and said, "This new . . . this guy . . . LeWitte, did you say?"

Bernie nodded.

"What's his job up there at the ranch?"

"Personal assistant."

Mr. Cuffy gazed across the room, into the fire. "What's that mean, the personal part?"

Bernie shrugged. "I assume he helps keep things organized."

"Like what?"

"The schedule. Travel arrangements. Dinner reservations. Things like that."

"What else?"

"What are you looking for, Mr. Cuffy?"

"Nothin'. And no one calls me that."

"What do they call you?"

"Sheriff, but I don't like that neither. I'm not the sheriff no more, haven't been sheriff since . . . since I don't know who was president. Who even cares these days? You get the president you deserve—ever heard that one?"

"Not till now," Bernie said. "What do you want me to call you?"

"Mitch. It's not short for Mitchell. My old man kept things simple. Mitch, that's it."

"All right, Mitch," Bernie said. "Tell us about the Teddy Leeford case."

"Who's us?" said Mr. Cuffy, now Mitch instead, on account of something about an old man, not Mitch, if I was getting this right, but some other old man.

"Me and Chet."

Mitch's eyes shifted in my direction. "But he's a dog."

"Very much so."

There's no fooling Bernie about things like that. He really is perfection.

Mitch nodded. "Makes sense." He sat back in his chair, almost like he was getting ready for a ride to some place far away. "The Teddy Leeford case never got solved. Stays open, of course, like all murder cases, but eventually it just fades away. Not that you give up. More like it gives up on you." He raised his empty glass. "Throat's getting a mite dry."

Bernie refilled it. Mitch gave the glass a little wiggle.

"Rocks, all the same to you," he said. "No rocks and folks might speculate about a drinking problem. Rocks and you're a solid citizen."

Bernie went to the fridge, again banged around with ice trays, and returned with some ice cubes which he dumped in Mitch's glass. I came oh so close to a thought about rocks and ice cubes.

"Much obliged," said Mitch, taking a sip. "Where were we?"

"Teddy Leeford," Bernie said.

Mitch nodded. "Basically a good kid. Big and strong, outdoorsman type—skiing the chutes, camping outdoors in all weather, rock climbing."

"And aside from basically?" Bernie said.

"Nothin'. Boys rough housed back then. It was expected. It's not like he had a mean streak. Didn't know his own strength—that would be more the way it was."

"So he got in a lot of fights?"

"Some, I'd say. Bar room stuff. Back then the drinking age wasn't enforced all that strictly up here in the mountains. The old west hadn't quite died out. Dead and buried now, of course. What we got now is—well, you can see for yourself. The city boy, version, actually more like the city gal." Mitch swirled his drink around. "Life was better then, and not just because I was young."

"Did Teddy Leeford have a criminal record?"

"No, nothin' like that. This was a peaceable county, just a touch on the wild side. And in the last few months of his life Teddy got himself straightened out. Matured, like, so he was still a fun guy, but within bounds."

"How did that happen?"

"Oh, it was Ariadne, for sure. He was head over heels."

"Did you know her back then?"

Mitch nodded. "I'd known her since she was so high, from being here in the summers. Ariadne was a great one for horses and Gina ran a small stable. Comanche—that was Ariadne's favorite."

"Who's Gina?" Bernie said.

"My late wife," said Mitch.

"I'm sorry."

"Don't be. Her health went to pieces. In the end . . ." He made a little sound in his throat, very, very little but I caught it: a sort of moan. Then he reached for his glass, but paused, and didn't touch it. "Anyways, we're off topic. The point is Teddy was on track. Not a surprise, Ariadne or no Ariadne. He came from good people. His dad taught gym at Bridger High and his momma was the nurse." Mitch shook his head. "He was the one fainted when I came telling them the news. She caught him before he hit the floor. I'll never forget that part."

"Are the parents still around?" Bernie said.

Mitch shook his head. "Died a few years back. One of those

deals where they go within hours of each other. Turns out to be a real thing."

He gazed into his glass and went on gazing until Bernie said, "What else do you remember about the case?"

The fire made a popping sound and some sparks flew out, landing not far from me. My tail—acting on its own, the way it does from time to time—flicked them away. Bernie rose and moved the fire screen closer to the fire. Mitch looked up.

"It was the same time of year as now," he said, "but there'd already been lots of snow, so I was on the road, making sure we'd chained off all the high passes, closing them down, when the call came in. Some snowshoers had spotted a body down at the bottom of Devil's Purse. I went out there with a deputy I had back then, expert climber, and we got ourselves down. Teddy Leeford, lying on his back, although I didn't ID him till I got the snow brushed offa his face. He was pretty much frozen already. Looked like a fall at first, an accident, but when we hauled him up and got his ski hat off, there was the bullet hole."

Mitch touched the back of his head. When he withdrew his hand he did it very slowly and his eyes had an inward look.

"And after that?" Bernie said.

"Forensics, canvassing for witnesses, timeline, all the usual. Came to a dead end."

"How about starting with the forensics?" Bernie said.

"Single round, I remember that. Can't say about the caliber, distance, none of that. A long time ago, like I said."

"That's okay," Bernie said. "It'll all be in the file. Is it online?"

Mitch shook his head. "They never got the funding for scanning that far back."

"Where's the paper original?"

"All that's down in the basement at the county office."

"We'll need to see it."

"They'll want to know why and they're not specially fond of PI's. And that's in-state PI's. Outta state is worse."

"Will they want to know why if you do the asking?"

"And leave you out of it?"

"You could say you were taking a little trip down memory lane."

"That's pretty feeble. Here I was—starting to think you were smart. And why would I want to leave you out of it in the first place? You paying me?"

"How much?"

Mitch leaned forward and wagged his twisted old finger. "That's an insult. I might notta done much in my life but I never took a goddam payoff."

"I take it back," Bernie said.

"Take it back? What are you? Some kid?"

"Then I apologize."

Mitch went on glaring. Finally, he said, "Okay, then," and sank back in his chair. He gazed at me. I gazed back at him. "I'll do it for Chet," he said. "Try out your pathetic memory lane theory."

"Thank you."

"Don't thank me. Didn't I just make that clear? Thank your big ol' buddy here. Maybe throw him a bone once in a while."

Up until that moment, I'd been going back and forth on Mitch Cuffy. But all at once it was obvious: he was aces.

"I promise," Bernie said.

What a nice day this was turning into! I moved slightly closer to Bernie. He didn't have a single bone on him right now, no treat of any kind, so my plan was to ease him on out of here and outside, where there had to be some sort of convenience store. Convenience stores display their bones, chewies, and other treats in different spots on the floor, but I always know where they are the instant I come through the door.

"You ever solve a cold case?" Mitch said.

"One or two," said Bernie.

"Run me through one of 'em," Mitch said. "Run me through one of them cold cases of yours."

"There was this faded country singer, a woman named Lotty Pilgrim who never made it big in the first place, although she did write one song that got a lot of play."

"What was that?"

"'How You Hung the Moon.'"

"Yeah?" said Mitch. "Gina loved that song."

Mitch got a look in his eye, like he was leaving for somewhere else. Bernie started in on the Lotty Pilgrim case, not easy to follow even if you'd been there, which I had. But there was no forgetting a horse name of Mingo who turned out not to be a team player. Oddly enough, when he got to the end, Bernie had told the whole story without mentioning Mingo.

At first Mitch was silent. It was very quiet in his little apartment, except for the crackling fire. Then Mitch plucked an ice cube out of his glass and tossed it into the fire, making a brief but very satisfying sizzle.

"Teddy Leeford was a moon hanger," he said. "They can leave a hole in people when they go, worse when they go so young."

"What do you mean?" Bernie said.

"He was a dreamer—the dreaming half of the team. And the dream came true, never mind that it turned out to have downsides he didn't think of. Anyways, he never got to see it."

"Are you talking about Ariadne?" Bernie said. "Were they a team?"

Mitch shook his head. "They were boyfriend and girlfriend. The team was Teddy and Drake."

"Who's Drake?"

"Teddy's big brother. Well, older brother, but not bigger, Teddy was six five, after all, built like a tight end. Drake was a smaller version, but you see that with older brothers sometimes."

"The two of them had some sort of dream?" Bernie said.

"Sure as hell did. There's lots of young men with dreams—familiar at all with the history of the West, Bernie?"

"Some."

"Then you know that ninety-nine point whatever you want percent, those dreams don't pan out. But when they do, well, Katy bar the door."

Ah ha! Sometimes you're just drifting along—completely out of the picture would be the truth—and suddenly *boom*! Back on track, in fact, leading the parade. I knew Katy, a biker gal who runs a biker bar—Katy's Bar—way out in the desert. And it has a door—swinging doors, in fact, somewhat shot up but still working, last time we were there. In short, I was all over whatever Mitch was talking about, so all over it that my mind felt free to wander to the subject of parades. I'd seen parades, of course, so often annoyingly led by a person on horseback. Why would a horse lead a parade? Why not some other . . . whoa! Why not me? Why not me, Chet the Jet, at the front of a parade? Oh, how I wanted that! No parades were happening here in Mitch's apartment, so instead of making any sort of fuss I simply filed the thought away, all set to go when the time was right. And one day—maybe tomorrow!—the time would be right. It's that kind of world.

"So," Bernie was saying, "what was this dream that came true?"

"All around you," Mitch said.

"I don't understand."

"Silver Mountain."

"You mean this town?"

"This town the way it is now, not the shabby little backwater it was. And not just the town—the ski resort, the condos, the hotels, the whole development, all built, run, and owned by Silver Mountain Development, meaning Drake Leeford."

"Where did the money come from?" Bernie said.

"Borrowed, mostly, as I recall. But the Leefords had land going way back to mining days, not useful land, at least at the time, no silver on it in spite of the name—basically the whole back side of the mountain, where all the black diamond runs are now. Teddy took a trip down to Taos and came back with the idea that they—him and Drake—had a similar layout. Potentially, I'm saying. Which is what they borrowed on to get started."

"Did they have any business enemies?" Bernie said.

Mitch shook his head. "Not that I got wind of, and I checked it out. Checked out everything—business enemies, personal enemies, some out of season hunter mistaking Teddy for game and then too lily livered to come forward—and came up with nothing." He turned to Bernie, his eyes suddenly angry. "So all these goddam years later, what makes you think you'll do any better?"

"I don't think that," Bernie said.

"Then what's the point?"

"To try anyway."

"Just based off this other body down there?"

"He's not dead yet," Bernie said.

Mitch rose, not easily, and made his way over to the fireplace.

He grabbed the poker and started jabbing at the fire, kind of fiercely, like he was trying to kill it. That doesn't work with fires, only makes them fierce, too. The flames shone in Mitch's eyes.

"I'll do it for Chet," he said. "Not you."

Hadn't he said that already? I watched Bernie, waiting for him to make some brilliant comeback. He kept his mouth shut.

Sixteen

Two dudes riding slowly down the main drag of this town—the town being Silver Mountain and the main drag called Bonanza Street, if my facts were right—taking in the fancy sights, those two dudes being Bernie at the wheel and me, Chet, in the shotgun seat, actually handling the steering, although it's hard to explain exactly how.

"What's going on with these names?" Bernie said. "Prada, Vuitton, Bulgari—they have a kind of magnetic power over people, but not all people. How come?"

Prada? Vuitton? Bulgari? Almost certainly perps of some sort. Did they know they'd end up breaking rocks in the hot sun, trying to look good in orange? What perps know and don't know is a huge subject, trust me on that, but there's no time to go into it now.

"But on the other hand," he said, popping the glove box open as we came to a stop at a red light. He took out the little purple box and had a look at the Desert Star. "What wrong with liking beautiful things? So the screw up must have something to do with the symbolism. If the symbolism is true then the thing is right."

Uh-oh. Where was this going? Nowhere good, that was certain. But then Bernie did something surprising. He closed the velvet box and put it back in the glove compartment. That wasn't the surprising part. The surprising part was that before he put the box in the glove compartment, he gave it a kiss. Just a quick kiss—you could almost call it shy—but I'd never seen Bernie kiss an object before. Charlie, yes. Weatherly, yes. Suzie, who came before Weatherly, yes. His mom, yes—she taps her cheek for where and when she wants a kiss every time she comes to visit. And me, of course, always on the top of my head, oh, so nice! And, oh dear, once or twice, Trixie! Why on earth? But forget that last one. The point is he'd never kissed an object, not in my presence. Not even the .38 Special. Wouldn't you want to kiss the .38 Special after it was done shooting spinning dimes out of the air for you? But no.

The light turned green, and someone honked behind us, maybe more than one someone.

"Honking comes with all the rest of it, Prada and those others," Bernie said, and we rolled on, him with a little smile on his face and me clearing my mind, which happened in a flash. I felt tip top.

"What we need to do is recon the whole area," Bernie said, "not just the ranch. We have to feel the pulse, as they say. And I'm not feeling it. How about we start with the skiing?"

That sounded great! Although if I'd given it a moment's thought I'd have realized I had no idea what he meant. But I didn't give it a moment's thought. My mind is on my side. It thinks to itself, Hey, Chet, don't you trouble yourself about a thing. Is that how your mind runs, looking out for you? I sure hope so.

We drove out of town and followed a wide and smooth road that curved up and up. Snow began to fall again, the flakes fat and fluffy. The wipers went back and forth, back and forth. Before my eyes closed completely, I caught a glimpse of a towering peak mostly bare but with snowy white ribbons twisting down its green face.

"Wakie wakie, big guy."

I opened my eyes. We were parked in front of a sort of rough-hewn wooden building with a huge wooden skier on the roof, a cowboy hat on his head and what looked like what we call a spliff in our business, a rather enormous one, between his lips. The tips of his skis hung over the edge of the roof and his eyes were the crazy type.

"This looks promising," Bernie said.

We went inside. The only guy around was a bearded dude rubbing a yellowish waxy bar along the bottom of a ski, the smell very pleasant. Skiing made a good impression on me from the get-go.

"Help you?" said the bearded dude.

"Looking to rent skis and boots," Bernie said.

"Good timing. We've got snow at last and there's a super big dump on the way."

Interesting, although you usually can sniff out an indication regarding big dumps, and there wasn't a trace of it in the air.

The bearded dude stuck the waxy bar in the back pocket of his overalls. "How would you rate yourself? Beginner, intermediate, advanced?"

"Well, I haven't skied in years."

Whoa! Bernie'd skied ever? Why was I just finding this out now?

"Beginner, then?" said the bearded guy.

"Whatever you think."

"What sort of skiing did you do when you skied?"

"It was on leave when I was in the service."

"Here in Colorado?"

"Mostly in Europe but once in Colorado."

"Here?"

"No," Bernie said. "Up at A-Basin."

"Cool. I love A-Basin. Remember the names of any of the runs you skied there?"

Bernie thought. "There's the one that starts off at one of those cornices."

"The Pallavicini?"

"Yeah, I think so."

"You handled the Pallavicini?"

"Well, not all of it. The snow was coming down pretty good and I took a wrong turn, ended up in some gullies."

"You skied the Gullies?"

Bernie laughed. "There was no choice."

The expression in the bearded dude's eyes changed, like he was seeing Bernie fresh. Then he seemed to notice me for the first time.

"This your dog?"

"We're more like partners."

"He looks like one of those avy dogs."

"Don't give him ideas."

Too late! Avy dog? Sounded great! My ears rose up on their own, ready for more on the subject, starting with what an avy dog actually did. But there was no more. Instead, we headed over to the ski boot area and then the skis area and poles area and the jacket and pants area and goggles, helmets and gloves area, and I began to learn that skiing was a very tiring sport.

"I can sell you a lift ticket, too," said the bearded guy. He checked his watch. "Half-day pass? Two day? Week? Season?"

"Half-day," said Bernie.

"Here's a trail map. Sick pow on the way but for now Figaro's Leap is your best bet, Mr. Pallavicini. Gnarly off the top and in spots, but you'll be fine."

We went outside, just me and Bernie. He put on the helmet. I was not cool with that but I kept the feeling to myself.

"Two things, big guy," Bernie said. "First, we can't afford skiing. Second, if this place was cut off from the rest of the world, they'd be speaking their own language in ten years."

I missed whatever that was, on account of how closely I was watching Bernie do all sorts of new things, like somehow clicking right into his skis, pulling goggles over his eyes—helmet and goggles, too? Like he was changing into someone else? Or . . . or hiding on me? Hiding on me! That was it! This was all a game!

And off we went, Bernie sort of skating along a flat stretch between the rental place and the bottom of the hill—skating on skis, can you imagine? The one and only Bernie. And me charging in circles around him as he glided along, round and round and round, raising a sort of snowstorm with my paws. The Little Detective Agency, ladies and gentlemen! Any questions?

We came to a sort of shed where chairs on cables were coming and going. A chairlift! I'd seen one before and remembered it well from a case involving something or other, no actual details available at the moment. No other skiers were around. A young woman wearing huge furry boots stepped out of the shed as a chair came around.

"That an avy dog?" she said.

"Not yet."

"Is he familiar with the lift? We don't generally—"

Familiar was what, again? Meanwhile here was the chair, now right behind us. What fun! A moving chair! You had to love Bernie, and I did. I hopped right on and Bernie joined me, perhaps somewhat awkwardly.

"He is now," Bernie said.

I barked a savage bark, for reasons unknown but very satisfying. The young woman's eyes opened wide.

"Get ready," Bernie said, as we approached the top. "As soon as it flattens out a bit and we're close to—"

And there was more, which I missed on account of the wind in my ears as I soared through the air—really like a bird, except in a much better mood than any bird I've ever seen—and stuck the landing the way I always stick landings, sticking them but good. Sometimes that sends a little jolt through your body but not in this snow-covered ground, soft like a pillow.

I turned to Bernie just in time to see him gliding away from the chair. He skated over my way—skating on skis again, so it was no fluke—and did a little half swing around, coming to a quick stop that sent snow spraying my way from the edges of his skis. It got all over me! How much fun was this? Leave it to Bernie, coming up with a brand-new game right out of the blue. Again, Bernie! Again! Snow shower me again!

But no. Instead, he looked all around and said, "Top of the world, Chet."

He was right, no surprise there. We'd found the top of the world. Nothing was above us and everything was below, even the tops of other mountains. Chet and Bernie, on top of the world at last! All our problems were gone just like that, poof!

Although we actually had no problems. Well, except for the finances part. Did this mean our finances were now in good shape? That was my takeaway.

Bernie pointed with his ski pole. "Way down there is the ranch. The roofs are all red—how did I miss that before? And just to the north, see that steep slope with the rocky cliff? Gotta be Mount Murdstone, and that ledge at the side must be the top of Devil's Purse. Just a mile, maybe a mile and half from here, as the crow flies. A kind of isosceles triangle, with us at the apex." He glanced at me. "Do some crimes have a hidden geometry about them? Maybe Euclid would have made a good cop."

Bernie looked all right but perhaps he'd suddenly gone feverish. Out of all that palaver, the only thing that stuck—aside from this Euclid fellow, probably not a perp if he was a cop, although not for sure—was the crow. I checked the sky and wouldn't you know? A black bird, circling high above. You might say, well, Chet, maybe not a crow, right? Unless, with those ears of yours you could hear it cawing even at this distance. Which I could have done in a snap if it had been cawing, except it was not. But unlike other birds, crows always have something on their minds when they fly, specifically something perpy. That black bird up there was flying in a perpy manner. So therefore: a crow. And what was this? I'd just done a so-therefore, normally Bernie's department? Did that mean he'd soon be doing things in my department, like . . . like peeing on hydrants, for example? But perhaps a bad example, since I'd already seen him peeing on hydrants, and more than once.

As we turned to go—we often move as one, me and Bernie—he suddenly paused and took another look into the distance, over toward Mount Murdstone.

"What's that dark patch?" He pointed with his ski pole. "Not far from Devil's Purse. A cave, maybe, tucked into the side of that hill? Maybe the entrance to some old mine?" He got an idea. "They sell calendars with abandoned mine photos, a different abandoned mine for each month. Might make a nice stocking stuffer. The ring plus the stocking stuffer—how does that sound?"

He'd lost me completely, but it didn't matter because now we were on the move again, over to a tree that stood at one side of a trail, a tree with a sign nailed to it, and on that sign two black shapes like you see on some playing cards. No time now to get into my one visit to Valley PD poker night, and not a big deal in the first place since that poker chip had ended up going right through me, no harm, no foul.

Bernie read the sign. "'Figaro's Leap, experts only.' Double black diamond." He gazed down the trail. "He said gnarly off the top but it doesn't look like much from here."

Well, perhaps not, but a very pleasant view all the same, a snowy trail without a track of any kind on it, sloping gently down with trees standing on either side, some with yellowish bark and leafless, others of the Christmas tree type, and then making a turn not too far away, the rest of the trail hidden from sight after that.

"I'll go first," Bernie said, "see if I can still carve a turn or two. You follow, but not too close. Got it?"

What was there to get? I took off down the trail.

"Um," said Bernie.

I didn't waste a second on that um—ums can mean anything. Instead, I ran down the trail, not close to my fastest, more like a ramble. The air up here! Fabulous. It made me want to ramble the whole day away in this snowy silence. And then I heard this soft whoosh-whoosh-whoosh from behind, those whooshes sounding quick and powerful and sure. I glanced back and there was Bernie, all at once the most graceful Bernie I'd ever seen, like a dancer! By which I don't mean like a Bernie dancer, since I'd seen Bernie dance on more than one occasion, and despite how much fun he had dancing you couldn't really call it graceful, even though that last time Weatherly hadn't needed a cast on her foot, according to the doc. The whooshing had to be the sound of turns when they get carved, but the look was dancing. He danced right by me, a big grin on his face, and whooshed around that first corner.

Hadn't he told me to lead the way? I had a distinct memory of that. I bounded after him and reached the first corner after hardly any more bounds at all, but what was this? Our gentle trail had disappeared? Well, maybe not disappeared but turned into something very, very narrow like . . . like a chute or a gully, with sharp-topped rocks poking through the snow all over the place, and what was more and where I probably should have started in the first place, the trail was now pointing pretty much straight down.

As for Bernie, at first I didn't see him at all, but only because I was looking in the wrong places, namely down among all the sharp-pointed rocks. But Bernie wasn't down there, all twisted up and hurt. Instead, he was in mid-air, soaring, his body relaxed and leaning over his skis. What a sight! Take that, you birds! Then slowly and smoothly he came back to earth, touching gently down on a patch of snow free from rocks, and right away—whoosh-whoosh-whoosh—he carved his way down this chute or gully and zipped around another bend with a cry of "Weeeeeoooo Mama!"

I tore off after him, my paws touching down, but not often. Mostly I was just steering myself through the air. Yes! Like a bird, but not a crow, or one of those tiny twittering types. No! Like an eagle! That was Chet the Jet this wonderful day on Figaro's Leap. I flew around the bend and oh, what a nice surprise! Figaro's Leap got even steeper and narrower. You might even think and more dangerous, too. But I did not and neither did Bernie. He was already way, way down there, his body relaxed and still with only his feet seeming to do any work at all, almost like the skis knew the way on their own. I caught up, of course, hardly bears mentioning, although where I caught up might not have been the best choice, since it seemed to be the narrowest, steepest, twistiest part of the whole shooting match, sheer cliffs rising high on both sides, close enough for me to touch at the same time if I'd wanted to, and I sort of did. We'll have to get into shooting matches another time, about which I have many, many stories, some bloody and some not, but you see the problem, with me going faster than Bernie and no room to pass.

So what did I do? You guessed it. Maybe you'd have done the same. Ha! Please pardon that ha. As for what I did, well, it was pretty simple. I flew right over Bernie, saw him like I never had, just the top of his helmeted head, his hands out front, his ski boots, and that was it. Just superb.

I stuck the landing, although for less than a moment, all the time it took for me to get airborne again, and meantime I heard Bernie.

"Oh my God! Chet!"

I bounded and flew, bounded and flew—there really wasn't much to skiing if you thought about it, no real skill involved but it sure was fun—and took another sharp turn. But that was pretty much the end because the trail began to widen and flatten out and all at once I was no longer airborne or bounding but just trotting along on a wide snowy slope, the snow not hard, not soft, just right, and the slope not gentle but not steep either. I turned around in time to see Bernie come flying out of the chute and onto this broad slope, the sun coming out at that exact moment, making a kind of glowing beauty—white, green, and gold—I'd never seen before. Bernie straightened slightly and began to laugh, a low, burbling laugh that went on and on like some lovely creek. He glided toward me in a long curve and stopped by my side.

"Gnarly, big guy—it's not like we weren't warned."

Then he fell down, just like that, *ka-boom,* and lay on his back—heels of the skis in the snow and the tips sticking out sideways—and laughed and laughed, pausing to say "gnarly," from time to time, which always got the laughing going again. Was he all right? I leaned down and licked his face. Which was when he started to sing. At least I thought it was singing but it made no sense.

"Figaro qua, Figaro la, Figaro su, Figaro gi! Fee-ga-ro! Fee-ga-ro!"

I was wondering whether or not this was worrisome, when two shadows, big and human, suddenly loomed over us.

Seventeen

Two human shadows suddenly looming over us? From out of nowhere? Suddenly looming and out of nowhere do not happen when Chet is in charge of security, and Chet is always in charge of security, especially when Bernie's on the premises, like now. I whirled around, whirling my whole body real quick the way I can, ready for anything.

Two men on skis stood over us, one big—about Bernie's size—and the other bigger. Behind them I could see a fairly wide ski trail, not too steep, with lots of skiers on it. Figaro's Leap seemed to have merged with this run, a run that continued after the flattish stretch we were on, so just from that my mind somehow knew these two dudes had come from up thataway. There are times when my mind pitches in, just one more lucky thing about me. But back to these guys, both wearing white jackets, orange helmets, and orange pants, with orange writing on the chests of their jackets. Those orange pants interested me, but there was no time to figure out how come.

The real big guy spoke. "Sir? You all right?"

Maybe I should have mentioned that Bernie was still singing his Figaro song, his gaze directed straight up at the sky, so suddenly blue. But now he shut that singing down pronto.

"Uh, yeah, fine thanks, just um." And somehow he scrambled out of that strange position—the heels of his skis stuck in the snow and all that—in a jif, and stood up.

"Oh, good," said the real big guy. He pointed with his ski pole. "For a moment there we thought you might have come out of Figaro's Leap."

"We did," Bernie said.

Both dudes gazed at Bernie, their eyes dark and not easy to read behind their goggles.

"How was it?" said the real big guy.

Bernie laughed. "Hard to say—it was over so fast."

Wasn't that funny? You get a feel for when humans are about to laugh, and I got it now, but there was no laughter from these guys.

Now the smaller of the two big guys spoke for the first time. His voice was deeper than the bigger guy's, more like Bernie's or even deeper, but not so . . . so musical. Whoa! Was Bernie's voice a kind of music? Why had it taken me so long to get here? And now the whole Figaro singing thing made perfect sense.

What the smaller guy said was, "Know this gentleman, Von?"

The bigger guy, almost certainly named Von if I was catching the drift, raised his goggles and had a good look at Bernie. And I had a good look at him. Von's eyes turned out not to be dark at all, but an icy blue. His face was tan and weathered, not in an old person way, rather in the way of a younger guy who spends a lot of time outdoors, Bernie being another example, although much nicer to look at, goes without mentioning.

"Nope," Von said.

"Me either," said the other guy. "And I thought I knew all the rippers on the mountain."

"I'm no ripper," Bernie said.

The smaller guy shook his head. "Figaro's Leap is the real deal." He raised his goggles, his eyes turning out to be even deeper and darker than they'd looked under them. He was older than Von, with salt and pepper hair and skin that was aged by time as well as the weather, but he talked and carried himself like someone younger. "First time here at Silver?"

"It is." Bernie checked the writing on their jackets. "You with the ski patrol?"

"No," said the dark-eyed guy, "but our ski patrol is second to none, won the state competition three years running. This here's Von Sikes, director of ski operations. I own the place. Name's Drake Leeford." He held out his hand.

Drake Leeford? The name meant nothing to me, or almost nothing, and it might as well have meant absolutely nothing because I couldn't get past the almost. At the same time I knew the name meant something to Bernie, although nothing showed on his face. But I can feel things going on inside him—perhaps? Was it possible?—one of the reasons for the success of the Little Detective Agency? Wow! Except for the finances, of course.

Bernie shook hands with Drake Leeford and Von Sikes, all of them keeping their ski gloves on, which seemed a bit strange to me, but so did clothing in the first place, so pay no attention.

"Bernie Little," Bernie said.

If folks have heard of Bernie—and we see lots of that, especially among the perp community—I know it right away. These dudes had not. We were far from home. That explained it.

"And this is Chet," Bernie went on. "He beat me down that run, and by plenty."

Then all eyes were on me. I was sitting nice and tall in the snow, perfectly positioned between these two dudes—super friendly, sure, but still pretty much strangers—and Bernie.

"Looks like an avy dog," Von said.

Avy dog? Again? Why? What did it mean? Nevertheless, my tail began swishing back and forth in the snow, so maybe avy dog was a good thing. Sometimes your tail sorts things out for you, as you may or may not know, but probably not. Whoa! All at once the whole clothing thing which came up so recently grew clear. If you have a tail clothes don't work. So they're instead of a tail. A poor substitute, to my way of thinking. No offense.

"He's not," Bernie said.

"Unfortunately," Von said, "we've got rules about non-avy dogs on the mountain."

"No doubt about it," said Drake, "but some rules are meant to be broken, and this is one. We want rippers on the mountain. The non-rippers—meaning the vast majority of our paying customers—see them and take lessons."

"Yes, sir," said Von.

"But you might be interested in our avy training program, Bernie," Drake said.

"There's a thought," said Bernie.

"Got one of those coupons, Von?" Drake said.

Von reached inside his jacket.

"And how about a couple of free drink tickets, good at any of our drinking and dining establishments?" Drake said.

"Sure thing." Von handed over some stuff to Bernie.

"Very nice of you," Bernie said. "A beautiful mountain, Drake. How long have you owned it?"

"Since the beginning." Drake smiled. He had those very white teeth you see a lot these days, kind of gleaming and all pretty much the same size. "It's my baby. Happy trails."

They skated away, heading downhill, bobbed over a dip and were soon out of sight. Bernie turned to me. "Sometimes Trudi Tremaine asks questions she knows the answers to. What did she call it? Her modus? I should do more of that."

What? Why? And who was Trudi Tremaine? A perp? For some reason I thought not.

We drove up the red and green brick road and stopped at the gatehouse. The tall dude—Santa's gatekeeper, if I remembered right—leaned out with a smile, a smile that would have been a lot bigger except he had a candy cane sticking out the side of his mouth.

"Chet! And, uh, Bernie! Enjoying the snow?"

"Very much," said Bernie.

"Didn't realize you was a skier."

"Well, I'm really . . ."

But there was no denying it, since when we returned the rental ski equipment, the bearded dude said something about a sale and the next thing I knew we were buying new skis, boots, poles, pants, jacket, gloves, helmet, goggles, plus a special ski rack that would work on the Beast, the bearded dude very nicely making sure it fit just right. True, there was a bit of an issue with our credit card when the time came to pay, but then deep in his wallet Bernie found another credit card he'd forgotten about and never used.

"It's like striking gold," Bernie said, and the bearded dude laughed and laughed. You can't beat the holidays. That was my takeaway.

Meanwhile, back to Santa's gatekeeper, who'd reached out and was running his hand gently over the tips of one of his skis. "Sweet boards," he said.

"Thanks," said Bernie, in that shy way he sometimes surprises you with. All I know is that Bernie's surprises are always good ones.

"Let it snow, let it snow, let it snow!" Santa's gatekeeper sang. Then he tapped the roof of the Beast and raised the gate.

We followed the red and green brick road to the ranch, soon caught up to a car-hauling trailer, the kind we often see on the highways except instead of cars this one was carrying . . . well, I didn't know what.

"Santa's sleigh," Bernie said. "Just look at it."

I looked and saw a sort of very big red—not chair, but . . . but loveseat. I'd sat on a loveseat once. This was in the More part of Livia Moon's Coffee and more place, specifically in Livia's office in the More part, where we were working a case and Livia wanted Bernie to stick around for something or other, the actual reason never clear in my mind. All I really remember was her sitting on her red love seat and patting the space beside her, and of course I'd jumped right up. Livia had flashed me a big smile but under her breath she'd said, "Not you, darlin'." Very confusing, and still more so when back outside Bernie had said, "Thanks, big guy." For what? Here might be a good place to add that when it comes to how men and women get along I often end up being puzzled. These things are arranged much differently in the nation within.

But back to Santa's sleigh, which looked a lot like Livia Moon's loveseat, except for the fact that it stood on what appeared to be very long and wide skis that curved up high at the front end. Santa, if I was in the picture, was Hal, so I knew Santa. I also knew Livia Moon. Did Hal know Livia? Would she be sitting up there next to him anytime soon? Just one more thing to look forward to.

We tailed the sleigh hauler all the way to Cratchit house, where we stopped, the hauler continuing in the direction of the big house down the street, named the North Pole if memory serves—a big if.

We went inside. "Hungry?" Bernie said.

Famished.

"Skiing will do that," he said, and right away started cooking up a big juicy steak. He cut it down the middle.

"Even Steven."

A bit of puzzler. Did that mean even Steven was in for a bite or two? Anyone else? But how could it be Steven, when the only Steven we knew, Steven "The Weevil" Bole was far away at the moment, safely behind razor wire at Northern State Correctional, something to do with a scam he had going, perhaps involving the sale of lunar panels to elderly homeowners. But there was no knock on the door from Stevie Weevie and soon Bernie and I were chowing down, my share nicely cut into bite size chunks.

While Bernie ate he got busy on the laptop. "What I'm going to do now, like some possessed social climber, is check out where all these people went to college—Cole Samuels, Georgette Eliot, Maddy DeFarge, Missy Havisham." He tapped away at the keys. After a while, he closed the laptop and shook his head. "All of them the kinds of places you'd expect, but not Big Green."

A puzzler for sure, but I was suddenly a little too tired for puzzlers. I lay down on the floor and got comfortable.

"Tuckered out, big guy? Skiing'll do that, too."

And he might have added a little something or other to that but if so I missed it.

Eighteen

Next morning we were polishing off breakfast—bacon and eggs for Bernie, kibble for me, plus a scrap or two or more than two of bacon he tossed my way—when a delivery dude showed up with a box. Bernie read some writing on it. "From Georgette." He brought it to the table and pulled out a book with a picture of a Christmas tree all decorated with the usual decorations except for one, which happened to be the very first thing that caught my eye, namely a knife hanging from a branch, a red drop or two on the shining blade.

"*Yuletide's Ebb*," Bernie said. "Doesn't sound very cheery, but . . ." He opened the book and began reading to himself, eating at the same time. That's something Bernie loves to do, read while he eats. He gets so content. I can feel it, and not only that but I get content, too. I licked my empty kibble bowl and lay at his feet.

"This is interesting, Chet," Bernie said after a while. "Trudi Tremaine is visiting Potherington Manor on what she thinks is a missing peacock case. The peacock's name is Sammy and Lady Potherington was planning to give Sammy to Lord Potherington for Christmas. Lady Potherington seems very disturbed about Sammy, but Trudi knows something that would be much more disturbing—Lord Potherington is having a top secret thing with what Trudi calls an 'on the QT cutie' who works as a barmaid at The Fox and Vulture in the neighboring village of Mycroft. So while Lady Potherington is filling her in on Sammy—physical description, when last seen, all that—Trudi starts . . . well, I don't know what to call it? Kind of having doubts about her work in general? Something like that."

Bernie licked his lips and turned the page. "'Lady Potherington poured more tea, first for Trudi, then for herself. The teapot was nineteenth-century Wedgwood Jasperware, as Trudi knew from watching Antiques Roadshow, not the American version, which was all about money, but the British, also all about money but in the British manner. "I feel so malheureux," Lady Potherington continued. "Alistair so loves peacocks and here we are three days from Christmas and poor Sammy tout perdu." Trudi sipped her tea. She suppressed a vagrant desire to blurt out a very unprofessional observation, such as "Alistair so loves peahens, too, milady." She kept that to herself. But what was the job? Was it always to stay within the boundaries of the case, at present, for example, to establish the whereabouts of Sammy and round him up, as the Americans say? Would it be wrong to widen her scope, to watch out for the welfare of the client in a more general way? What if Sammy was connected, perhaps psychologically or even unknowingly in Lady Potherington's mind with Lord Potherington's dalliance? "You don't find the tea to your taste, my dear?" said Lady Potherington. "Oh, no." Trudi looked up quickly. "Delicious. Is it lapsang?" "Oh my, no," said Lady Potherington.'"

Bernie folded his hands on the open book and gazed out the window. A few snowflakes were in the air, not falling, exactly, more like wafting around. As for all this Sammy business, well, I'd dealt with peacocks before. This was in the cactus garden behind Rancho Grande, one of the nicest hotels in the whole Valley. Peacocks roamed the cactus garden, as I discovered on my very first, and only, visit. I also discovered that they were birds and that they could fly. But, unluckily for them, or at least one of the Rancho Grande's peacocks, they're a little sluggish in the take-off department, probably on account of those tails, which really are something, and I'm what you might call an aficionado of tails. But basically they were just birds. Were birds on Bernie's mind right now? For how long? I was considering various ways of interrupting when noises started up outside. I hurried over to the window. What was this? Down the street, not far from the North Pole, we had some action going on. Do I like when action goes on without me? You know the answer. Barking arose in Cratchit House, loud and fierce.

"What's up?" Bernie came over and saw what I was seeing: the trailer from yesterday was parked near the North Pole and several big guys with enormous beards were climbing out and shifting the sleigh off the trailer. At the same time, a bunch of folks started gathering, some from inside the North Pole and others from here and there on the ranch. In short, a crowd, a crowd in a good mood, always the kind of crowd you want to be in, and very, very soon we were.

"Chet! Hey, Chet! How's it going, Chet?"

There was lots of that, and I'm sure lots of "Hi, Bernie," too, certainly from Georgette. Guys and gals took turns sitting in the sleigh while their pictures got taken: Hal, of course, being Santa, and even though he wore padded overalls and a hat with stick out flaps instead of a red suit, he was still Santa for sure, just on a day off. Then we had all those people from Ariadne's team, like Cole Samuels, Maddy Defarge, Missy Havisham, the city folks dressed in fancy outdoor gear and eager to get back indoors, and the locals dressed any old way and happy to stay out all day. Bernie and I were like the locals, of course. We usually are.

Finally, Ariadne appeared. She came out of the North Pole wearing enormous sunglasses and a black cape with a black hood that shaded most of her face. The crowd parted. She came closer and slowly walked beside the sleigh, once reaching out to touch it but not quite doing it, her bare hand hovering over the shining red paintwork. Her hand looked colorless, maybe from the cold. She spoke to Hal in a husky voice, like she'd been crying. "Thank you, old friend. It's lovely."

"I didn't do anything," Hal said, taking her cold hand in both of his. "You can thank these boys from Alaska."

Ariadne took a step or two closer to the guys with the enormous beards, the halfway down the chests and way out to the sides kind of enormous.

"Thank you, gentleman. It's a thing of beauty."

They touched their caps, all of the hunting type.

"Sit in it, Ariadne," said Georgette. "I'll take your picture."

Ariadne shook her head.

"Pretty please," Georgette said. "It'll be huge on social media."

Ariadne shook her head much harder.

Georgette tried one more time. "And it'll make a nice souvenir for these gentlemen."

Ariadne seemed to fix Georgette in a very long stare, although the sunglasses made it hard to be sure. Then she turned to the bearded guys.

"Would it?" she said.

The bearded guys nodded.

"Very well," Ariadne said, and she climbed onto the sleigh and sat on the seat at the back. A sort of bench seat, I now saw, but not an el-cheapo kind, instead velvety and puffy. Plush, that was it. Santa's seat was plush. I remember having that thought, very clearly.

Then comes a period of time, maybe short, from which I remember nada. My next actual memory has me sitting nice and
comfy on Santa's plush seat, right beside Ariadne, and laughter
rising up all around in little breath clouds. What a fine moment in my career! Georgette loomed in over the front of the
sleigh, taking pictures. Then someone said, "Too bad the reindeer aren't here. They could take Ariadne and the pooch on a
little ride."

That gave Georgette an idea. I could see it on her face. Her
eyes found Bernie in the crowd. Not a real big crowd, to be ac-
curate. We stick to the facts in this business.

"Bernie?" she said. "Do you think Chet would go for getting
harnessed up to the sleigh? We could make it look like he's pulling Ariadne."

"Nice idea," Bernie said. "But not his kind of thing."

Bernie's always right of course, so I pretended I hadn't heard
him. Because—and what does this tell you about life? Let me
know if you come up with something. Because almost before I
knew it, I'd jumped off Santa's sleigh and was standing in front
of it, close to where the leather harnesses hung from a hook underneath.

The biggest and most bearded of the Alaskan boys went over
to Bernie.

"Sir?" he said.

"Maybe his kind of thing today," Bernie said.

My Bernie! Never wrong! In no time at all the Alaskan boys
had me all harnessed up to the sleigh and pictures were happening out the ying-yang. I considered howling at the moon, but
there was no moon. In fact, we had a beautiful sunny day going
on, with fresh white snow on the ground, in the trees, on the
roof of the big house. The only thing we didn't have was action.

I thought, what the hell, and strained a little on the harness, just testing the pressure against my chest, if you take my meaning. And right away I knew: yes, doable. So I did what I'm sure you'd have done in my place. I began to move. And so did the sleigh. Yes, I, Chet, was pulling this sleigh, normally pulled, if I was understanding right, by a bunch of reindeer, which I believe are a type of deer. So there you have it. On one side, a bunch of deer, rolling their big brown eyes and caught up in all sorts of other deer stuff. On the other side, I, Chet. Chet the mighty, if you don't mind me saying so.

Cheers rose up all around. I happened to glance back at Ariadne. She was smiling but a tear or two had rolled down from under her enormous sunglasses and frozen in icy streaks on her cheeks. To help her out—well, really just to have some fun, which I believed was the whole point of the holidays—I turned it up a notch, advancing to a trot. Not quite my go-to trot, but close enough. I trotted that sleigh round and round in the pure white snow in front of the North Pole and would have continued forever if Bernie hadn't come running up. There's always fondness in Bernie's eyes whenever they're on me, but now there seemed to be some concern or even worry as well. What could there possibly have been to worry about?

"No sense overdoing it, big guy," he said. "I've got some of those special biscuits you like, the ones from Rover and Company."

I missed the first part of that but got the second. Biscuits from Rover and Company. There you have it, the brilliance of Bernie. I came to a halt.

Not long after that, back in Cratchit House, Bernie's phone buzzed.

"Bernie?" said the man on the other end, easy for me to hear even though we weren't on speaker, and on top of that I already knew who it was, being a professional, as you must know by now. "Mitch Cuffy, here. That matter we discussed? Got time for a quick confab?"

"Where and when?"

"Muley's. It's a roadhouse on the backside of Mount Murdstone, just past mile seventeen on the old state highway. You at the ranch?"

"Yes."

"Should take you forty-five minutes. See you then."

Muley's was a little wooden joint, some of the boards blackened like they'd been through a fire or two. There was snow on the roof and out front a sign with a kicking mule. I'd shared a few moments with a mule name of Rummy in a case involving a gold nugget which had finally ended up in my possession. There's nothing sluggish about the kick of a mule. That's one difference between mules and peacocks. No time to get into any of the others because we were on our way inside.

There was no one to see except the bartender, eating peanuts at the bar, and Mr. Cuffy, sitting by a woodstove in the far corner.

"Hey!" said the bartender, "you didn't say nothin' about no hound."

"So what?" said Mr. Cuffy. "You like dogs."

"That's not the point," the bartender said.

He was right about that. Hound was the point. Some folks talk about my appearance right in front of me! Can you believe it? But that's how I know I'm a mix of some sort. Was hound part of it? Not that I remembered. Now comes a little joke I once heard Bernie say: "One thing's for sure—zero percent chihuahua." How all the barflies had laughed and laughed, some falling down, and of the falling downers some of them not getting up! There's fun to be had in this business. Perhaps I haven't made that clear.

"Hey, Bernie," Mr. Cuffy said. "Say hi to my uncle Lou, owns this godforsaken hole."

"Hi, Lou," Bernie said.

"No one actually calls him that," Mr. Cuffy said. "He's Uncle Hum in these parts, 'specially this time of year. Stands for Humbug."

"Hi, Uncle Hum," Bernie said.

Uncle Hum was a very old dude, with a patch over one eye, blurred tattoos on his arms, and a cane in the hand that wasn't busy with the peanuts. Shelling and eating them with one hand, by the way. I've seldom met a human who didn't have at least one talent of some kind.

"No free drinks around here, amigo," Uncle Hum said. "No free drinks, no credit, don't ask."

"Can I ask for a beer?" Bernie said. "Plus whatever your nephew here is drinking? And something for yourself?"

"Hmmf," said Uncle Hum.

He went over to the beer taps, his back now to us, and filled two glasses and then one more, making . . . oh, how frustrating. I was so close.

"The dog's a fine lookin' specimen, so at least there's that," Uncle Hum said.

"I told you," said Mr. Cuffy.

"Hell you did."

"I did."

"You din't."

"Did too."

And there might have been more of that, but Bernie interrupted.

"His name's Chet."

"Did I ask?" said Uncle Hum. He turned and plunked the full glasses down on the bar, a hard plunk although somehow not a drop got spilled. "Three times four and quarter makes twelve seventy-five, call it fifteen with tip."

"Tip?" said Mr. Cuffy. "You're the owner. Not supposed to tip the owner."

"What the hell are you talkin' about?" Uncle Hum said. "Bank's the owner, always has been always will be."

"Fifteen it is," Bernie said, laying some bills on the bar. "My compliments to the bank."

"Ha!" said Mr. Cuffy.

"Everybody thinks they're funny," said Uncle Hum, pocketing the money. "That's what's wrong with the world these days. List as long as my arm of what's wrong, but that's on it for sure. Funnymen. Pah!"

Bernie picked up two glasses, clinked one against the glass that remained on the bar, and headed over to Mr. Cuffy by the woodstove. I was about to follow when Uncle Hum made a tiny little hiss in my direction. *Pssss.* Like that. I looked his way. He looked mine, with just that one eye, but it was suddenly shining bright. I sat, not for any particular reason. I just did it. Uncle Hum nodded, that sort of nod humans do when they turn out to be right about something. The next moment a biscuit came spinning over the bar. I snapped it up and scarfed it down in one motion.

"Merry frickin' Christmas," Uncle Hum said, and disappeared into a back room. I went over by the woodstove and curled up in the warmth.

"That's my uncle," Mr. Cuffy said. He was the same guy as before: mostly bald except for a few bone white hairs sprouting here and there, and all shrunken except for the big hands, but for some reason he didn't look quite so old today.

"I got that," Bernie said.

"My ma's brother. She was just like him. But tougher."

"Ah."

Mr. Cuffy took a long swig of beer. "I looked into that matter."

"Thanks."

"Regarding the Teddy Leeford case. You wanted to see the file. I told you I'd go over to county records and nose around. On account of we didn't digitize that far back. Nobody cared. Didn't even ask what I wanted. I went down to the basement all by myself. Sub-basement, goin' that far back. Everything's in paper files. A month on every shelf, each year on a bank of shelves. Cases in file folders, separate folder for every case. In order of the day the case opened. Got the picture?"

"I can almost see it."

"Not in the order of the case gettin' closed. Open only. That's the system. So supposing there's a larceny under seven-fifty on a December twenty-four and an assault with a deadly on December twenty-six, and on December twenty-five you got a homicide, then that file should be between the larceny and the assault. You follow so far?"

Bernie nodded.

Mr. Cuffy raised his hand. "So you're pokin' along the shelf." His hand made wavy motions. "All the dates is on little tabs—like twelve twenty-four, twelve twenty-five, twelve twenty-six—stickin' out tabs, color coded for whoever caught the case. Red. That was my color." He gazed into his beer.

"You're poking along the shelf," Bernie said after a while.

Mr. Cuffy glared at Bernie. "Don't rush me."

"Sorry."

"Nobody does their best work when they're rushed."

"Agreed."

"I'm just trying to sort this out, that's all. Course in the old days I coulda dusted for prints, but now . . ."

His voice trailed off. Meanwhile Uncle Hum had reappeared behind the bar and was eyeing Mr. Cuffy. He shook his head.

"Maybe I can help with the sorting," Bernie said.

"Don't see as how," Mr. Cuffy said. "As for dust, like the ordinary kind, there was plenty of that on the shelf except for . . ." He shrugged his bony old shoulders.

"You're telling me the file was gone?" Bernie said.

Mr. Cuffy nodded. "Dust all around, years of it, 'ceptin' for that one space."

"Did you report it missing?"

"Nope."

"Why not?"

Uncle Hum spoke from behind the bar. "Can of worms."

"Is that it?" Bernie said to Mr. Cuffy. "What could be in that can?"

Wasn't worms the answer? Could we move onto something else? Birds are big on worms, which I've only tried once, enough to know they're of no interest to me.

"It's not that," Mr. Cuffy said. "I just didn't see the point."

"Now you're makin' sense," said Uncle Hum. "Things go on and get themselves lost. That's how it's always been in these mountains and always will be."

"You're wrong," Mr. Cuffy said. "It's changed. Look around."

"I do. And what I see is a real thin—what's the word?"

"Veneer," said Bernie.

"Bingo. Veneer. Veneer of so-called civilization. Blow on it like this—poof, and it's gone. Gone with the wind, Mizz Scarlet."

"Don't listen to him," Mr. Cuffy said.

And I was with him on that. The case—about Rudy the missing reindeer, right?—was turning out to be way too complicated already. Did we really need Mizz Scarlet, whoever she may be, in the mix?

Nineteen

"In this basket," Bernie said as we drove back through Kringle Ranch, confusing me from the jump, since we had no baskets in the Beast, and had never had one, although once there'd been a basketball I'd . . . come across, let's put it like that, and quickly made manageable. If you don't make them manageable, basketballs are very hard to deal with, as you may have discovered on a playground at sometime in your life. A big problem for you—and I feel bad about this—is that you really don't have the teeth for the job. But there are other great things about you, so chin up!

". . . we have facts," Bernie was saying. "Fact—Rudy the reindeer is missing. Fact—Ariadne has writer's block. Fact—Teddy Leeford, a long-ago romantic interest of hers, was the victim in an unsolved homicide. Fact—Chaz LeWitte, her young assistant now in a coma, was found in the same place as Teddy's body. Fact—the file on the Leeford case is missing."

Wow. How in the world did Bernie hold all that in his head? He had a beautifully shaped head, of course, and not at all one of those small heads you see from time to time, but also not one of the real big ones. Take Fritzie Bortz, for example, earlier in his career a motorcycle cop on the highway patrol and now sheriff of a county quite near the Valley and possibly soon to be running for governor, if I'd heard right, but back in his motorcycle days—and he'd never quite gotten the hang of riding one— they'd had to order a special helmet for him, on account of his head being too big. But forget Fritzie. My point was Bernie and all those mountains of facts. How does he do it? You tell me.

Bernie leaned forward and wiped away some fog that kept forming on the inside of the windshield. Outside snow was still coming down. My, my, what a place! Who had said, and very recently, "Let it snow, let it snow, let it snow!"? Whoever that was knew a thing or two.

"The problem," Bernie went on, or perhaps starting up on something new, "is this theorizing machine inside the human brain."

I stuck out my tongue as long and as far as possible and gave my whole muzzle a good, thorough lick. I couldn't think of anything else to do. This was such a shock! A machine inside the brain? Did it hurt? Was it the cause of all those headaches humans had? Here I'd always thought it was about the booze! And what about the fact that women seemed to get more headaches than men? Did it mean the machines in their brains were bigger? Or did they need oiling more often? What about white wine? Women seemed to like white wine quite a bit, in my experience. But that was as far as I could take this on my own.

"The theorizing machine is impatient," Bernie said. "It doesn't like to wait until all the facts or in—or, and this happens a lot—it fails to recognize the facts that are out there in plain sight. For example, the book Ariadne is working on now is number one hundred. Is it possible the number alone is freezing her up and all the rest of this, starting with Rudy, is irrelevant? People always say that words have power, Chet, but so do numbers. In any news story everybody's age gets noted. Numbers pack a punch."

Punch? Punches were now involved? Have I mentioned Bernie's sweet, sweet uppercut yet? If not, I've really messed up.

It's so quick, comes out of nowhere, and lands on the point of the chinny chin chin not with a thump, but a click. Just a click but then comes dreamland. I hadn't seen that uppercut in way too long. As for the power of numbers, I went over what I knew. One. Two. Yes, they had power, especially two.

"On top of all this, there's the timeline question. You might think that later events can't have an effect on earlier ones, but I'm starting to re—"

At that moment something flashed right in front of us, or more like bounded. Bernie hit the brakes, maybe a bit too vigorously, although he's the best wheelman in the Valley. Once a cartel gentleman offered Bernie big green to drive for him, and couldn't believe it when we turned him down. He couldn't believe it so hard he just wouldn't let go of the idea. We ended up making it very clear. I was thinking about all that—especially the night we made it clear—as we spun and spun across the road, finally coming to a stop by a big snowbank.

"That's what I get for running my mouth," Bernie said. I wasn't really listening, instead had my eye on something else, namely the reindeer standing on top of the snowbank, a big reindeer with breath streams rising from both nostrils. I barked a just between the two of us bark to get Bernie back on track. He looked where I was looking. The reindeer looked down at us.

"I don't believe we've seen this one before," Bernie said. He pulled out his phone, peered at the screen. "Rudy or nor Rudy? It's hard to tell from Ariadne's picture."

We got out of the car, nice and easy, which is how you handle these things when you don't want anyone getting spooked. Bernie held out his hand.

"Rudy?"

The reindeer showed no sign of recognizing the name, but

also no sign of not recognizing it. None of that mattered, at least not to me. Hadn't I smelled Rudy's scent on our visit to the barn? One sniff is all I need. This was not Rudy.

"You hungry, Rudy?" Bernie said. "How about we all walk over to the barn, let you belly up to the trough?"

This not-Rudy—certainly the biggest reindeer we'd seen so far—just stood there, watching us and breathing. Also I could hear the heartbeat, slow and surprisingly strong. The strongest heartbeat I've heard in my career belonged to Peanut the elephant, perhaps no surprise. Like that booming bass drum you see in parades. Which reminded me of how badly I wanted to be in one! But this was not the time for wants of my own. I'm a professional.

Not-Rudy turned and walked down off the snowbank, knees crack crack cracking with every step. What was going on with that? Was Not-Rudy somehow like Uncle Hum? In need of a cane? Right away I knew that was a bit on the crazy side. I promised myself to do better.

Meanwhile we were now following Not-Rudy, who was walking right down the middle of the red-and-green brick road, now snow-covered, and seemed to be in no hurry. Dickens House appeared off to one side, half hidden in a grove of trees. Not-Rudy went that way. We followed, and there in the big window sat Ariadne at her desk, gazing at her laptop screen, her hands motionless over the keyboard. Not-Rudy paused right by the window, gazing in, but Ariadne didn't look up. I should have mentioned that the snow now lay pretty high all around Dickens House. Still, the ease with which Not-Rudy leaped up onto the roof was almost impressive. Then Not-Rudy just stood there, mouth making chewing motions and eyes vacant. We had now had a view of Not-Rudy from underneath.

"Um," Bernie said. Was he finally getting it? That was my

take. Bernie always gets it eventually. And then it hit me: eventually was the key to our success! Wow! The Little Detective Agency, simply the best.

Ariadne's head came up. She looked out at us in surprise. Bernie gave her a little wave. Ariadne half-waved back, then patted her hair, kind of wild at the moment, and rose. She walked away from her desk and disappeared from view, but a few moments later the front door opened, and she stepped outside, wearing baggy sweats and unlaced furry boots.

"Bernie? Is something wrong?"

"Didn't mean to bother you." Bernie pointed up at the roof. "But is there any chance that Rudy is a she?"

Ariadne glanced up at Not-Rudy and shook her head. "That's Vixen."

"Ah," Bernie said. "I didn't notice the . . . the female aspect until just now. I thought it might be Rudy from the size and all."

"Very understandable," Ariadne said. "Vixen's something of a giantess, but still smaller than Rudy. And her antlers, too, are smaller than his—even at this time of year, when the males shouldn't have antlers at all."

"No?"

"They're supposed to lose them in November, but ours don't seem to." Ariadne smiled one of those quick and not happy smiles you see from time to time. "Just another of life's mysteries."

"Could it have anything to do with the fact they've been transplanted from Lapland?" Bernie said.

Ariadne turned to him. The sun was shining bright, making it look like her face was more lined than it really was, if that makes any sense.

"A lot of men promote themselves as problem solvers," she said. "You actually seem to be one."

"I wouldn't say that," Bernie said.

She smiled again, another of those here-and-gone ones, but not so unhappy this time. "No, you wouldn't," she said. "Care for tea? I could do with a break."

I shot a quick glance up at Vixen as we went inside. Nothing had changed, eyes still vacant, mouth still chewing. Her female smell was unmissable and had been from her first appearance on that snowbank by the road. Bernie has no weaknesses and his nose couldn't be called small for a human nose, but . . . I'll leave it there. But, simply, but.

"Excuse the Spartan conditions," Ariadne said.

We were in her writing room with the big window, but there wasn't much in it. No couch, no comfy chairs, no rug, no Christmas decorations or decorations of any kind for that matter, just a desk with a swivel chair, and a card-table chair that Bernie pulled up to the desk.

"It was all chintz and maple in here until a few weeks ago," Ariadne went on. "I thought banishing the clutter might help."

Bernie said nothing.

"You're not asking the obvious," Ariadne said. "Specifically, what banishing the clutter might help with."

"Well, Chaz did mention that your productivity isn't up to your usual standard. He thought—he thinks that the Rudy situation is the cause."

"He thinks?" Ariadne said. "Do you believe people in comas have thoughts?"

"I don't know," Bernie said. "It was more like I just didn't want to speak of him in the past. But the thing is I actually wasn't thinking about clutter."

"No?"

"None of my business, but I was thinking this whole ranch is all about Christmas but here in the, um, engine room, there's nothing Christmasy."

Ariadne gave Bernie a look, not long but deep, if that makes any sense. A deep look from green eyes that themselves seemed deep, like you could dive in and sink down and down. A rather scary thought that I hoped would not come around again.

"In all these years of writing about a sleuth," Ariadne said, "I've never taken the trouble to actually sit down and talk to one."

"It's no trouble," Bernie said. "Not to us."

"Us meaning you and Chet?"

"We're a team."

Ariadne looked at me. I was curled up on the floor quite close to Ariadne's desk and . . . let's not call it gnawing, more like just getting to know the desk, specifically its nearest leg, a little better. I should point out that the desk was wooden, and the wood very old, possibly making the desk itself what they call an antique. The older the wood the better the mouth feel, a little fact you might or might not know. But I hadn't actually started in on anything, so I might have been exactly what I looked like, just ol' Chet up to nothing special.

"He really is magnificent," Ariadne said. She turned her deep green gaze on Bernie. "I like your Christmas question. I get asked the same questions all the time, but not from you. There are two answers, somewhat contradictory. The first is that if there's no Christmas in the room then the writer is forced to imagine it. As opposed to reporting—as a journalist, if you will. And what's been imagined—meaning cooked up from a mixture of thought, memory, and the inexplicable—ends up on the page, invisible but there."

Bernie gave that some thought. Then he said, "What's the second answer?"

Ariadne laughed. Then she made that little come-with-me finger waggle and led us to a big side window, me getting there first, as you probably would have predicted. She pointed way up in the sky, and there was the blimpy wreath thing, like a drifting green cloud.

"It's tethered to this house?" Bernie said.

"To a custom-forged hook anchored in the foundation, to be specific," Ariadne said. She looked about to say more, but at that moment, the kettle on her desk whistled, and she got busy with a teapot, cups and saucers, sugar and cream bowls, little silver spoons.

Bernie pointed to the teapot. "Wedgwood Jasperware?"

"My God, no," Ariadne said. "Pottery Barn close-out sale." She poured, at first watching the tea flow from the spout, but then looking up at Bernie. "You've been reading *Yuletide's Ebb*?" Her hand seemed to know when the cup was full and stopped pouring by itself. That was the moment I decided Ariadne was pretty magnificent herself.

"Guilty as charged," Bernie said.

"And?" said Ariadne.

"And?" said Bernie.

"And what do you think of it?" Ariadne said. "Writers hate when readers say they're reading one of their books and then go silent. Doesn't that strike you as you rude?"

"Maybe those readers feel shy about offering opinions."

"Those days are in the past," Ariadne said. "And you're not shy." She clinked her teacup against Bernie's and took a sip.

"Your writing is great," Bernie said. "You must know that."

"I most certainly do not. Popular, yes. But great? What's great about it?"

Bernie set his cup back in the saucer, doing it with care, the cup so dainty and his hand so big and strong. "Like when Trudi thinks about Alistair and peahens but doesn't say it out loud."

"That's great?"

Bernie shrugged. "I'm no expert. But you've got experts. They must have told you."

"I've got experts?"

"Georgette. Cole. Missy Havisham. Maddy Defarge."

"I've never had a conversation like this with any of them. As for Missy, she despises my work and doesn't take much trouble to hide the fact. That's what I like about her. I'm tempted to add it's the only thing but that would be overegging the pudding."

Bernie laughed, at the same time giving Ariadne one of those second looks of his. As for pudding or even just eggs there were neither in this room and hadn't been for a very long time, perhaps even never.

"What about Chaz?" Bernie said.

"That's different. He's biased."

"How so?"

"First I need your word that my response will remain confidential."

"You have it."

"I'll trust you," Ariadne said. "Do you know why?"

"No."

Ariadne didn't say anything. She pointed at me, lying close by and doing basically nothing, other than contemplating those furry boots of hers. Bernie just nodded a slight nod, like whatever was going on made sense.

"My answer," Ariadne said, "is that Chaz is biased in the unrealistic manner of the young. You may have noticed the rather large age gap between him and me. And please don't say age is a state of mind, or you're only as old as you think. The clock is relentless."

"What about living in the moment?" Bernie said. "Throwing caution to the wind?"

"Don't you think that's a bad look after a certain age?" Ariadne said. "Say, thirty-five, give or take?"

"But you're an artist."

"That's not carte blanche to play the fool," Ariadne said. "Although it is a license to give curiosity free rein. I've been thinking of that friend of yours—the one who can rope and ride."

"Weatherly Wauneka."

Ariadne nodded. "Is that an Indian surname?"

"Navajo," Bernie said. "Why have you been thinking about her?"

"Maybe not easy to believe, but once I, too, could rope and ride." Ariadne shrugged, just a slight movement of her shoulders. Despite her baggy sweats, and not wearing make-up, and her hair seemingly thinner than it had been at the dinner, there was still something about her, something special, maybe even grand.

"I believe it," Bernie said.

"Thank you," said Ariadne. "So what are you getting her for Christmas?"

Bernie turned to her and began, "What makes you think it's that kind of—?"

But Ariadne interrupted. "Bosh!"

For a moment Bernie came close to looking a bit—I don't even want to name it—sheepish, but then he laughed and reached into his pocket. "The truth is I'm a bit worried about it." He laid the little velvet box on the desk. "I saw some of those window displays in Silver Mountain—Bulgari and all the rest—and, well, she deserves better than what I, um . . ."

Ariadne read the writing on the little velvet box: "'Singh's American Dream Pawnshop.'" She opened the box. Ariadne had opened a lot of little velvet boxes. You could just tell from the movement of her fingers. And there was the Desert Star, glowing like the middle of nowhere at dawn.

"Like, ah, an engagement ring," Bernie said. "I read you're supposed to spend ten percent—or maybe twenty—"

"Bosh," Ariadne said again.

"More?" said Bernie. "Or do you mean it's the thought that counts?"

"Certainly not. Taste is what counts. And this—" She pointed to the Desert Star. "—is just the ticket."

"Blind luck," Bernie said.

"Let's not overdo the modesty, shall we?" Ariadne said. She opened a desk drawer, took out a bottle and filled their teacups. "I was engaged once myself."

Bernie looked at her. His expression changed very, very slightly, going from Bernie not working to Bernie working. "Who to?" he said.

Ariadne placed her elbow on the table and her chin in her hand. What a nice chin she had, strong and gentle at the same time. The human chin is a big subject we can maybe get back to later.

"It was a long time ago," she said. "And we didn't have time to get to the ring stage."

Bernie just sat there. That's one of our best techniques at the Little Detective Agency, simply sitting and keeping our mouths shut.

Ariadne reached out and touched the Desert Star. I thought she was about to take it out of the box and try it on, but all she did was touch it. Her finger lingered there. Then she picked up her teacup and drank.

"He was very good with his hands," Ariadne said. "And with tools of any kind. Once—this was with a chainsaw—he carved a sculpture of me from a block of aspen. It took him less than an hour."

"Where is it?" Bernie said.

My ears went up. Something was moving on the roof. My mind checked in: that would be Vixen, shuffling around, cracking her knees, rolling her eyes, the whole reindeer thing. My ears went down.

"A good question," Ariadne said. "I actually haven't thought of it in years." She made a soft grunt, picked up a pen and made a quick note on one of those yellow notepads.

"Um," Bernie said, "did you just get a writing idea?"

"You never know," Ariadne said. "But there's a big distance between the ideas and the writing. In dreams begin responsibility, and all that." She drank again from her teacup. "I don't want to talk about writing. I want to talk about Teddy." She glanced at Bernie. "It's something I never do."

"Teddy was the boyfriend?"

Ariadne nodded. "Teddy Leeford."

"The T.L. you dedicated *Bad or Good* to?"

"That's right." Her deep green eyes narrowed. "Are you way ahead of me, Bernie? Asking questions you already know the answers to?"

"I wouldn't go that far," Bernie said.

"Why not? Trudi does the same thing—asking questions when she knows the answers. So it's good to know I've stumbled into reality." Her fingers made strange little motions, almost like she was typing in midair. "Go on, please," she said.

"Where to?"

"A summary of what you already know."

"Fair enough," Bernie said. "I don't know much. Teddy and his brother Drake were from a local family that was cash poor but land rich. They came up with the idea for Silver Mountain—the skiing, the resort, all the rest of it, but Teddy never got to see it. He was murdered on a Christmas Eve, his body found at the bottom of Devil's Purse, the crime unsolved."

Ariadne sat very still.

"That's about it," Bernie said.

Ariadne nodded. "It seems so . . . so orderly the way you put it."

"I didn't mean it that way."

"That's all right. It's almost refreshing."

Now Bernie picked up his little teacup. For a moment I thought it was going to get crushed in his hand but that didn't happen. He took a little teacuppy sip. "Did you ever suspect anyone?"

"No."

"I heard he got into fights sometimes."

"That was just youthful roughhousing, and besides it was over by the time we got together. Everyone liked him."

"Women, too?"

"What are you getting at?"

"Nothing, really," Bernie said. "Just speculating. Suppose, for example, that there was another woman who had her eyes on him but got rejected because of you." He raised his open hands.

"And killed him out of jealousy?" Ariadne said.

"It happens."

Ariadne shook her head. "There was no woman like that. Not that I knew of. I suppose it can't be ruled out."

She thought for a moment or two. I could feel her thoughts. To my surprise, they felt a lot like Bernie's—big, heavy, and rising and falling like waves. I knew waves from our visit to San Diego. We'd surfed, me and Bernie. What a life!

"I suppose," she said, "that you've already taken the next logical step and shuffled the chess pieces around."

"What do you mean?" Bernie said.

"Queen to pawn two," Ariadne said. "Woman X is the true love and I'm the jealous one."

"Hey," said Bernie. "Hadn't thought of that." He stretched out his legs. "Any truth to it?"

Twenty

"What do you think?" Ariadne said.

"You're not the jealous type," said Bernie.

"How would you know a thing like that?"

"We run into jealous types in this business. You don't fit the description."

"How not?"

"They all—men and women both—have holes inside that need filling. You don't."

Men and women with holes in them? Bernie was right. We saw that for sure, and way too much, but it comes with the territory, the territory being jam packed with guns and knives, not to mention forks, scissors, nail files, and even twigs if they're sharpened, all very good at making holes in people. There wasn't a trace of blood on Ariadne. That was Bernie, right again.

Meanwhile, Ariadne was giving him a long look. "Do you have any children?"

"A son."

"What's his name?"

"Charlie."

"I love that name." Her eyes glistened. "That was what Teddy and I had picked out—Charlie for a boy or a girl. After he was gone, I actually prayed—on my knees—that somehow my birth control had failed, but of course it hadn't."

"So you never had children?"

"Correct."

"Did you ever get married?"

"I did not. There were—I suppose you would call them lovers, each turning out to be unsatisfactory, as I'm sure I was to them." She closed the velvet box and handed it to Bernie. He put it in his pocket.

"What did Chaz know about all this?" Bernie said. "Teddy, the murder, Devil's Purse?"

"Nothing," Ariadne said, "until quite recently. It was all long ago, before my career, and I've never seen the point of having the whole story in the public forum. I get interviewed quite a bit, Bernie. They're always looking for hooks to hang their stories on. I didn't want Teddy, or some shallow sympathy for me, to be a hook. But, quite separate from that, during this past fall Chaz was out hiking—not that he does much of that, being an indoorsy type—and he happened upon Devil's Purse. He came back in a state of high excitement, thinking he'd found a wonderful crime scene for Trudi. I pointed out the unlikelihood of finding such a place in the Cotswolds, and then for some reason couldn't leave it at that, and blurted out, well, not the whole story, but enough."

"What was his reaction?"

"He took my hand and held it in both of his. I don't fancy being the object of anyone's sympathy, but Chaz is a sweet-natured young man. The gulf between sympathy and empathy grows deeper and wider the older I get. Sorry, Bernie—I can be such a bore."

"I've missed that so far," Bernie said.

"Oh, good!" Ariadne laughed. "Then I'll add one more tedious aperçu—Christmas is all about empathy, not sympathy. That's the appeal. Meanwhile I'm way off topic. Feel free to edit me, Bernie. What I should have gotten to already was what Chaz said after he took my hand. He asked if I had a picture of Teddy."

"And?"

"And I did. I do." Ariadne paused, maybe waiting for Bernie to say something. When he didn't, she sighed and went on. "Trudi does that same exact thing, just keeping mum until some truth or semi-truth comes out. But I hadn't realized until this second how irritating it is to be on the other end."

She rose, crossed the room, and opened a narrow closet. In fact, it looked a lot like a broom closet, although you usually found broom closets in kitchens. Almost always broom closets have brooms and mops and dustpans and that kind of stuff inside, nothing important. But then there was the one broom closet that was different, namely the broom closet in the Gail Blandino case, the one case we didn't solve.

The point is I get edgy when broom closets are in the picture, and was all set for who knows what, the muscles bunching in my back legs, when Ariadne opened the door. But there was nothing scary inside, hardly anything at all, not even a broom—only a few bare hangers on a rail and a low stubby safe on the floor. Ariadne crouched before it, her knees cracking, but not in that irritating reindeer way that goes on and on, more in the older human way sometimes accompanied by a wince that makes you a bit sorry for them, although there was no wince from Ariadne. She tapped at the buttons, opened the door, reached inside, and came back with a framed photo. Ariadne handed it to Bernie. He gazed at it, holding it so I could see, too. We're a team, me and Bernie. It shows up all the time.

There were two people in the photo, a young man and a young woman. They both had big smiles on their faces, wore shorts, T-shirts—sleeveless in her case—and hiking boots, and looked strong and healthy. The man—a real big guy, but not the mean-looking type of big guy—had long blond hair. The woman's hair was short and dark. She held a bundle of split logs. He had an arm over her shoulders, his hand resting lightly on her bare arm. In his other hand he held an ax, hanging loosely at his side. Maybe I should mention that it wasn't just me and Bernie taking a close look at the photo. Ariadne was doing the same thing.

"I didn't look at this for decades," she said. "Then, after Chaz asked about it, I've been taking a peek almost on a daily basis." She pointed to the smiling young woman. "Nowadays she seems like more of a stranger that he does." Then, very quietly, she added, "'When old age shall this generation waste, Thou shalt remain, in midst of other woe.'"

"What's that?" Bernie said.

"Keats," Ariadne said. "A hopeless romantic to modern taste and of course he never came close to old age to see if he was right, but I look at this—" She nodded toward the photo. "—and can't help thinking he was. But if so, Bernie, what's the point of anything? You're smart. Tell me what the point is."

"Is there anything left in that bottle?" Bernie said.

Ariadne stared at Bernie for a long moment, then threw back her head and laughed and laughed. Her eyes welled up and tears rolled down her face. She opened her arms like she was about to embrace Bernie, but she did not, instead wiping away the tears on her sleeve.

"There sure as hell better be," she said, opening the desk drawer and taking out the bottle. She filled the teacups. The drink was not bourbon or scotch—I think I've already pointed out the difference—but rum, one of the very easiest smells out there, burned sugar plus something close to maple syrup, and charcoal, a combo impossible to miss. I have reason to believe that parrots like it, having come across a few parrots in my career of whom two—Cap'n Crunch and Davy Jones—both called for it incessantly in their croaky and very loud voices. "Yo ho-ho and a bottle of rum," over and over and over. It makes you want to figure out a way to get them out of their cages and—well, no time for that now.

Ariadne leaned the photo against the desk lamp. "We did a lot of camping that summer. This photo was taken on the near side of Mount Murdstone. It was wild country back then, almost like from a previous century. There was no one around but a few old prospectors, still not willing to believe there was no silver in these mountains. Right there behind that poplar you can just make out the entrance to an abandoned mine. Teddy and his brother Drake had been exploring it since they were kids. I remember ducking in there when it rained the next morning."

"Is that who took the picture?" Bernie said. "One of the prospectors?"

Ariadne shook her head. "Drake took it. He and his wife Nellie were with us."

"Drake was Teddy's brother?" Bernie said.

Didn't we know that already? But maybe not. Keeping track of everything or even less than everything is not so easy, and if Bernie was asking there had to be a reason. I felt nice and calm inside, my mind moving to other things, rawhide chews, for example.

"Correct," Ariadne was saying. "They were partners in SMD—Silver Mountain Development. They actually came up with the name on that camping trip. We took a vote on it, around the fire."

"What were the other contenders?" Bernie said.

Ariadne cocked her head to one side, a move you see when someone's trying out a new angle on Bernie. "Where do questions like that come from?" she said.

"I don't understand," Bernie said.

"What went on in your mind before you asked it?"

"Nothing special," Bernie said, which of course wasn't what we call the truth, the whole truth, and nothing but, since everything that goes on in that head of his is special. So right now Bernie was just being nice. You can count on him for that.

"Apologies if I'm being intrusive," Ariadne said. "Trudi asks a lot of questions like you do, but I always have them connected to some pattern forming in her mind."

Bernie smiled. "She's way smarter than me. I've already read enough to know that."

What was it with this Trudi person, all of a sudden? My teeth were looking forward to meeting her. Oh, dear, what a bad thought! I squashed it at once. Meanwhile Vixen was shifting her position on the roof and Ariadne was pouring more rum.

"The readers like Trudi for her smarts most of all," Ariadne said. "I'm not so sure that would be the same in real life. As for your question, there was only one other contender—Two Big Lugs and Company. It was Nellie's idea. She could be very funny."

"Are they still married?" Bernie said.

"Nellie and Drake? No. The marriage didn't last very long. Drake had several more—I'm not sure of the exact number, haven't seen him in a long time. He got very rich, of course." She drank from her teacup.

"So did you," Bernie said.

Ariadne set the teacup back in the saucer, perhaps a little unsteadily, from how it rattled around a bit. "That I did," she said. "But it was never a plan. Drake and Teddy getting rich—well, only Drake, as it turned out—was the plan from inception. All I wanted to do was see if I could write a novel good enough to be published. Not even that. Just to write a novel, full stop. A story with beginning, middle, and end that made sense." She looked at Bernie. "Here's something I haven't thought of for ages. When I finally came to the very last sentence of *Holly Jolly Homicide*—the first in the series and the worst of all the titles—a sentence I'd had in mind for months so there was nothing left to do but type it down in its place, I suddenly could not. A feeling overwhelmed me, and I burst into tears, cried like I'd never cried before or since." She took a deep breath. "Why the hell I'm telling you, I can not imagine. The simple point I was trying to make is that I never did this with money in mind. The money was partly luck and partly due to the enthusiasm of one well-respected and highly competent gentleman in the marketing department, now long gone, who was determined to spread the word about Trudi. Not that I'm unhappy about the money. It's lovely having piles of the stuff—although lovely's not the right word, because, unlike with so many of the rich, the money itself is not a love object for me."

Bernie sat very still through all that, listening so closely I could feel it. After Ariadne was done he just sat there, very still like he was still hearing something.

"Bernie?" she said. "Something on your mind?"

Bernie gave himself a little shake. That made perfect sense. We're a lot alike, don't forget. He smiled. I'd never seen a smile like this from him—or from anyone. Not happy but not unhappy, and in other ways impossible to describe, at least for me, the Chetster. I can only do so much.

"I was just thinking that now I can stop trying," he said.

"Trying to get rich?" Ariadne said.

Bernie nodded. "Because now I know what it would be like."

Ariadne smiled, too, also a not happy and not unhappy and otherwise impossible to describe smile.

"How old are you, Bernie?" she said.

He told her. The number—neither one nor two—did not stick in my mind.

"And Weatherly is age appropriate?"

Bernie nodded.

"Please invite me to the wedding," Ariadne said. "I won't come but I'd like to send you something nice."

"She hasn't said yes yet," Bernie said.

Ariadne laughed. Bernie laughed, too. They clinked teacups.

"I'd like to see Chaz's room," Bernie said. "But before that, this dropped from your pocket in the hospital." He handed her the little notebook I'd found in the waiting room.

"I won't ask whether you looked inside," Ariadne said.

"The answer would be yes," Bernie said.

Ariadne didn't seem at all upset. Not only that, but she wasn't—I can feel when people try to hide their upsetness. "Anyone good at your job would have to be rock hard somewhere inside," she said.

At the big house—called the North Pole if I understood right—Ariadne took us up a broad curving staircase and along a broad hallway lined with Christmas wreaths. I'd been in this hallway the night of the dinner party, but I'd come from the other end, following Chaz up the back stairs. We passed Ariadne's bedroom, with the big silver bell on it, and stopped at the next door, which had two silver bells, but much smaller.

"Chaz's room," Ariadne said. She pointed to the keypad. "The code is nineteen, one, fourteen, twenty, one. I'll leave you to it."

Bernie tapped the buttons. "Nineteen, one, fourteen, hmm . . . nineteen is S . . . one is A, hmm . . . Santa," he said in that soft voice he uses for talking to himself, with me always included, goes without mentioning. I heard Ariadne, already walking away, pause in mid-step.

The door opened, the two silver bells tinkling. The tinkling of bells is one of the nicest sounds out there. If I'd bothered to think about it I'd have realized I was already in a pretty good mood and now with the sound of those bells it was even better. But I didn't bother because once we were inside with the door closed Bernie started looking around in a way that told me we were reconning the joint. Reconning is one of our specialties at the Little Detective Agency and we're real good at it. For example, I already knew there was no blood in Chaz's room, fresh or otherwise, and also no dead bodies. Plus no food of any kind, not a scrap. The truth is that the food situation was the part I knew first. So no food, no blood, no bodies. Were we done?

Perhaps not, because Bernie seemed to be doing one of those thorough searches of his, going through the closet and the chest of drawers, even getting down on the floor to check under the bed. I joined him on that part, squeezing in close as close could be right beside him and stretching my head way, way underneath. The fun you can have in detective work never ends. There turned out to be nothing under the bed except for one gym sock, the white athletic kind, maybe ready for the laundry. I snatched it up as we wriggled out from under.

"What you got there?" Bernie said.

He took hold of one end of the sock and gave it a gentle tug. At least that was most likely his plan, but I did one of those real quick head tosses of mine—but smooth, smooth being the real payoff when it comes to the head toss and so many maneuvers—

easily keeping the sock away from his grasp. But not far away! Oh no. Quite the opposite. In this sort of situation, you keep the end of that sock dangling real close, right there for the taking, encouraging your playmate to try again. Why be discouraging in this life? I just don't get that.

In this case Bernie didn't take another swing at it, something of a disappointment. "Chet? Are you planning to eat that sock?"

What a suggestion? When had I ever eaten a sock? I'm not saying it had never happened. That wouldn't be reasonable. Socks were always lying around. You saw them everywhere. In the meat drawer of some perp's fridge, for example. I have a very clear picture in my mind of that sock, also a gym sock, also overdue for the laundry, lying beside a nice—very, very nice, as it turned out—salami roll, although nothing else about the case remained in my mind. The point I'm making is that—

"Chet? We've got work to do, big guy."

I dropped that sock immediately. I forgot all about it, now and forever, and trotted swiftly around the room, totally professional, sniff-sniff-sniffing in every corner, picking up Chaz's smell—typical youngish male plus just a touch of toe fungus—but nothing else of interest.

Meanwhile, Bernie was sitting at the desk and going through the drawers, which he always did the same way, starting at the bottom drawer and working his way up. From time to time he stopped to read some sheet of paper, open a notebook, flick through check stubs, all the usual. Humans wrote lots of things down and we take a look-see at their writings—Bernie handling the actual look-see part—because perps are humans and write things down, things that we sometimes read back to them, Bernie handling the actual reading. Like this: "But Ziggy, here you seem to have written, quote if I ever get the chance I'm going to blow that lousy bar to smithereens. End quote." The pant leg grab came soon after.

But right now, Bernie wasn't laying anything aside, just replacing everything and closing the drawers. He came to the top drawer, opened it, gazed inside, and took out a laptop. He set it on the desk, opened the lid, tapped at a key or two, then paused.

"Password protected," he said.

I had no idea what that meant but it didn't sound promising. Bernie sat back and thought. I sat on the floor beside him and watched him think. We get some of our best work done that way. On the screen a tiny line went blink blink blink, on and on. Humans are capable of making lovely things, like silver bells. They also make lots of machines, some of which—cars, for example—are off the charts. Others, such as laptops, well, as Bernie's mom puts it, if you don't have anything nice to say don't say it. But I've heard her say, among other things, that Bernie should find another barber. And just look at Bernie's hair, the best you'll ever see on a guy! It just doesn't get rumplier than that. Bernie's mom is a piece of work. That should be your takeaway.

Meanwhile Bernie thought, the tiny line went blink blink blink, and my eyelids started getting heavy.

"Is he a numbers guy?" Bernie said.

I perked up. Was he talking about me? I'm certainly a numbers guy if we're stopping at two.

"I don't think so," he went on.

So probably not me, but now my sleepiness went pop for reasons unknown, and I was all ears. Whoa. Better stop right there. All ears is one of those human expressions that grabs your attention. If only my ears were the size of my whole self then I'd be hearing properly at last! That's what's in their minds when they talk about being all ears. But if my ears, already superb, grew to the size of whole me, well then . . . I don't actually know, and in fact don't want to, since it sounds kind of scary.

"Chaz is a word guy, of course. He loves the Trudi Tremaine series. That's what led to his job with Ariadne."

Bernie's fingers went tap tap tap on the desk. Human hands can be like little people, helping out with the thinking. For a while we had the tap tap tap and the blink blink blink going on at the same time. Then suddenly Bernie sat up straight.

"How about we try this?" His fingers went to the keyboard and did their tapping on it. "'*Holly Jolly Homicide*', first letters in caps." On the screen the blinking line disappeared and a photo of a house appeared, a snow covered house I recognized, all decorated for the holidays with a bunch of reindeer on the roof, with a big front window, and although no one was sitting in that window I knew right away I was looking at Dickens House. Two things were for sure at the moment. First, Bernie was still and forever the smartest human in the room. Second . . . well, the second thing may come to me later.

"Bingo," said Bernie. "We're in."

My tail started swishing back and forth across the floor. Now was great and the future was greater. Who could ask for more?

Bernie tapped, paused, tapped. All kinds of things appeared and disappeared on the screen, way too many to keep up with so I didn't even try. Keeping up with stuff like that can tire out your mind in no time flat, and what good is a tired mind to anybody? My eyelids knew that all by themselves and began getting heavier again, but at the very last instant, sleep looming before me like a pillow of cloud, a voice came out of the laptop, a man's voice, in fact the voice of Chaz. A nice voice, by the way—cheerful and friendly.

"Hi, there, Sheriff. My name's Chaz LeWitte and I—scratch that."

"Hi, there, Sheriff—or whoever's at the desk, find out their name if possible—my name's Chaz LeWitte and I work for Ariadne Carlisle. She sends her—maybe not. Find out whether they've met, but not from her. Hal, maybe?"

"Hi, there, Sheriff, or possibly Stell or Greg, my name's Chaz LeWitte and I work for Ariadne Carlisle, who I'm sure is looking forward to meeting you one day. Meanwhile, here's a signed copy of—dig through the boxes in the lower storage room to find one we've got lots of. I'm actually here on a research assignment. Ariadne needs help with . . . but what if . . . hmm."

"Hi, there, Sheriff, Stell, Greg, et cetera. My name's Chaz LeWitte and I work et cetera. Here's a signed copy of *Upon a Midnight Fear*, which Hallmark is basing a brand-new series on. Currently I'm helping Dame Ariadne with a bit of research. She's writing a scene that takes place in a small town police station in an old English village, and she needs to know the exact—nope."

"Hi, there, blah blah blah. My name's et cetera. *Upon a Midnight Fear* blah blah. She's writing a scene that takes place in a small town police station in an old English village, specifically in the room where the files on all the old cases are kept. Dame Ariadne's a stickler for accuracy and since this is the nearest old police station around, I'm asking if I could grab a quick—take a quick peek at your file room. No photos or anything like that. Just a quick peek so I can give her a verbal picture. Then the magic begins. Unh unh. Scratch that. Dame Ariadne will . . . will take it from there. Take it from there or . . . Yes, take it from there. Good enough. So please and thank you, et cetera, et cetera."

Bernie closed the laptop. He rose, dug through his pockets, and took out the Swiss Army knife. Wow! I hadn't seen the Swiss Army knife in a long time, not since Bernie had used it for some emergency work on the car, not the Beast but several Porsches before, all our Porsches being older as they got newer, if you see what I mean, the Beast being the very oldest. The particular Porsche in question, possibly the purple one with yellow doors, had lost most of its oomph on a dirt desert road far from anywhere—exactly our favorite kind of road, but not at night with no oomph, a cartel situation, and very strong snaky scents in the breeze. Bernie had tried every single one of the thingies on the Swiss Army knife, a finally the toothpick had done the trick. Bernie has quite a lot of mechanical ability, a fact unknown to a surprising number of people, including Weatherly. But my point is that if the Swiss Army knife was making an appearance, something was up.

"The file wouldn't take up much space, big guy," Bernie said. "We're going to do the whole thing all over again, this time for real."

He began by taking everything out of the desk, then opening the Swiss Army knife and unscrewing this and that until the desk was all in pieces. Then he took the chest of drawers apart the same way, stripped the bed, checked the mattress carefully, flipped it off the bed frame, took the bed frame apart. After that he got to work in the closet. Then came the bathroom, where he checked the toilet tank first thing. We'd come up big with toilet tanks before in our career, but not today. In the end everything that could be in pieces was in pieces.

Bernie looked at me. I looked at him. We had zip. He put

everything back together, me helping as best I could. We made that room look exactly like before. That's how things work at the Little Detective Agency. Bernie stuck the Swiss Army knife back in his pocket and brushed off his hands.

"Chet? What you got there?"

Oh my goodness. Not another sock? How was that possible?

Twenty-one

We left Chaz's room—Bernie closing the door behind us and the two silver bells tinkling softly—and headed down the hall on our way to whatever was coming next. I could hardly wait. You'd be the same if you worked here at the Little Detective Agency but that's not in the cards, no offense. As we passed the door with the single silver bell, Ariadne's room if I remembered right, and how could I forget, since this is where I'd come upon a somewhat—what would you call it? Emotional? Close enough. I'd come upon an emotional back and forth between Ariadne and Chaz, about what I had no idea. My point is that now as we passed by I heard faint sounds from within, emotional sounds like sighing or sniffling or snuffling or even outright crying, although muffled. I stopped where I was and took up a stiff position facing the door, slightly ajar. We call that pointing where I come from, just one more of the techniques we've invented, me and Bernie. Another is Bernie biting a Slim Jim in two, tossing one half to me and keeping the rest for himself. There are many more and I hope to get to some of them later.

Meanwhile Bernie was looking down at me. I looked up at him. "Something up?" he said, cocking his head to the door. "I don't hear—" He pressed his ear to the door. How wonderful he looked at that moment! He gave me a little nod, then knocked softly. "Ariadne?"

No answer from inside.

He knocked again and the door slowly swung open.

Silence. Well, not silence if you're counting the sighing, sniffling, and all the rest, and that's exactly the kind of thing we count in this business. The little sitting room where Ariadne and Chaz had had their little—scene, would that be it? Close enough. The sitting room was now empty. Two big furry boots lay on the floor, not lined up the way Esmé leaves her shoes when she comes to visit but more how Charlie does it, kicked off here and there. Through the doorway on the far wall I could see part of the bedroom, dark and shadowy like it was night, although it was still day outside the windows, but heavy clouds were sliding in across the sky, almost black. Ariadne was not in sight but she was in sound, if that makes any sense, and the sound was muffled crying, for sure.

"Ariadne?" Bernie said, his voice as low as I'd ever known it, almost as though he didn't want her to hear. But what sense would that make? I moved forward.

"Chet? I don't think—"

By then I had crossed the sitting room and entered the bedroom. Ariadne had a huge bed. It stood off to one side under a big skylight, now covered in snow, so that light coming in wasn't really light at all, but something else that made me uneasy. Ariadne lay on the bed, curled up in a ball, facing away from us and wearing her ratty robe. I didn't know what to do. I just stood there, a few steps from the bed, and made no noise. The muffled crying grew fainter and fainter and finally faded away. Ariadne lay motionless in a ball, her hands between her knees, breathing. Yes, I could hear the soft in and out of her breathing. So this was some form of sleep, and sleep was good. That was as far as I could take this situation on my own.

Bernie came up behind me. "Chet," he said softly. I waited for some—well, not command, more like a suggestion from him, but none came. His gaze was on Ariadne and he looked worried. Ariadne's eyes were closed, her cheeks tear-stained, her lips slightly parted. She wasn't wearing makeup and her hair was all askew, but for some reason she looked younger than at any of the other times I'd seen her, younger even than at the bookstore, where she'd been the top dog. Uh-oh. Not top dog. I didn't mean to go there. All I'm trying to get across is that she was far from top anything at the moment but still looked so young. I went over all the cases I remembered—perhaps not many—and found nothing to compare. Then a strange thought hit me: This was a Christmas case. Did that explain it?

The curtains over the nearest window fluttered, meaning the window was open. Was it cold in the room, cold for humans? Ariadne's feet and the lower part of her legs were bare, not covered by the ratty robe, and neither were her hands. On the covers lay pieces of something that at first I couldn't put together in my mind, and then could. It was a picture frame, taken apart. The picture itself lay close to her face, like maybe she'd been looking at it. Bernie reached down and picked up the picture.

He held it so we both could see, a photo of a man, the same man I'd seen in the other photo, only now he was alone, maybe walking away on a snowy trail. He had a wrapped present under one arm and had turned his head to look back, maybe at whoever was taking the picture. A big blond guy, not smiling as in the other photo, but I got the feeling he was about to smile any second.

Bernie gazed at that photo for what seemed like a very long time. Then he glanced down at the floor. A worn leather suitcase lay open, overflowing with a whole jumble of stuff, all smelling of mothballs. You can't miss that mothball smell, people, one of the strongest there is.

Bernie leaned forward and laid the photo back down where he'd found it, on the pillow by Ariadne's face. She breathed, her breath gently raising the near edge of the photo, even rippling it a bit, like it was coming alive.

"Remember all those facts, big guy?" Bernie said. "Rudy, missing. Ariadne, writer's block. Teddy, victim of an unsolved homicide. Chaz, found in the same place as Teddy's body. Case file on the Leeford case, also missing."

No, I did not remember all those facts. Also I did not not remember. My mind was neither here nor there. Was I on top of the situation? Possibly not, but pretty darn close! I waited for Bernie to go on. Meanwhile, we were back in Silver Mountain, cruising down that fancy main street.

"Now we've got one more fact," Bernie said. "Although it's more of an opinion, or—what was that word Ariadne used? Aperçu?" He laughed to himself. "Can't wait to try that out on Weatherly. But call it whatever you want, here it is. In that photo of Teddy Leeford walking away he had his head turned to look back in a way that reminded me of her photo of Rudy. Also walking away and looking back. Remember?"

Again, I did not remember and did not not remember. I was in a groove. That was my takeaway.

"It was uncanny, at least to me," Bernie went on. "Not that I'd want to defend it in a court of law, but there are more things in heaven and earth, Horatio, than are dreamt of in your philosophy."

Horatio was in the picture? The only Horatio we knew was Hammerin' Horatio Herrero, a jackhammer specialist who'd dug tunnels under the safes of numerous banks until one night he'd popped up in a bank where we were waiting, me and Bernie. And then the fun began, extremely noisy fun I'll try to get to some other time. But if he was back on the street, or under one, such as this street in Silver Mountain, then . . . then this case was about more than Rudy! How exciting! Especially since although reindeer kept turning up out the ying-yang none of them was ever Rudy. Why did that have to be?

"Chet? Howling? Really?"

If howling was going on—and from the expressions on the faces of some folks on the sidewalk it was clear that something was up—then it was my job to put a stop to it, even if I myself was perfectly innocent. I'm a professional and that means you have to dig deep—and if you know me you know that digging's one of my best things, no jackhammer needed.

"That's more like it," Bernie said.

I planted a quick lick on the side of his face, my tongue perhaps not aiming with its normal accuracy. But Bernie gave himself a bit of an eye rub and we were good to go, parking in front of a fine stone building. Bernie read the writing on the big window. "'Silver Mountain Development, International Corporate Office.'" We went inside.

"We'd like to see Drake Leeford," Bernie said.

The woman at the front desk eyed Bernie, then me, and back to Bernie. Sometimes their eyes come back to me once more. Those are the eyes of what's known as a dog person, although they look just like any old human, nothing dog-like about them. This woman was not a dog person.

"Do you have an appointment?" she said.

"No, but we met him on the mountain yesterday." He handed her our card, the one, as I may have explained that Suzie designed, with flowers on it instead of the .38 Special or the single shot .410, neither of which we had on this trip. Now, as the woman studied our card, I had a very strange thought: maybe the flowers were better. Whoa! How crazy was that! I mushed the thought down at once. "We're happy to wait," Bernie said.

The woman rose and disappeared up a broad wooden staircase, the wood blond and highly polished. I should have mentioned that this was a fancy-looking office, reminding me of a fancy ranch where we'd once worked a case involving stolen snakeskin cowboy boots that had belonged to someone by the name of Tom Mix who I don't think I got to meet, the whole case over and done with before they'd even finished telling us what it was about, snakeskin being a smell I don't miss even if the boots happen to be stuck up a fireplace chimney. What I'm getting at is that this office reminded me of that ranch, except for the lack of the heads of various creatures hung on the walls, which made it even better. Just my opinion.

The woman came back down the stairs and motioned for us. "Mr. Leeford will see you now." She sounded surprised.

Drake Leeford was waiting for us at the top of the stairs, our card in his hand. "As soon as she said dog I knew it was you two," he said, a big smile on his face. "Chet, right? A champ on the mountain, for sure. You've changed your mind about the avy dog program, Bernie?"

They shook hands, Drake turning out to be one of those powerful handshakers, an older guy, yes, but the still strong type. Except for his close cut silvery hair, hidden by his helmet when we were on the mountain, he didn't look that much older than Bernie.

"Chet's already got a job," Bernie said, "which is actually why we're here."

"Ah," Drake said. He glanced at the card. "You didn't mention you were a private eye."

"It didn't seem relevant," Bernie said.

"But now?" Drake said, still smiling. He seemed slightly bigger than he had on the mountain, perhaps a tich bigger than Bernie.

"Maybe just slightly relevant," Bernie said. "We're at the gathering information stage."

"Well, come on in. Sit down. Something to drink? I'm having coffee myself, more like self-defense—a lot of drinking goes on at this time of year. But we've got everything."

"Coffee's fine, thanks."

Drake poured coffee into two mugs. I waited for him to say, "Water for Chet?" But he did not. Instead, he pointed to a big screen on one wall. Things were happening on it, different-colored blobs on the move, none of them making sense to me.

"My new toy," he said. "Granular meteorology of the Rockies in real time. See that purple part, kinda looks like a giant teardrop? That's a check in mail, Bernie. Snow that gets measured in feet, not inches. Maybe even yards, not feet. Stick around for three days, maybe four, and there'll be enough to challenge even a ripper like yourself."

"I'm no ripper," Bernie said.

Drake shook his head. "There's no fooling me when it comes to skiing. I grew up on boards. And one thing I know—the real rippers, the back country boys, are humble about it."

He motioned for us—well, maybe just Bernie, but us was what he meant—to sit. Bernie sat on a couch beneath the big screen. Drake pulled up chair and sat nearby. I sat on the floor between them, nice and comfortable and at the same time doing my job.

"I didn't grow up on boards," Bernie said, sipping his coffee. "I'm a city boy, born and raised in the Valley."

"A happening place," Drake said. "Fourteen point five percent of our lift tickets were sold to folks with Valley addresses in our last fiscal year."

"I understand you built the company from scratch," Bernie said.

"I hired good people," Drake said. "And had some luck along the way. But the potential was always here. The mountain was waiting to happen."

"How did you get the idea?" Bernie said.

Drake set his mug on a side table, slowly and carefully, although a drop or two spilled anyway. "It was obvious, like I said. So what can I do for you, Bernie?"

"Maybe nothing," Bernie said. "The case was initially about a missing reindeer."

"Assuming that's not a joke, who's the client?"

"It's not a joke," Bernie said. "The reindeer's name is Rudy. Normally we don't reveal the client's name, but it'll be impossible to have this discussion that way. The client is Ariadne Carlisle."

"Ariadne," Drake said. "Our most famous resident, at least part time. I haven't seen her in years, maybe decades. I hear she sticks pretty close to that ranch of hers when she's here. Please say hello for me."

"Will do," Bernie said.

"Is she still writing?"

"Every day."

"I've never read any of her books. Not much of a reader, I admit. Murder mysteries, are they?"

"And all with a Christmas theme. I think that's why she keeps some reindeer, including Rudy—for the atmospheric effect."

"Whatever works," Drake said.

"She also likes the reindeer just for themselves."

That part, liking the reindeer for themselves, didn't seem to interest Drake. He shrugged, picked up his mug, drank more coffee. At that moment Bernie turned to check the big screen. Drake took a real close look at him.

"I'm guessing you'd like my mountain staff to keep an eye out for Rudy," he said.

"That would be helpful," Bernie said, "but it's not why I'm here. The person who originally contacted me was Ariadne's assistant, Chaz LeWitte. Do you know him?"

"No."

"Does the name ring a bell?"

"No."

"Chaz LeWitte was the man rescued from Devil's Purse the other day. Chet and I found him."

"Ah," Drake said. "I heard something about a skier falling in there. I didn't know about the Ariadne connection. But that's state land. If it was ours that whole section off the north side would be roped off. You can be damn sure of that."

"No one's suggesting your company's at fault," Bernie said. "And Chaz was snowshoeing, not skiing."

"Very rough country for snowshoeing," said Drake. "Or for any kind of skiing. How's he doing?"

"In a coma at the hospital, last I heard," Bernie said.

Drake swirled his coffee around. "Do they expect he'll come out of it?"

"I don't know."

Drake shook his head. "Poor bastard. Did he have much back country experience?"

"Not to my knowledge," Bernie said.

Drake looked up at Bernie, their gazes meeting. "Then what the hell was he doing in a place like that? Don't tell me he was searching for the reindeer, Ruby, was it?"

"Rudy," Bernie said. "As in Rudolph."

Drake smacked his forehead. "Of course! I'm an idiot. The shiny nose and all that. I better get into the Christmas spirit and fast or my wife's gonna kill me."

"Your wife Nellie?" Bernie said.

"Whoa there, buddy." Drake sat back. "The divorce was decades ago. How do you know about Nellie?"

"I don't really know anything about her," Bernie said. "Her name came up."

"I'm starting not to follow you," Drake said.

"My fault," Bernie said.

That caught my attention. Something was Bernie's fault. Not possible. Therefore, some kind of trickiness was in the works. Whoa! Had I just done a so-therefore, normally Bernie's territory? And then came the most astonishing thought of my entire life. Maybe I, Chet, was the tricky one! Not just astonishing, but also scary. Did I want to be the tricky one? I did not. Could you be the tricky one even it you didn't want to? I rose, stepped over to a big potted plant, and curled up behind it, or at least mostly. I could still keep an eye on Bernie. He glanced at me, perhaps with a somewhat surprised expression on his face, and then went back to something he seemed to be in the middle of, me possibly missing the beginning.

". . . my impression that she seemed disturbed not just about what had happened to Chaz but also by where it happened. That led to a discussion about your brother Teddy. She showed me a photo of him—the two of them, actually—taken by you on a camping trip. Apparently, your wife Nellie was there too, which is how I know about her and all I know about her."

Drake rose and stood by a window, his back to us. Outside a few strands of tinsel went flying by in the wind. Drake's shoulders rose like he was taking a deep deep breath, and fell. He turned to Bernie, his face hard but his eyes misty.

"I understand," he said.

And then silence, a silence with a strange feeling in the air, a kind of soundless buzz. That's a signal to keep your trap shut, which we did, me and Bernie.

Drake put his hands together the way humans do when they're praying. I've witnessed human praying now and then. A complete mystery, but not one of those mysteries—like the ones we solve—with something bad at the bottom. That was my impression, based on nothing. Next Drake stuffed his hands in his pockets. It was like he didn't know what to do with them, an expression you hear from time to time. You never hear "his hands don't know what to do with him." But why not?

"I understand Ariadne's reaction," he said. "Meaning the Devil's Purse part." He shook his head. "I'm just shocked."

"At what?" Bernie said.

"At myself. Or maybe about how goddam old I am. When you said Devil's Purse, I didn't even think of . . . of what happened before. It was so long ago." He put his hands to his face, or they went there by themselves. "God help me."

"By what happened before you mean . . . ?" Bernie said. Wow? Had he just left a question hanging in the air? One of our very best techniques. Why didn't he use it more often?

Drake's hands dropped down to his sides, for just an instant curling into fists, but then relaxing. "What kind of a question was that?" he said, obviously unfamiliar with the hanging in the air type, rare, as I believe I already suggested. "I mean the death of my brother Teddy, which you clearly know about."

"We don't know much, beyond the fact that he was murdered, and the crime was never solved," Bernie said.

Drake came forward, sat on his chair, took a big drink from his mug, like he was very thirsty. Normally you see that more with water than coffee, but lots of things you see turn out not to mean anything, at least to me. I've been lucky all my life, especially since I met Bernie. There's a whole story about that. Was a cat involved? But no time for any of that now. I ambled over and found a spot on the floor between them.

"Sorry," Drake said. "I didn't mean to be a jerk. It just took me back, that's all. A long way back." He set the mug on the table, steadily this time. "I don't remember the photo you're talking about. Where was it taken?"

Was that a question? When that happens, when somebody in an interview—and I was pretty sure that was what we had going down here—asks a question, Bernie says this works better if we ask the questions, but now he did not.

"On Mount Murdstone," Bernie said. "I don't know where exactly. There seemed to be some sort of cave or mine in the background."

Drake nodded. "Caves we got, natural and manmade. The occasional prospector still turns up, believe it or not. Teddy had a thing about them."

"What do you mean?"

"He thought they were fundamentally destructive, not stewards of the land. We saw ourselves as stewards. We had a lot of land, dating way back, but there was no silver on it, no valuable minerals of any kind, not commercially viable at all. My folks tried to sell off some when I was a kid for twelve dollars an acre, and got zero offers."

"And now?" Bernie said. "Per acre?"

"Ha!" Drake said. "I couldn't even tell you. The market would set the value but it's not for sale." He waved his hand in a broad gesture, sort of at everything. "This is my dream. You don't sell your dream."

"When did it first occur to you—developing the mountain, the skiing, the resort, all of it?"

"Couldn't tell you," Drake said. "It was like I was born with it."

"Was Teddy born with it, too?"

Drake's head went back a little. For a moment I thought he'd decided not to like Bernie. But what sense would that make?

He held up one finger, not quite pointing it at Bernie, not quite waving at him, just a hint of both. "Here's one thing to get straight, Bernie. The dream was mine. Teddy got it from me. Understand?"

Bernie nodded. "But," he said, "do you ever think the whole development is at least partly a memorial to your brother?"

Drake thought about that. "No," he said. "And—not telling you how to do your job—I don't see what this has to do with a missing reindeer."

"Probably nothing, like I said," Bernie told him.

"Is Ariadne paying you to look . . . to do whatever it is you're doing?"

"We've been hired to find Rudy, full stop. But when we run into an unsolved murder we can't help getting interested. Call it an occupational hazard."

Drake smiled. "I'll do that." He checked his watch.

Bernie rose. "Thanks for the coffee. Before we go, do you have any thoughts about what happened? Did Teddy have enemies? Someone else interested in Ariadne, for example?"

"No enemies. Everybody liked Teddy. He was one of those popular kids. As for Ariadne, I'm sure there were plenty of guys with fantasies, but I never heard of the kind of thing you're suggesting."

"Then what? What could have happened?"

"If I had to guess I'd say he ran into some crazy old mountain man up there, got himself in an argument."

"Did you pass that idea onto the sheriff?"

Drake nodded. "Mitch Cuffy was the sheriff. The last old-time type sheriff we had, and a pretty sharp guy despite his country ways. He looked into it, turned up nothing. Not a single damn thing." He sighed. "It was a long time ago."

Up on the screen the purple blob shuddered and began growing again.

Twenty-two

In the Beast and headed who knows where. How exciting was that?

"Maybe I can get the audio version, pick up where I left off," Bernie said.

That sounded both great and incomprehensible at the same time. I could listen to Bernie talk forever and even longer. Meanwhile he eased us off the road and began monkeying around with his phone and some of the buttons on the dash, doing exactly what I didn't—whoa! Monkeying around? What was up with my mind? Why does it go places like that? Were baboons monkeys? If so I knew monkeys, having had an experience with a baboon during the Peanut case, the baboon and I both finding ourselves prisoners of some real bad guys, although not for long. I'd had no problem with my baboon buddy and wouldn't have wanted to. And neither would you. Have you heard baboons hoot? Once is more than enough. And I won't even mention their teeth. What I'm getting at is that Bernie's no baboon. I've never heard him hoot, not once, and as for his teeth compared to baboon teeth— well, that's just not fair.

A voice came out of the speakers. "Chapter Nine."

"Ah," said Bernie, pulling back onto the road. "She does her own audio."

And the voice continued, a voice I knew, of course. Once I've heard your voice I've got it in me forever.

"Rain poured down in buckets, washing away the recent snow, meaning this Christmas would not be white. Trudi, in a gloomy mood already following her inconclusive conversation with the new vicar, raised the hood on her mac, unfurled her brolly, and trudged into the graveyard that lay behind St. Eustace's, her wellies squishing in the spongy damp sod.

"The older graves, stumpy and eroded, were found closest to the church, so as Trudi moved along she was also advancing in Potherington history, from ancient times to last week, when Mr. Fergus Willin, one-time beekeeper who enjoyed his pint perhaps overly, was laid to rest. Tremaines, her people, began showing up in the years following the Glorious Revolution. Her aunt Roberta was continually pestering Trudi on the subject of securing her own plot. St. Eustace is running out of space, my dear. It's this dreadful population explosion. Back of my hand to St. Eustace, Trudi had thought to herself. She was in no hurry to formalize her own denouement, perhaps in a magical way putting off the actual event.

"In a few steps she entered the Great War, row upon row, followed by two sparse decades, and then the next popular section, which she knew was coming although the interred had not. Soon she entered the fifties, her goal, and followed a row of Greenloughs and Fortescues down to the end, where, by a stone marked Miranda Greenlough, 'who lived and loved,' she found she was not alone. A tall man wearing a wide-brimmed hat rain and a long black slicker stood motionless by the stone, his back to her.

"'Doctor Fortescue?' Trudi said. She wasn't the least surprised. Trudi had stopped believing in coincidences.

"Dr. Fortescue turned slowly toward her. He had the face of one used to mastering any—"

A strange little screech came through the speakers, like things were colliding, followed by the voice of Nixon Panero.

"Hey, Bernie, it worked."

"What did?"

"Telling Rui to kill somebody. Unblocked him just like that. We're all set to ship on the twenty-fourth. Where to—your place or Leda's?"

Bernie thought that over. "Make it Weatherly's." He gave Nixon the address.

Bernie parked the car and shut everything down. "Can't wait to see his reaction," he said, losing me completely. Meanwhile, I saw we were parked across from a very plain building, brick with no decorations of any kind, not Christmas and not Hanukkah. Hanukkah came easily to me this time, and with it the fact I knew the plain brick building was the sheriff's office and had even been inside. Funny how the mind works. Was Hanukkah somehow the key? I looked forward to finding out more—or anything—about it.

We sat. The sky darkened. Sometimes in this business you sit on folks, almost always perps in my experience. You don't actually sit on them, although that does happen, but it usually means waiting outside some place—a bar, say, or surprisingly often a strip club—for someone to come out. Were we sitting on the sheriff's office? That would be a first. There's no one like Bernie for coming up with firsts. A gift, really. Could it somehow be turned into money? I was putting my mind to work on that question, with no progress so far, when Bernie said, "I get why she reads her own stuff. Her voice is amazing."

Uh-oh. He'd lost me. Amazing voices was the subject? There was no voice more amazing than his own. Some—well, many—human voices are a bit on the thin side, like there's not enough

power pushing out the sound. Not an issue with me, amigos! Or
Bernie. With him the sound comes out like a deep stream, held
back, if anything, and with plenty of oomph in reserve.

We sat. Bernie thought at the same time. I was happy just to
sit. After a while he got busy with his phone and the dash buttons again, and through the speakers came: "Trudi had stopped
believing in coincidences."

Ah, Ariadne. She had a nice voice, too! Well, well. Who was
keeping up, maybe even getting his nose out front? Not too
shabby on the part of ol' Chet, not shabby at all! Just sitting and
sitting yet somehow on a roll. Life hands out little treats from
time to time, especially to me. What have I done to deserve it?
Any point dwelling on that? Not that I could see.

Bernie played Ariadne a few more times, more than two for
sure. But why? Who was this Trudi person? A perp? Would she
look good in an orange jumpsuit? Then came a crazy idea. Trudi
would look good in anything! What a thought! I hadn't even be-
gun to deal with it when the door to the sheriff's office opened
and a solidly built woman stepped out. Bernie started us up,
switching off the sound at the same time, just at the "stopped
believing" part.

The woman wore a beige uniform, had a gun on her hip, and
was shrugging herself into a red and white puffy jacket. This had
to be Deputy Sheriff something or other. Stell? That stuck in my
mind. She and Bernie had had a discussion involving cats. You
don't forget things like that.

Deputy Stell walked down the street, very soon entering a
store. Bernie read the sign on the front window: "'Fun Toys For
One and All.'" I got ready to hop right out, but that didn't seem
to be happening. We kept sitting. After not too long, Deputy Stell
came out, now carrying a gift-wrapped package. She walked to

a nearby car, small and boxy, and got in. So many people drove cars with no pizzazz. What was the point?

Deputy Stell pulled onto the street. We let a car or two go by and then followed. We can follow in any way you like—from close behind, far behind, one lane over, many lanes over, even from in front. And once from in front while going backward! The Little Detective Agency, ladies and gentlemen.

The small boxy car led us out of the center of town and up into some hills, curving higher and higher, the houses up there looking nice and big. But Deputy Stell turned into a driveway long before we'd have gotten that far. She parked and went to the front door of a small but cared for house, opened up with a key that flashed in the last of the fading light and went inside. We kept going, pulled a U-ee, and parked across the street and a few doors down in front of a house much like hers.

We sat. Soon the door opened and Deputy Stell, no longer wearing the puffy jacket, stepped out with a teenage girl beside her. They were talking. Bernie slid down the windows.

". . . mostly we just watched cartoons," the girl was saying.

"Peppa?" said Deputy Stell.

"What else?" said the girl.

"I wish I could hear what they're talking about," Bernie said.

Oh, dear. Meanwhile Deputy Stell was handing the girl some money and they were saying goodbye.

"I think the girl just said goodbye," Bernie said.

Wow! Was he upping his hearing game at last? We really were unstoppable. The girl went to a car, also of the small and boxy type, parked across the street, not even glancing at us, and drove away. Deputy Stell went back in her house and shut the door. All this—the sitting, the tailing, the watching—is like a dance, Bernie says, the steps always the same but the music different. When he tried that one out on Weatherly she said, "You've had too much to drink, boyfriend." I'd never allow myself such a thought but Weatherly really was a gem.

"Okey doke," Bernie said. We got out of the car, crossed the street and knocked on Deputy Stell's door, Bernie doing the actual knocking, which is how we usually handle this part of . . . of the dance. Yes, the dance. Perfect.

Sometimes in this business a knock on the door gets answered with silence, even though you know there's someone inside, even lots of someones. Sometimes you get a voice saying who is it, maybe a scared voice, maybe angry, maybe sleepy. Sometimes you get a line of bullets ripping through the door. And sometimes, like now, and my preference, someone simply opens up and looks out.

"Yes?" said Deputy Stell, now barefoot and gunless, wearing jeans and a sweatshirt and holding a sippy cup. "Ah, Bernie, was it? And Chet? You were the one looking for Mr. Cuffy?"

"And we found him, thanks to you," Bernie said. "But some questions came out of that and maybe you can help us."

"Questions about what? Are you a cop?"

Bernie handed her our card. She studied it, making no mention of the flowers. I took that for a good sign. "Can anyone vouch for you?"

"Do you know Albie Rudge?" Bernie said.

"The rescue pilot?"

"Yeah."

Deputy Stell looked a bit surprised. "Wait here." She closed the door.

We stood on the front step. Down the street, Christmas lights came on at a house, and another and another. What a lovely sight! Maybe not so lovely were the giant puffy things—giant white puffies with big black smiles and tall black hats—popping up on some of the lawns and leaning this way and that in the breeze.

"Easy there, big guy," Bernie said. "It's just Frosty the Snowman. Lots of inflatable Frostys."

Just Frosty the Snowman? What did that even mean? But I latched onto the inflatable part. Inflatable meant that if you sank your teeth into whatever the object, a balloon, for example, then—

I felt Bernie's hand on the back of my neck, not heavily, just there. Meanwhile the last remaining daylight was checking out fast, headed where I had no idea, even though I'd watched Bernie explain the whole thing to Charlie and Esmé, drawing with a stick in the playground dirt. After it was done Esmé said, "Why doesn't Earth spin the other way?" and Charlie broke the stick in half and used the sharp end of one part to dig a worm out of the dirt. What a clever kid!

The door opened.

"Albie says you're a stubborn and uncooperative son of a bitch," Stell said. "But Chet's the best crime fighter in Arizona. Come on in."

How nice of Albie! Somehow, he'd left out the part about Bernie always being the smartest person in the room, but who can think of everything? We followed Stell through the front hall, small and tidy, with two jackets on hooks, her red and white one, and another just like it but much smaller, and into a living room of what I believe is called the cozy type. The furniture—a couch and a couple of chairs—looked comfy, the rug felt soft under my paws, and a steady little fire burned in the fireplace. The gift wrapped present lay under a small Christmas tree, strung with soft lights and a bit of tinsel. I took all that in without really knowing it. What actually caught my attention was the boy in the wheelchair.

The wheelchair stood between the comfy couch and one of the comfy chairs. The boy's eyes were on the TV screen, hanging on the opposite wall. Some sort of cartoon seemed to be happening on the screen, a cartoon involving pigs. Charlie liked to watch this same cartoon. I didn't get the appeal. I knew pigs. The boy himself seemed to be of about Charlie's age. He even looked like him.

"Timmy?" said Stell. "This is Mr. Little and Chet."

"Hi, Timmy," Bernie said. "And call me Bernie."

Timmy didn't call Bernie anything, didn't speak at all. His eyes stayed on the screen, didn't shift our way even for an instant, like we weren't even there. Those eyes were light blue, maybe the lightest blue I'd ever seen, like one of those days when the sky seems farther away than usual. Bernie says I can't be trusted when it comes to colors, so forget this part. But had I ever seen human eyes more beautiful? That's what to remember.

"Have a seat," said Stell. She went over to Timmy and handed him the sippy cup. "Thanks, Mom," Stell said quietly. Timmy was silent. He took the cup without looking but didn't sip from it, just held it in his hands. The pigs talked in odd human voices, something about a picnic.

Bernie and I sat, Bernie on the couch and me between him and Timmy. Stell sat on one of the chairs.

"What can I do for you?" she said.

"It's about Chaz LeWitte," Bernie told her.

Stell was silent.

"The man who—"

"Yes," she said. "I know."

"Did you also know Chet and I were the ones who found him?"

"I didn't when you came to the office. I do now."

"How did you find that out?"

"This is a small town. It just doesn't look that way."

Bernie smiled. "Small towns are the toughest."

"What do you mean?"

"They cling to their secrets."

Stell nodded a very slight nod.

"Do you know Chaz LeWitte?" Bernie said.

Stell said nothing.

"Or have you ever met him?"

She didn't answer that one either. Maybe she was thinking of answering it, but while that was going on or not I kind of began shifting a bit in Timmy's direction. Why? Hard to say. For one thing I'm a big fan of kids in general. What is it about them? I don't know, but whatever it was Timmy had it big time. There was something about him, a very skinny kid now that I had a closer look, nothing extra on him at all, except for his hair, on the long-ish side, and also wonderful, more like silk that hair. Timmy was a fine fine specimen, no doubt about that at all. Those high sky eyes, his beautifully shaped even if quite weak-looking hands with their loose grip on the sippy cup, that silky hair: they didn't come better than this. I got real close. Any closer and we'd be touching. I sat beside him, both of us watching those annoying pigs. I got the feeling that Stell was checking me out, but I didn't look at her. For this little while I was no longer on the job and didn't even feel bad about it.

When Stell spoke her voice sounded a bit thick, like emotions were happening inside her. "Yes, I met Chaz LeWitte," she said.

"He came to the office while I was on duty, asking to see the file room, something about doing research for Ariadne Carlisle. You know—the famous author. Pretty much the whole of the high valley is hers. She'd sent him to get some details right for one of her stories. He brought some signed copies for the staff. I didn't see why not so I took him down. That's about it."

"How long was he there?"

"Couldn't have been more than ten minutes."

"Were you with him the whole time?"

"Until the last couple of minutes—I had to go upstairs to take a call. It was the week before Thanksgiving and things were busy."

And maybe there was more back and forth like that, but by then I'd leaned over a bit and laid my head on Timmy's lap. The strangest thing, really, like I was the one in need. But it felt right. After not too long he let go of the sippy cup and rested his hands on my head, even stroking it a little. His eyes never strayed from the screen. It got very quiet in the room, except for the pigs, maybe discussing a trip to the beach, although even the pigs seemed quieter. And if I did happen to tune in to what Bernie and Stell were talking about it seemed to be coming from far away.

"I'm not sure what all this is about, Bernie. What are you getting at?"

"Right now, I'm just trying to establish a timeline."

"Mind sharing it?"

"Not at all. Sometime last fall Chaz found out about the murder of Teddy Leeford. The week before Thanksgiving he came to your office looking for the case file. The day after Thanksgiving, Rudy—Ariadne's favorite reindeer and maybe even a sort of talisman for her—disappears. Last week he hires us to find

Rudy. Two days ago, we find him at the bottom of Devil's Purse, where Teddy's body was also found."

"What's the implication of all that?"

"I don't know. I just know there has to be one. That's enough for us."

"Enough for you to what?"

"Work the case."

"You mean the Rudy case?"

"Partly."

"What else?"

"The Teddy case. And if it turns out that Chaz's fall was no accident, then that, too."

"You don't believe in coincidences?" she said.

"Less and less," said Bernie.

Around then I felt Stell's gaze on me. And maybe not just me, but on Timmy as well. I didn't look to make sure. I trusted the feeling.

"What can I do to help?" she said.

"If there's anything you know that could be at all relevant, now's when to share it."

"Actually, I have more of a question. If I went down to the file room looking for the file, would I find it?"

"No," Bernie said.

"How do you know?"

"I won't tell you that."

"That doesn't seem fair," said Stell.

Bernie didn't answer. After a long, long pause, Stell spoke again.

"You're saying Chaz stole it in those two minutes I left him alone?"

"He's the leading candidate."

"Are there others?"

"Possibly."

"Like who?"

"No idea."

"So if you're right, Chaz himself was working the Teddy Leeford case?"

"Yes."

"Does he have any law enforcement background?"

"His background is in English literature," Bernie said, all of this still far away. The nearby world was just me and Timmy, my head on his lap, his hand resting on my neck, little fingers making little movements now and then, and his eyes on the TV, although from the look in them he was seeing much farther than that, seeing far far away. "Did you tell anyone about Chaz's visit to the file room?" Bernie went on.

"A few people—when I handed out the signed books."

"Did you mention that Chaz was on his own down there for a few minutes?"

"No. Why would I? It didn't seem at all remarkable at the time."

"Do you remember who got the books?"

"Sheriff Monk, for one. I could go back and check the duty list, maybe figure out the others."

"That might help. You've got our card. And for now—on account of all the unknowns we seem to be dealing with—I'm hoping you'll keep this conversation to yourself."

There was a long silence. During this silence—not including the pigs, of course—Timmy murmured very softly. How softly? So soft that even I couldn't hear.

"Agreed," Stell said at last, "but I'll find my own reasons."

I looked up. Bernie was nodding. Then he was on his feet,

holding out his hand for shaking, but Stell gave him a very quick hug instead, her head turned away. I don't remember me getting up at all, or moving across the floor, or leaving the house. All that's a complete blank, like it never happened. But it must have because the next thing I knew we were outside, me and Bernie, headed down Stell's walk, the door to her house closed behind us. That was when I heard Timmy speak from inside the house.

"Bye-bye, Chet."

That was it. Bye-bye, Chet. And perhaps very softly, because Bernie didn't seem to hear. But I had a feeling that Stell had heard, because through the door came the sound a human makes when she claps a hand to her chest, right over the heart. And she said, "Oh, my God. You spoke."

But Bernie didn't seem to hear that either. We got in the car. Bernie turned like he was going to tell me something, but right then a squad car came slowly down the street. Bernie waited till the taillights disappeared and then he said, "You did us proud. You're the brains of the outfit, no doubt about it."

Me the brains? That had to be one of Bernie's jokes. He can be very funny at times. If I were the brains how could the Little Detective Agency be so successful, except for the finances part? Still, it was nice to hear. If only I knew exactly what I'd done I could do it again, and then hear Bernie say "You did us proud," once more. Or even more than once! But you can't have everything, which kind of makes sense, because who could possibly carry everything? You could have it, but you couldn't go anywhere. What would be the point of that?

We took off into the night.

Twenty-three

We drove back into the center of town. Nighttime now but Bonanza Street was all lit up and there was plenty of action, especially shopping but also eating and drinking. Even though it was on the cold side for humans, the restaurants and bars had outdoor set-ups, warmed by fire pits, glowing heaters, and some tall clear chimneys with flames shooting up inside them, a lovely sight.

"What do you think?" Bernie said. "Hungry?"

Famished was the answer. When had I last eaten, even the smallest morsel? I couldn't remember, and in any case small morsels or even oversized morsels do not do it for me. The next thing I knew we were nicely set up at a sidewalk table beside one of those flaming chimneys and a waiter with earring bells that tinkled with every movement was saying, "What can I get for this handsome fellow? And for you, too, sir?"

Soon we were chowing down, Bernie on burgers and fries with a big frosty mug of beer and me with steak tips and water. Singers came strolling down the street and stopped right in front of us to sing a very cheerful song, possibly about jingling bells. What with the cheerfulness and also the waiter's earrings, who wouldn't have felt at least a little excitement, even enough to spark some of that crazy running that pops up in one's life now and then, possibly not enough? Meaning the time to make up for that shortfall had arrived! And with a bang! Yes, a real bang, having to do with a chair—unoccupied, which was a good thing, and also one of those happy accidents—that suddenly went flying into the street, somewhat like a tumbleweed although noisier—a happy accident followed with some hard cuts, swerves, and other specialties of the house, talking about my house, amigos, the house of Chet the Jet, where nothing, at least nothing physical is off the table and every day's a brand-new—

"Ch—et?"

Not long after that, everything was back to the way it had been before, nice and peaceful, with us chowing down again, the singers gone, and folks at nearby tables enjoying drinks Bernie had sent them. He's the generous type and it was Christmastime, so that explains that. Meanwhile shoppers kept passing by, all in good moods, all carrying brightly wrapped packages, one or two of those packages somewhat oddly shaped, quite a lot like shotguns or rifles. I took note of that, being a professional.

I was licking the bowl, a fine way to end a meal, as you may or may not have discovered, when two couples walked by, an older one and a younger one.

But they didn't quite walk by, because the older guy suddenly stopped and turned to us.

"Hey," he said. "You still here?"

I stopped licking the bowl and stood up. It was something to do with the guy's voice, hard to nail down exactly what. This guy—beefy, apple-shaped, with a bulby reddish nose—looked familiar. And so did the younger guy, an outdoorsy type with icy blue eyes. I remembered him from . . . from Figaro's Leap! Yes, that was it, up on the mountain, where we'd first met Drake Leeford, owner of the whole shebang, if I'd gotten it right. This dude was Von Sikes, Drake's ski guy, and the older fellow with the unpleasant voice was . . . was—

"Evening, Sheriff Monk," Bernie said.

Right! The sheriff. Not Sheriff Cuffy, the sheriff from long ago. We had no problems with him. This was the sheriff now, and we maybe had problems with him, starting with that voice.

Von Sikes came closer. "Hey, there. Bernie, right?" For just the slightest moment he didn't look friendly, and then just like that he went to looking very friendly. "You two know each other?" he said.

Sheriff Monk turned to him. "Huh?"

"Met Bernie here—and this champion pooch of his—over at Figaro's Leap," Von said.

"What the hell's that?" said Monk.

"For God sake, Pop," the younger woman said. "Figaro's Leap is the most famous run on the mountain. Everybody knows about it."

Monk swung around toward her, in the same motion sending a wave of his breath my way, the booziest breath I'd smelled in some time, and boozy breaths are one of those human things you get to know well in our line of work.

"Did I ask you to stick your nose in?" he said to the younger woman, his daughter, if I'd gotten hold of the right end of the stick, an expression that makes no sense, but perhaps I've gone into this already. Meanwhile the older woman, who'd been arm-and-arm with Monk, now blinked—one of those long blinks where the eyes seem to stay shut for too long—and then moved slightly away.

"Hey, now," Sikes said.

Monk took a breath, tried to control himself. "Sure, easy to say hey now, but I'm sheriff of this godforsaken town and here comes this private eye from outta state claiming he's searching for some goddamn reindeer. What am I? An ignorant fish who swallows any stupid story?"

That was so interesting! Why? Because at that moment I really could see him as a fish! A fat fish-faced fish who'd had too many. My my. Something new, and I like new things. I also like old things. I like new and old. But that's just me.

"But Pop," the younger woman said. "It's not a stupid story. It's true. Mizz Carlisle lost one of those reindeer of hers. The *Weekly Miner* wrote about it."

"Who reads that rag?" Monk said.

"I do," said Sikes. "We own it."

"Huh?" said Monk.

"Silver Mountain Development," Sikes said. "Lock stock and barrel."

"That's not what I mean by we," said Monk.

"No?" said Sikes.

He said it quite softly but Monk looked down and seemed to . . . to deflate a little, as though he was one of those inflatable snowmen and someone like me had done what he wanted to do.

Sikes came closer. "Nice running into you again, Bernie. Good luck with the reindeer and if you ever change your mind about the avy dog program reach out. Happy holidays."

They shook hands. Then Sikes gave Monk a very slight push in the small of the back, hardly more than a touch, but it seemed to propel him anyway and they all moved down the street. Bernie watched until they were out of sight.

"It's a small town, just like Stell said." He downed the rest of his beer. "So's Potherington," he added, losing me at the very end.

Next thing, Bernie was going to get up and we'd be out of there. He hadn't gotten up but I knew he would. I could feel his legs getting ready even though I wasn't touching them. But they were almost my legs in a way, impossible to explain so I suppose I shouldn't have even started on the whole thing. But what I'm trying to get to was my surprise when the waiter came with the check, those bell earrings jingling, Bernie said, "I'll have another, and more water for Chet." He sat back, stretched out his legs, and gazed around, first at the fiery glass chimney and then at the night sky.

"There's a glow tonight," he said. "I'm not imagining it."

I myself saw no glow, but if Bernie said there was a glow, then that was that. The waiter came. Bernie sipped his beer, set it down very carefully on the table, like everything was about to break.

"Remember that part just before the graveyard scene?" he said. "Trudi's thinking to herself about how she's really a kind of engineer. How does she put it? She reconstructs bridges. Sometimes all she has is one section, often the end, sometimes the middle, never the beginning. So the job's always about going backward. But at the same time you're on another bridge yourself, and that one only leads forward. And then, just when she parks and the rain starts coming down and she reaches for her umbrella she pauses and says to herself, 'Is my sense of balance up to the job?'"

Bernie took another drink and was silent for a long time. "I think she's talking about the fear of falling off, but she never says it." He reached over and patted my head. More! More! That was my thought but evidently not his, because the patting came to a stop—too soon, always too soon!—and he said, "Trudi's real smart, big guy, way smarter than me."

Which made no sense. Had he perhaps had one too many? Not quite two beers? A big guy like Bernie? Come on! I went on high alert, waiting for what he'd say next, but he was done speaking, perhaps because the singers were now coming back the other way.

There seemed to be more of them now, and . . . and—could it be? They were singing a song about Rudy! What was this? He had a red nose? And it was shiny? It even glowed? Why were we just finding this out now? Red? Shiny? Glowing? These were what we call something or other in our business, the term escaping me at the moment but the point was they were important facts, especially if you were looking for Rudy, and we were. There was big money involved, if I remembered right, and big money is the best kind of money. Never forget that, my friends! Big money! Big money! Big money!

"Chet! What's that barking? Cut it out!"

Barking? There was no barking that I could hear, possibly just the faint echo of far distant barking, coming from the mountains above the town. I could see their rough shapes over the rooftops, somehow blacker than the night. But if there was far distant barking going on, surely it was someone's job to bark back? And I've never been afraid of work. I love work! I took a quick deep breath and—

And at that moment, the very last singer—straggling slightly behind the others, which was maybe why his singing wasn't quite keeping up either, but also lagging, so he was still singing about the shininess of Rudy's nose when the others had moved on to the glowing part—noticed us and stopped. A real old guy in a watch cap, wild eyebrows, and the smell of something going wrong inside him. That all added up to Mitch Cuffy, the sheriff before this other one who didn't seem real fond of Bernie, if I was reading the situation right. I can't actually read, of course, and wouldn't have time in any case.

"Bernie?" Mitch said.

"Hi, Mitch," Bernie said. "You can sing."

"Bullshit," said Mitch, all at once leaving the parade and plunking himself down at our table. "What's to drink?"

"Anything you like, on us."

What he liked was bourbon. He clinked his glass against Bernie's mug, then glanced at me. "Chet, right?"

"Correct."

"He's enjoying himself."

Bernie just smiled.

"Do you think he knows it's Christmas?"

Bernie's smile got bigger. "Nothing about him surprises me anymore."

Mitch thought about that, nodded, and said, "You're a lucky son of a bitch." He took a nice long swig and licked his lips. "Christmas drinking is better. Ever notice that?"

"Better how?" said Bernie.

"Mentally." His eyes went to the singers, now farther along Bonanza Street. "How're you making out?"

"With Rudy?"

Mitch waved that idea away with the back of his hand. "With the Teddy Leeford case. Gettin' anywhere?"

"I'm not sure we've even taken the first step," Bernie said. "But we are learning that this is a small town."

"Tell me something I don't know."

"I doubt I can. But small towns always have a web of connections that's hard for outsiders to penetrate."

"What are you getting at?"

"For example, tonight we found out that a guy we met on the mountain is married to the current sheriff's daughter."

"Talkin' about Von Sikes?"

"You know him?"

"Wouldn't go that far," Mitch said. "Met him a few times."

"And?"

"And what? Spoon-feed you?"

Whoa! The conversation had taken a strange turn. Yes, there was a spoon on the table, unused since Bernie had handled his burger and fries without silverware, no problem. But Bernie was perfectly capable of feeding himself. The only time I'd seen anyone feed him was at a bar where Weatherly took a cherry from her drink and popped it into Bernie's mouth. And thinking back, from the looks they gave each other, the whole thing wasn't actually about food. Whatever it was about I'll leave to you.

"Time may be a factor," Bernie said.

Mitch got a faraway look in his eyes, not just faraway but even a bit frightened. He shook it off and said, "You're right about that, my brother."

Some humans—and I like just about every single one I've met, even most of the perps and gangbangers—get big things wrong. For example, they say one more won't hurt. For another example, Bernie has no brother. But I gave Mitch a pass. That's just about my go-to move when it comes to human . . . what would you call them? Failings? Close enough.

Mitch rubbed his hands together, those big hands that looked like they'd once been very strong, but now were all misshapen, fingers bent, knuckles swollen. "Von Sikes ain't from around here, not originally. He's from back east. But he came here from way more east than that. Yemen, I think it was. Some place I probably couldn't find on a map. This was ten years ago, maybe a little more."

"Is there skiing in Yemen?" Bernie said.

"Ha!" said Mitch. "No idea. But skiing is just one of his areas of—what's the word?"

"Expertise."

"Yeah, expertise. He is an expert skier—a college champ, one of them Ivy League places, I think it was. But I guess you'd say he's really a kind of organizer, keeps everything running smooth for the company."

"What was he doing in Yemen?" Bernie said.

"Like I said, might not have been Yemen. Coulda been some other hell hole where wars break out from time to time."

"You're saying he was a mercenary soldier?"

"Well, not soldier. More like an organizer of soldiers. Commanding them, like."

"Mercenary soldiers?"

"I don't know the details."

"Was he trained in the military?"

"If you mean ours," Mitch said, "I don't think so. But he must've learned somewheres. I saw him in fight once. This was at Muley's."

"Your uncle's bar?"

"Correct. Kind of a dive, like you must have seen. Not the kind of dive where rich folks sometimes drop in. Just a dive, period. So it was a bit of a surprise when Sikes and a couple of girls showed up. Women, I should say, city type women. They weren't asking for any trouble but it came to them." Mitch shot Bernie a quick narrow-eyed look. "Fella like you knows how these things unravel."

"Tell me anyway."

"Ah, same old shit. Some guys from a road grading crew were in the place, Friday night, spendin' their paychecks, and by total accident one of Von's lady guests spilled a little wine on a road grading boy. This road grading boy—typical big rough badass— overreacted, the way his kind always does. Next thing, even before my uncle could grab the twelve gauge he keeps under the bar, wave it around some just to calm things down, Von laid that road grader out, flat on his back, eyes rolled up. Then his pals jumped Von, so predictable, two of them as I recall but mighta been three, and he done for all of them, too. Causing considerable damage to what he used as weapons, a couple of barstools and such. He went through the pockets of one of them boys for the cash to pay for the damage and handed it over to my uncle. After that he walked out, them women, now more like girls, on either arm." Mitch raised his hands, then dropped them down on his lap. "So, you get the idea."

"I'll be careful not to spill," Bernie said.

Mitch threw back his head and laughed. He had some teeth, but not the full set a human needs. Even with a full set, they're still at a real bad disadvantage when it comes to teeth. But that's not the important point, which is that before Mitch was even done laughing Bernie said, "Looking back, is there anything you'd like to do over in the Teddy Leeford case?"

Mitch stopped laughing stone cold. For a moment I thought he was going to blow up at Bernie, but the force seeped out of him real quick. "That's the reason I went looking for the file," he said. "To make sure I'd left no stone unturned, like they say."

"A stone such as . . . ?" Bernie said.

Mitch shook his head. "Don't know. That's why I went down there."

"But if you had to guess?" Bernie said.

Mitch lowered his head. "I'm a real bad guesser. That's one thing I've learned in this life."

Twenty-four

Next morning, back at Cratchit House, we were up at dawn. More accurately, I was up well before dawn, feeling a bit restless, and when I'm restless I like to get outside. I'm sure you're the same way. But Bernie needs his sleep and his needs come first so I didn't wake him until the first lightening of the far edge of the sky, or just slightly before.

His eyes opened. "Hey, big guy. Something up? Need to go?"

I gazed down at him. My Bernie. Did I mention that I was mostly on the bed? Standing above him? My front paws on his chest? Sorry if I skipped that part. Maybe now you can picture it. As for needing to go, there were two answers. First, if he meant did I need to pee, the answer was sure, but not desperately, no rush. Second, if he meant did I need to simply go outside, the answer was yes, desperately, big rush.

Bernie's a quick dresser, has a knack for grabbing whatever's on the floor from last night and just throwing it on. This time I helped him go even faster, mostly by prancing around him while he buttoned his shirt, fastened his belt, tied his boot laces, and all rest—how complicated! I do none of that. Just imagine if all of you were like me, totally ditching the clothes part, except for a collar. What a world that would be! I should add that the other way I helped him go faster on this particular morning was by making a sort of squeaking noise in the back of my throat. Like I needed oil! I didn't need oil, of course, although once I drank a whole puddle of olive oil which had somehow ended up on the floor. But no point in dwelling on memories like that. The point is it turned out that in fact I did need to pee, and desperately, after all. How do you like that?

Very soon we were outside, the early morning air still and cool, perhaps even cold, although not to me, both of us making breath clouds but only me making yellow holes in the fresh white snow. That was when I knew this day would be something else. Digging had always been one of my best things, but now I, Chet, had discovered how to dig holes with pee. Life, already good, just keeps getting better. That's one of my core beliefs.

I was considering holding on to a small pee supply—always handy if any marking possibilities cropped up, but in this case to conduct more yellow digging experiments—when Ariadne appeared on the red and green brick road. She was walking from the direction of the North Pole, dressed in her furry boots, a long Indian blanket coat that went down almost to her ankles, and a cowboy hat, not the right off-the-shelf kind you see so often on tourists back in the Valley, but worn and battered like the cowboys wear. Weatherly has a hat a lot like Ariadne's with the same black and white feather stuck in the hatband. She wasn't walking fast, just steadily, her face hidden in the shadow of the cowboy hat brim, a long, thin breath cloud trailing in the air behind her. She came closer and closer but didn't see us. Finally, when she was right opposite Cratchit House, Bernie spoke.

"Uh, good morning. Don't mean to interrupt your thoughts, but . . ." His voice trailed away.

Ariadne stopped and turned slowly to us, revealing her face, a tired, puffy face with dark shadows under the eyes. "I'm not having any thoughts. That's the whole point."

"Don't let us stop you," Bernie said.

"Stop me from not having thoughts?" Ariadne said. "You just did."

"Um," said Bernie.

Ariadne tilted her head to one side. "You're an unusual man. There's nothing unusual about an inarticulate man. It's the default, if anything. And there are also articulate men around, especially in my line of work, god knows. But you're the first one I've met who is both."

"I don't know what to say," Bernie said.

That turned out to be funny. Ariadne was silent at first, but then she chuckled, a chuckle that grew into a laugh. But she cut that laugh off before it was done, in my opinion, kind of strangling it. She came forward, off the road and onto the snow-covered lawn at Cratchit House.

"Are you going to find Rudy?" she said. "Tell the truth. You'll be paid no matter what."

"It's not about the money," Bernie said.

At that moment it hit me, something huge. It wasn't about the money! That was one of our best techniques at the Little Detective Agency, a reason—maybe the most important of all the reasons—why we were so successful. Wow! What a thought! Really too much to take in, so I hoped it would disappear as soon as possible.

"It turns out to be more complicated than Rudy," Bernie was saying.

"Oh?" said Ariadne. She stood quite still, no particular expression on her tired face. But she'd had a sudden rush of fear inside her, smellable by me right away, of course. Some humans—Bernie's the best at this, off the charts—are good at controlling inside fears. Most are not, in my experience. Ariadne was in the Bernie group, but not up at his level, which would be impossible.

"First," Bernie said, "any news on Chaz?"

"No change as of last night, according to Dr. Woodcourt. But what are the complications?"

"They could be only in my mind. That's an occupational hazard. You'll never have all the data, or it would take too long to find it, so you have to make a mental leap. That's where mistakes get made in this business."

Ariadne's green eyes seemed to get a shade brighter for an instant.

"I'm sure," Bernie added, "from the little I know of Trudi so far that she's aware of this problem."

Ariadne smiled a little smile, almost shy. For an odd moment I saw her as a young girl. How strange! But so was the ranch, all this snow, reindeer on the roof. I got ready for anything.

"She is," Ariadne said. "Although she doesn't think in terms of data. Her mind doesn't work that way. But I wonder," she began, and then went silent, her gaze rising to the mountaintops. All that only lasted for a heartbeat or two—Ariadne's heartbeats, I mean. I could hear them—no surprise there— but I seemed to be quite tuned in to her, out here on this quiet morning. She gave herself a little shake, a first-rate move in many situations, although not many humans had the knack. Ariadne was turning out to be aces. "But let's jump right to your conclusion," she said.

"Before we get to that," Bernie said, "do you know anyone who went to Dartmouth, or had any connection to the school?"

"Probably."

"Who?"

"I'd have to think."

"Anyone from around here?"

"No one who comes to mind. Why? Is it important?"

"I can't say for sure," Bernie said. He looked down at her with a very interesting expression on his face, like he admired her. "To quote Trudi, I feel something stirring in the dark part of my mind."

"You like that line?" Ariadne said.

"I do."

"Well, that's welcome feedback. When I wrote it I remember worrying that it was maybe a bit much."

"What do you mean?"

"Edging too close from drama to melodrama. With melodrama as a cliff to be avoided."

Ariadne was right about that. To take just a single example of cliff problems in our career, there was the time when an earlier old Porsche of ours went zooming off of one, never to be seen again. And then—and this took me a bit by surprise—came the image of Chaz LeWitte, lying still at the bottom of Devil's Purse, meaning we had cliff problems in the here and now. At that moment I knew for sure Ariadne had plenty going on upstairs.

"I don't know anything about that," Bernie said. "Do readers even care?"

Ariadne smiled one of those mixed smiles, happy and unhappy. In the nation within our tail does that one for us, not up and stiff, not down and droopy, but in between.

"Critics do," she said.

"Boy oh boy," said Bernie.

"Meaning?"

"Meaning I wouldn't want your job."

Ariadne laughed, reached out and touched Bernie's arm. Her

laughter faded away but her hand stayed where it was. "Tell me about the dark things," she said.

"I think there may be a connection between Rudy's disappearance and the Teddy Leeford case."

Ariadne closed her eyes in what might have been a very long blink. "I knew it," she said. Her eyes opened. I saw something in them that was very dark for sure. "Maybe not consciously, but I knew it, knew it the moment I heard where you found Chaz. What are you going to do?"

"What we're already doing," Bernie said. "Finding out who killed Teddy."

"How?" said Ariadne.

"For now we'll follow in Chaz's footsteps. During that talk you had with him, after he learned about Teddy, did he give any indication of what he might do next?"

"Maybe, although I didn't see it that way at the time. He asked if there was still anyone around from those days."

"And?"

"And Hal Pelgotty was the only one I could think of."

"Where can we find him?"

Ariadne pointed. "Turn right at the corner. It's the cabin on the lake, Trotwood House."

Trotwood House looked pretty much like Cratchit House, but smaller, and with a wraparound deck. Smoke curled up from the chimney, carrying many smells, of which I singled out bacon right away. Bernie knocked on the door, not nearly hard enough in my opinion.

But the door opened right away, which was what I'd had in mind, and there stood Hal, wearing—ah, sheepskin moccasins.

I hadn't had a crack at . . . let's just say that sheepskin moccasins are a particular interest of mine. That wasn't all he was wearing, of course. He also had on boxers with Santa decorations and a huge baggy sweatshirt with a big Santa on the front.

"Hey, hey, hey," he said. "Chet! And also Bernie. What brings you here?"

"A couple of questions, if you've got a minute."

"Of course, of course. Come on in." He stepped aside, closed the door behind us and then called toward the back of the house. "Sam! The pooch I was telling you about? Save some of that bacon!"

Some starts are promising and some are not. This was the most promising start of my career and it wasn't even close. I found my own way to the kitchen, thank you very much, where a small silver haired man sat at the table busily sewing, a couple of little pins held between his lips. If I can go back to that silver hair of his for a moment, I'd like to add that it grew down to a sort of point in the middle of his forehead, making him look like an elf, even though he wasn't wearing a costume, in fact was dressed in a black robe with a pattern of golden candle holders. Had I seen candle holders like that before? Had Bernie even helped with the matches and the lighting? Perhaps at a dinner having to do with Hanukkah? I couldn't quite remember. Meanwhile the elfish man's eyes shifted my way, although his hands kept sewing.

"Well, well," he said, "even a stopped clock, as they say." Or something like that, hard to tell with those pins in his mouth.

Bernie and Hal came in.

Sam flipped over what he was working on, which seemed to be an enormous pair of red pants and stabbed it once, twice, with the pins. "You were right about this fellow, Hal. But just look at him. So obvious. What's his name again?"

"Chet," said Hal. "And this is Bernie Little. Bernie, say hi to Sam Wellerman."

"Hi," Bernie said.

"Pleasure," said Sam. "Coffee?"

"Sounds great," Bernie said.

"And a rasher or two for this god of the canine world?" Sam said. "Is that permitted?"

"There's no other way," said Bernie.

"Ha!" Sam said. "Hal, if you please? And when you're done with that, try these on. I've let them out as far as they'll go." He rolled the red pants into an enormous ball and tossed them on the counter. "And start listening to your doctor. I'll be extremely pissed off if I lose you on account of that appetite of yours."

"But for other reasons it's hunky dory?" Hal said, pouring coffee.

Sam thought that was pretty funny. His laughter spread to Hal and finally Bernie, whose laughter was perhaps a little uncertain at first but soon steadied itself. No pissing happened although I was under the impression it was supposed to. I shifted over toward the stove, where bacon was sizzling in a pan. It had been sizzling this whole time, dominating the whole room, in fact, the world.

Rashers! What a lovely word! You don't hear it often enough. Rashers of bacon! Wow! Rashers and rashers of bacon. Well, I actually had two to start with and one more after I . . . let's not say begged, more like I made clear to the cook—Sam, was it?—that I wouldn't refuse another.

"Another convert," Hal said. "Everybody loves Sam's cooking."

Converts loved Sam's cooking? Then call me a convert, end of story. Hal tried on the red pants—"Perfect!"—and we sat around the island in this warm kitchen full of delicious smells— the humans on stools and me on the floor, getting my front paws up on the island top only once and very briefly, a momentary misunderstanding—and enjoyed the nicest breakfast I'd had in a long time. What were the chances of getting invited back for dinner? Was simply hanging around this kitchen till dinnertime in the cards? Wouldn't that be the easiest?

Hal sat back, wiped his mouth with a napkin. A little blob of scrambled egg that had been snagged in his bushy white beard came loose and fell to the floor, but it was only there for the briefest of instants. He turned to Bernie.

"You've got questions?"

Bernie nodded. "Did you know Chaz was looking into the Teddy Leeford case?"

"I did not," Hal said.

Sam raised a spatula. "True, Hal, as far as it goes, but the Talmud frowns on silent deception."

"What deception?" Hal said.

"Don't you remember? When he dropped in? The night be-fore the Halloween party? And after you said, 'I wonder what he's up to'? So you can tell Bernie here that you didn't know, or you could say you didn't know but aren't surprised."

How baffling was that? Hal and Sam glared at each other. Maybe they, too, were baffled.

"Um," Bernie said. "Can we back up a little?"

Sam pointed the spatula at him. "How far?"

Bernie smiled. "Are you a lawyer, Sam?"

"I'm retired."

"From the law?"

"From the restaurant business. But getting to the night be-fore Halloween, Chaz came over and out of the blue asked Hal what he remembered about the murder of Teddy Leeford. The answer to which is nothing. Hal was still working at Vail at that time. The arrangement with Ariadne came later."

"Mind if I tell my own story?" Hal said.

"You'll botch it," said Sam. He sighed. "But in your own inim-itable way, God help me."

Sam took a sip of coffee, gazing into the mug. Hal did the same with his.

"Um," said Bernie.

Sam and Hal set down their mugs. "Exactly right," Hal said. "I was still at Vail. I don't recall how I first heard about Teddy. It might have been on the news. Which is what I told Chaz. Then what? I think he asked if I'd known Teddy. We were probably at the same school—Pioneer Elementary—but he was quite a bit younger and I was finishing seventh grade when we moved to Vail, so I really didn't remember him."

"What about Drake?" Bernie said.

"He was two years behind me. I knew him a little. We were actually on the same hockey team, the ten and unders, even though he must have been only eight at the time."

"You played hockey?" Sam said.

"Of course," said Hal.

"That explains a lot," Sam said.

"Damn straight," said Hal. "I was the goalie, if you want even more explanation."

Sam smiled and said nothing.

"What did Drake play?" Bernie said.

"Center," said Hal. "How I remember that I couldn't tell

you. But I can even picture him. He was a scrappy kid, the kind who just can't stand losing. They say that's what makes a great competitor—it's not so much the love of winning."

"What about the love of the game?" Sam said.

Hal turned to Bernie. "What do you think about that? The love of the game?"

"I'm tempted to say it's for the fans," Bernie said. "But that's cynical, and when I played I loved the game."

"What sport?" Hal said.

"Baseball."

"Were you any good?"

"So-so."

So-so? He must have said so good, and I'd simply missed it. He pitched for Army before his arm blew out, and can still throw a tennis ball a country mile—take it from me—which is longer than a city mile, by the way.

"So was that it?" Bernie was saying.

"Not quite," Hal said. "Chaz wanted to know who else might have been around at that time. There was Drake, of course, and he also asked about Nellie, Drake's first wife. I told him she'd moved away decades ago and I had no idea where she was, and that maybe Drake would know."

"How did Chaz know about Nellie?"

"I don't know."

"Did he mention anything about the sheriff's office? Old case files?"

Hal shook his head.

"Did he end up talking to Drake?" Bernie said.

"He did. I asked him that, mostly because I was interested in Nellie. She and I were in the same class from kindergarten till we left. Little Nellie—that's what everyone called her. The cutest thing. I do believe I came close to having a schoolboy crush on her."

"But no cigar," Sam said.

"No cigar," said Hal, reaching over to pat Sam's hand.

"What did Chaz find out about Nellie?" Bernie said.

"Nothing. Drake thought she'd gone down to Texas somewhere but he'd lost track of her. So that was that, except for one odd thing."

"What's that?" Bernie said.

"Nellie's back in town," Hal said. "Since the summer, but I only found out last week—happened to be talking to one of the custodians, also a former classmate, and he told me, thought I'd be interested."

Bernie was leaning forward on his stool, just the slightest amount, but I'm aware of pretty much every move he makes. "Custodian of what?" he said.

"La Plata," said Hal. "It's an assisted living place. I guess Nellie's in pretty rough shape and some cousin of hers works there, helped get her in at a reduced rate."

"Did you pass that onto Chaz?"

Hal nodded. "He said he was going to try and set up a visit."

"And did he?"

"If so, he didn't tell me."

"What's her last name?"

"I think she's gone back to her maiden name. It's Trent."

After that came a bit of a silence. Then Sam said, "Bernie? What's going on?"

Bernie rose. "We'll let you know."

I was already at the door.

Twenty-five

On the way to wherever we were going we stopped at a florist and bought some flowers. A man buys flowers when there's been some screw-up with a woman. The fun part is when he hands them over because the handing over never goes as planned, and then you get to see all sorts of amazing reactions on the guy's face, as reality comes sinking in. We handle all this quite differently in the nation within. I'm not saying better. Just differently. So I was already looking forward to the handing over of the flowers part. Who was going to get them? Ariadne? Stell? Georgette? That was as far as I could take it on my own.

Pretty soon after the florist's shop, the flowers lying on the dash, stems held together with string, we pulled into a parking lot in front of a long, low brick building and headed inside. Our flowers—the color of the sun—carried the smell of spring back in the Valley, and this place needed it. What a strange thought! Not me at all! I hoped nothing like it would ever come again. Me is the only way I know how to be. I'd . . . I'd be lost without me.

We went to the desk. I couldn't get there fast enough.

"Welcome to La Plata," said the clerk. "How can I help you?"

"We're here to see one of your residents. Her name's Nellie Trent."

"Is she expecting you?"

"No."

"Then let me check. Meanwhile, please sign here." She

handed Bernie a clipboard and got busy in front of a screen. "And dogs are welcome, of course," she said, fingers tap-tapping away. "We encourage—" Her fingers went still. "Oh dear." She turned to Bernie. "I see that Ms. Trent had some sort of medical issue last night. She was ambulanced to the hospital shortly after four this morning. I'm sorry."

"What sort of medical issue?"

"I'm afraid we don't share information of that kind."

"Okay, thanks," said Bernie, and turned to go. I followed, but at the same time saw that the clerk was now studying the clipboard. She took it into a back office and closed the door.

We entered the waiting room at the hospital, the same place where Bernie had told Ariadne the news about Chaz. The waiting room was empty now but as we moved to the desk, Dr. Woodcourt came walking by, wearing scrubs and a round blue hairnet.

Bernie turned to her. "Dr. Woodcourt?"

Her eyes—dark and with even darker circles underneath—showed no sign of remembering him. Not remembering Bernie? How was that possible? Her gaze moved to the flowers, then back to Bernie. "You're the one who found Chaz LeWitte?"

"Yes," Bernie said. "How's he doing?"

"He's breathing on his own," said Dr. Woodcourt. "That happened a few hours ago, frankly a surprise. But he's still in a coma—and may not ever come out and even if he does . . . What I'm trying to say is that there's really no point in visiting." She pinched the bridge of her nose, something you see only from very tired humans. "But it's very nice of you."

"Thanks," Bernie said, "but we're actually here to see a different patient. Her name's Nellie Trent and she was admitted during the night."

Dr. Woodcourt nodded. "I've just seen Ms. Trent."

"What's wrong with her?" Bernie said.

"Are you a friend?" said Dr. Woodcourt.

"Friend of a friend."

Dr. Woodcourt looked at me, then at the flowers, finally at Bernie. "I don't see the harm. I'll take you there."

Dr. Woodcourt led us down a hall smelling strongly of wax, which is just one of the many smells you get in hospitals, all of them adding up to a place where you don't want to hang out. As we passed an open doorway I happened to glance inside, and there was Chaz, tubes sticking into him here and there, his eyes closed.

"She had a fall at her nursing home last night and broke her hip," Dr. Woodcourt was saying, "which still hadn't healed from a previous fall." Dr. Woodcourt put her hand on a doorknob, paused and shook her head. "Which it won't. Her bones are riddled. And that's not all, far from it." She glanced at Bernie. "But all she wanted to know was whether this is Christmas Day. She's a bit confused. She's on a slew of medications."

Dr. Woodcourt opened the door and we went in. A tiny white-haired woman was sitting up in bed. There was a lot going wrong with her inside—I smelled that immediately—and she also smelled old, but the skin of her face was smooth and unblemished, not like any old person's face I'd ever seen, and very nice to look at.

"Hello, doctor," she said. "Did you get to the bottom of it?"

Her voice was what I think of as a very small voice, but clear and pleasant, at least to my ears. My guess is you yourself might have had some trouble hearing her, but I could be wrong.

Dr. Woodcourt put her hand to her ear. "Sorry?"

Nope. I wasn't wrong.

The tiny woman took a deep breath and tried again, that deep breath possibly making her wince slightly. "Did you find out? Is it Christmas Day?"

Dr. Woodcourt shook her head. "Tomorrow's Christmas Eve."

"So it's the twenty-third?"

"Yes."

"December twenty-third?"

"That's right," said Dr. Woodcourt. "You've got visitors. This is—" She glanced at Bernie.

"Bernie Little," said Bernie, approaching the bed. "And this is Chet."

The tiny woman looked my way and smiled, her teeth small, even, and very white, unlike the teeth you usually see on old folks. "Oh my," she said. "My, my, my. Very nice to meet you both." She took another of those deep, wincing breaths. "I'm Nellie."

"Nice to meet you, too, Nellie," Bernie said. "We're friends of Hal Pelgotty."

Nellie's eyes opened wide, and for a moment seemed to be looking far away. Then, slowly she came back to us. "Is he here with you?"

"No, but I'm sure it can be arranged."

Dr. Woodcourt's phone beeped. She glanced at it. "I'll check back later, Ms. Trent."

"Nellie. My friends call me Nellie."

Dr. Woodcourt left the room.

"Are those for me?" Nellie said.

Bernie laid the flowers on the bed where she could reach them.

"Sunflowers," she said. "My favorites." Her hands—twisted and bruised—emerged from under the covers and took hold of the flowers. "Did Hal send these? We were in kindergarten together. Can you imagine?"

"Would you like to see him?" Bernie said. He got busy with his phone.

"Who?" said Nellie.

There was a little pause. Then Bernie said, "Hal."

Nellie smiled a very bright smile. "I don't know any Hals."

"Hal Pelgotty," Bernie said.

"Hal Pelgotty," said Nellie. "There's a blast from the past. We were in kindergarten together. Can you imagine?"

Bernie smiled a gentle smile. "I'd like to talk about those days." He pulled up a stool and sat down.

"My kindergarten days?" said Nellie.

"Yes," said Bernie. "What school did you go to?"

"Pioneer Elementary. That's up in Silver City, Colorado. Miss Edwards was the teacher. She started every day with a prayer. I didn't come here until later in life."

"Here?" said Bernie.

Nellie gestured at the room around her. "Here. San Antonio."

Bernie nodded. He has many different nods, as I may have mentioned. This was the most thoughtful one. "What brought you down to Texas?"

"Oh, the usual," Nellie said, and then did some very rapid eye blinking. "Personal catastrophe." Her hands tightened their grip on the stems of the flowers.

"What kind of catastrophe?"

"D-I-V-O-R-C-E," said Nellie, her voice sinking away to almost nothing. I heard, as you might have guessed, but Bernie did not.

"Sorry, I missed that."

Nellie took another of those deep, wincing breaths, this one the deepest and the winciest. I didn't want to see another. "Like the Tammy Wynette song," she said.

"D-I-V-O-R-C-E?" said Bernie.

Nellie nodded. She was starting to look very tired. "I didn't know him."

"In what way?"

"I didn't know what he was capable of. That scared me. Wouldn't you be scared, too? They had the most terrible fight. I heard them in the woods. Someone had to be the boss."

"What do you mean?"

"Fifty-one percent. That makes you the boss. Fifty-fifty means no boss. But would you care to know what I think?"

"I would," Bernie said.

Nellie looked at him. "You're very nice. Are you a doctor?"

"No."

She reached out with that bruised and crooked hand and patted Bernie's. How could two human hands be so different? "That's all right, dear. Nurses do all the work—every patient knows that."

Then her eyes closed, and she just lay there breathing—perhaps not with the kind of oomph you like to see—and her hand resting on Bernie's. "Who was fighting in the woods?" he said.

More silence. Nellie's hand moved slightly, maybe trying to squeeze Bernie's. "What I think is that fifty-fifty is right."

"Is that what Teddy wanted?" Bernie said.

Nellie nodded. "But Drake wanted fifty-one. That horrible fight, all over one percent."

"What happened in the fight?"

"Well, Teddy was so big and strong."

"Drake got beat up?"

"Eye swoll shut."

"What did he do about that?"

Nellie laughed a tiny laugh, almost a giggle. "Took it out on me."

"He hit you?"

"My fault. I tried out the fifty-fifty side, you know, making the case, only trying to help."

"It wasn't your fault," Bernie said. "Don't say that. Don't think it."

There was a long silence. Then Nellie said, "Okay." But again, so faint.

Bernie leaned closer. "I didn't catch that, Nellie."

This time she didn't make another try.

"Do you want to sleep now?" Bernie said.

"Oh no," she said right away, her eyes remaining closed but her voice becoming a little stronger.

"Then maybe," Bernie said quietly, "you can tell me if Drake ever took it out on Teddy, too."

"No," Nellie said. Her eyelids quivered like they were trying to open but didn't quite get there. "I can not."

"Why not?" Bernie said.

"I left the next day. Wouldn't you?"

"The day after the fight in the woods?"

Then, so soft and weak I almost missed it myself, Nellie said, "I didn't know what he was capable of."

"Didn't quite catch that either," Bernie said. "Did Sheriff Cuffy try to reach you after you went down to Texas?"

I felt Nellie's tiny body gather all its tiny strength. Her lips moved and she spoke, but this time a little stronger. "I was unreachable."

"Meaning he tried to?" Bernie said.

Nellie's lips moved again but no sound came out, none at all. The whole room quieted down, even all the hospital sounds muffling away.

Bernie turned to me. "We'll let her sleep."

Fine with me, but at that very moment I picked up a smell I've familiar with from our line of work. It comes at the very end and right away, in case you didn't know.

"See you a little later," Bernie said softly, sliding his hand out from under hers.

We walked down the hall, soon coming to the open door to Chaz's room. I ambled right in, who knows why. Maybe just the open door was enough to do it. You see an open door, you go in. Some things are simple.

I kept ambling, right up to the bedside.

"Um, Chet?" Bernie said, lingering in the doorway.

Simply *um Chet*, which was far from Ch—et. So we were good. I stood beside the bed and had a good long look at Chaz. He lay on his back, eyes closed and tubes sticking out here and there. Had he gotten skinnier? That was my take. But maybe he'd made up for that by growing this scruffy beard. Did that make sense? If not, why not? Strangely enough, I found myself getting a little impatient with Chaz. He was a young guy, after all. Young guys should be up and at 'em! I growled a low, rumbly growl, not the aggressive type, more just to encourage him.

Chaz's eyes opened. That was more like it. I'd known he had it in him. I moved in a little closer, perhaps getting my face right in his, again, simply in an encouraging way. His eyes widened. No surprise there. I'd seen that look before, the look when some dude realizes ol' Chet's in his face.

"Chet?" His voice was so rough and croaky! He licked his dry, cracked lips with his dry, cracked tongue. "The mine," he said. Then his eyes closed.

"Oh my God," Bernie said. He hurried over to the bed. "Chaz? Chaz?"

No answer from Chaz, but his chest rose and fell in a deep and regular rhythm. Bernie ran out into the hall. "Dr. Woodcourt! Dr. Woodcourt!"

Not long after that, Chaz's room was full of hospital people surrounding his bed, Chaz himself back to just lying there with his eyes closed, and we were out in the parking lot, headed for the Beast. A familiar red pickup with a wreath on the grille pulled in and came to a stop beside us. The driver's window slid down and Hal looked out.

"Hey, Bernie. What's up?"

"A lot, actually." Bernie started to fill him in.

"My goodness," said Hal. "Should I tell the boss?"

"Ask Dr. Woodcourt."

"Gotcha. And how's Nellie?"

"They had to move her from La Plata but she's doing all right now."

Did I make a little squeaky sound? If so, it went unheard.

"I've been thinking," Hal said, "it's kind of ironic that she ended up at La Plata."

"Why is that ironic?"

Hal shrugged. "It's just that La Plata is owned by Silver Mountain Development. No surprise, I guess. They own the whole town."

Bernie turned slightly and gazed up at the mountains. "Got that Purdey with you?"

"Huh?"

"The side by side."

"How d'you know about that?" Hal said.

"Chet."

Hal looked at me, then at Bernie. "You know what you're doing?"

Bernie didn't answer. Hal reached under the seat and handed Bernie the shotgun through the open window.

Twenty-six

"Did he say 'mine' or 'the mine'?" Bernie said as we drove up a twisty mountain road I thought I remembered. Didn't it lead to Muley's, the bar run by Mitch's uncle Hum? Were we taking a little drink break, knocking back a few in the middle of the day? That seemed unusual to me, especially if we were working a case, which I kind of thought we were. Rudy, right? Missing reindeer? And possibly there was also an extra wrinkle or two. I tried to figure out what those wrinkles might be and felt myself getting very close. I wasn't quite on fire, but heating up for sure. I sat up high in the shotgun seat.

"If he said 'mine' then it could mean just about anything," Bernie said, possibly going on about whatever he'd just been going on about. "But if he said 'the mine' then it's got to mean just one thing."

I hoped it was that, namely the meaning one thing thing. All in all that's what I'm partial to—things that mean one thing. With things that mean more than one thing you start down some tricky roads.

As for the road we were on there was nothing tricky so far, other than a thin layer of snow and some icy patches here and there that didn't bother the Beast one bit. Muley's—with that kicking mule sign, something of a puzzle if, for example, you wanted customers—appeared, smoke rising from the chimney and quickly getting torn in strips by the wind, the strips shrinking as they were swept higher and higher. We didn't stop, not to knock back even one quickie, and drove up and up, finally coming to a fork, the road on Bernie's side paved and the road on my side snow-covered gravel.

That was the one we took, the back end of the Beast swerving the slightest bit and then digging in real hard, like it was sending this gravel road a message in no uncertain terms. Yes, a machine of some sort, but alive for sure. Were we starting to be buddies, me and the Beast? I got that feeling.

Up and up we went, following switchbacks that got tighter and tighter, the snow-covered gravel turning to snow-covered dirt until the road, already narrow, narrowed some more and then ended abruptly in front of a rusted oil drum. Bernie stopped the car and checked the screen on his phone.

"Should be up thataway, not far." He pointed into the woods, thickly treed and dark.

We got out, Bernie taking the snowshoes with him, and also the side by side. He broke it open, checked inside—I caught the coppery flash of two cartridge caps—and then snapped the shotgun closed, and strapped on the snowshoes. We set off, me in the lead, Bernie crunch crunching along behind, the shotgun in his hand, the muzzle pointed down.

At first it was very windy, a wind that made the trees wave back and forth and was probably what humans call a biting wind, although it didn't feel biting to me. As we moved deeper into the woods the wind ramped down, maybe screened out by the trees, most of the Christmas type. Were they on our side? That was my take. We made our way through this forest, now pretty much silent except for us, me and Bernie. Well, in truth, I was silent, too. The only sounds came from Bernie—the crunch crunching plus some huffing and puffing. Was doing this forever a possibility? I was all in.

Bernie came up beside me and pointed to a tree, or maybe the space between it and another. "Seems like a real old trail, Chet, not maintained. Feels right to me."

And to me. We kept going, side by side when we could, me in the lead when we couldn't, the trees rising so high above, snow sometimes thumping down as we passed by. Down into a dip we went, across a small frozen stream—I licked the ice, yes, frozen for sure but still quite tasty—then up a rise and into a small clearing. Snow lay thick in the clearing, pure white with not a mark on it. In the middle of the clearing stood the tops of some rocks, sitting in a sort of circle.

"Remains of an old fire pit," Bernie said. Then he pointed to the far end of the clearing, where the ground sloped up, a slope covered with small bushes except for in the middle, where there was a black hole, like an open garage doorway. Not a garage, of course—this was an abandoned mine with a cracked and weathered beam along the top, holding things up, as I'd learned possibly more than once. We've been in many mines, me and Bernie. It was a kind of hobby of ours, out in the desert. You can find all kinds of things in abandoned mines, broken old wheelbarrows, crushed beer cans, used toilet paper, to name just a few.

"Drake was standing just about where we are now when he took that picture," Bernie said. "Was Nellie right beside him? Saying 'everybody smile'?"

Whatever that was all about I'll leave to you. We went closer. The wind rose and the snow, which had been falling lightly, now came slanting down, harder and harder. Bernie took off the snowshoes. We entered the mine, but only for a step or two before Bernie stopped, turned, and watched the snow fall, whitening the whole world, including our footprints. In almost no time they were gone. We headed into the mine.

The air is always different in a mine, cooler for one thing, at least in all the mines I've been in. But not this one. It was warmer here, no snow on the bare ground, and a distant trickling sound like water was running over the rocky walls somewhere deeper in. Water can be a problem in mines, and that's not the only one. There's fun to be had in this business, perhaps a subject for later on. Now, after a few more steps, we'd moved beyond the daylight. Bernie switched on his phone light and we kept going. After just a few more steps I found something, a small white thing that looked like a snowball but was not, and took it to Bernie.

"What you got there?"

He turned it in his hand, held it to the light. "A pom pom." He nodded to himself and stuck it in his pocket. "What would I do without you?"

I didn't understand the question.

We moved on. The air got warmer, if anything, a faint warmish breeze coming from inside and carrying lots of interesting smells, including one like almonds. That almond nuttiness scent got me thinking of a drink called the almond tequila fling on a night south of the border, which reminded me of—My tail rose, straight up and high.

Meanwhile Bernie was shining the light here and there—along the rocky walls, on an old rusty wheel, and the ceiling, also rocky with a few cross beams, some bowed in the middle, running from one side of the mine to the other. And in the distance, what looked like a tunnel, narrow but fairly high, high enough for a man to walk in without stooping. The almond smell came from somewhere back there, and so I headed that way, but Bernie suddenly stopped and shone the beam on a small mound on the cave floor and off to the side.

He went over and knelt beside the mound. A pile of ashes. That was what it looked like to me. There'd been a fire here, but some time back, no heat at all rising up. Bernie stuck his hand in, let the ashes run through his fingers.

"Cold ashes," he said. We agree on so much, me and Bernie. He turned to me. "You know what I think we're looking at?" I had no idea, couldn't wait to hear. "The file, big guy. The Teddy Leeford case file, stolen by Chaz from the basement of the county office. Can't prove it." He rose. "Not yet." We moved toward the tunnel, Bernie still carrying the side by side, but now with the muzzle pointed dead ahead. He spoke again, his voice hardening as we entered the narrow tunnel. "Nellie was in that file, Chet. Nellie and the fact that Cuffy reached out to her—maybe not trying hard enough, leaving the stone unturned, but—"

Bernie went silent and still. Something big and dark had moved, somewhere deeper in the tunnel. Bernie killed the light at once. We just stood there waiting for whatever was next, almost certainly something bad. But nothing bad happened. Nothing happened at all, except that the almond smell grew stronger.

Bernie switched the light back on, the beam reaching down the tunnel, revealing rocky walls and the occasional floor to ceiling support beam. We moved forward. And now it wasn't only the almond smell getting stronger, for example, there was a certain funkiness and—

I barked. Yes, a savage kind of bark, a bit scary, even to me. I bounded forward.

"Chet! Chet!"

Bernie ran after me, the bouncing light illuminating this and that and then: two shining eyes. Big eyes, rolling somewhat, even doltish, all of that adding up to—

"Rudy!" Bernie said.

Yes, Rudy. Here was the smell I'd first picked up in his empty stall, somewhat like Blitzen's only funkier and with this odd nutty almond add-on, but now at the source, and so much more powerful. Bernie shone the light around, pointing out a bucket of water, another bucket with some of the reindeer food I'd seen in the trough in the barn, and the rope around Rudy's neck, tying him to an upright beam. What I did not see was the slightest sign of redness on his nose. Colors are not my best thing, according to Bernie, but could I be missing it completely? And also there was no trace of shininess. I was good on shininess, couldn't possibly be missing that. I realized that my understanding of the case might not be perfect. In fact, I didn't know the first thing about it. But maybe that didn't matter. Our cases ended when I grabbed the perp by the pant leg. Rudy wore no pants, of course, but was a pant leg type grab of one of his legs the right move now? Why not? Soon we could be picking up our check and hitting the road. I began studying Rudy's legs. Your normal perp has two, but Rudy had more than that, making my next move a bit of a puzzler.

Meanwhile Bernie approached Rudy. Rudy didn't like that and backed away, his knees cracking in the reindeer way, except much more loudly than any of the others—Blitzen, Vixen, Prancer, the whole dimwitted crew. But Rudy couldn't go far, not tied to the beam the way he was. Bernie reached out and placed his hand on Rudy's neck, firm and gentle at the same time. I knew that one.

"Been through the mill, huh, fella?" he said. "Kidnapped, tied up, used as bait for Chaz." He patted Rudy's neck. "It's over now. We're taking you home." Bernie moved over to the wooden beam, shone the light on the rope, began to untie it.

At that moment, I heard a sound coming from the mouth of the mine, a soft squeak, like a boot on packed snow. I barked my very lowest rumbly bark, for Bernie and Bernie only. He cut the light at once. For an instant or two we had pretty much total darkness. Then a glimmer appeared, faint and yellow and on the move, coming toward us from the mouth of the mine.

We waited, absolutely still, absolutely silent—even Rudy, who wasn't part of the team. Wasn't that a bit odd? Something to think about later, perhaps. Right now, we had that yellow light coming closer and closer, the soft sounds of quiet footsteps on the hard-packed dirt of the mine, the scents of two strong men. The edge of the light reached the entrance to the tunnel and kept coming. Closer and closer, and then I could see the men, mostly just dark man shapes, except for bright things lit up by the light—the lantern one was carrying, a gun pointed down in the hand of the other—and their eyes. They seemed to be having a conversation, kind of relaxed.

"Looks like he's a no show."

"Maybe he drove up the back way."

"But no prints in the snow. Wouldn't matter where he parked. There'd be prints."

"It's blowing pretty good out there."

"Von. Don't overthink. We're gonna shoot the goddamn reindeer—like we should have shot LeWitte—and get back. Missing the office Christmas party is a bad look."

"But we didn't shoot him because it had to look like an accident. Now what if he wakes up?"

"Stop worrying. He never saw us." Then came a laugh and: "Never knew what hit him."

Closer and closer they came, the front edge of the lantern glow flowing toward us like a wave, and just as it was about to reach our feet and light us up, Bernie spoke.

"That'll do it, right there."

He stepped forward into the light, the shotgun up and ready. I stepped right up with him, and now got a clear look at the two men, Von Sikes with the lantern, Drake Leeford with the gun.

Bernie took aim at Drake, but with a shotgun at this very short distance, practically reach out and touching range, not a whole lot of aiming was necessary. One shot halfway close would probably do for both. I know. I've seen.

"Drop the gun."

Drake dropped the gun.

Bernie shifted his aim over to Von.

"Set the lantern down, Von, nice and easy."

Von set the lantern down, nice and easy.

"Now—two steps back, both of you."

They took two steps back. Most bad men, in a situation like this, start some sort of talk going. A few do not. Those are the dangerous ones, in my experience. Drake and Von kept their mouths shut.

"Twelve gauge, in case you're wondering," Bernie said. "Pre-war Purdey, collector's item, add some class to your demise."

"You'd shoot us down in cold blood?" Drake said.

"Unless you can convince me otherwise."

"How?" said Von.

Drake smiled. That was the first scary moment. "Thanks, Von, I'll handle this."

"Nope," said Bernie. "We will." His eyes shifted to Von. "I hear you're an Ivy Leaguer."

Von nodded.

"Which one?" Bernie said.

"What difference does it make?" Von said.

With one hand Bernie kept his grip on the side by side, nice and steady. With his other he reached into his pocket. "This here—" He held it so everyone could see, green and gleaming in the light. "—is a Dartmouth class ring. Yours, Von? Kept it a secret from Drake? When did you notice it had gone missing?"

Von said nothing. Drake gave him a look, not disappointed, not angry, but way more than any of that. It was murderous. I began to understand the case.

"Would've been after you took Rudy out of the barn and brought him up here," Bernie said. "Chet found the ring in the straw in Rudy's stall. Think back. Did Rudy put up a bit of a struggle? That's when it slipped off. So there's a tidy chain of events, the kind any D.A. likes to have in the bag. Not that there's necessarily a trial in your future. A trial is your best hope."

"What do you mean?" Von said.

"Shut up," said Drake.

"What I mean," Bernie said, "is if you start talking you might get out of here alive."

"What kind of talking?" Von said.

Drake glared at him, his eyes on fire in the lantern light. "You think you can make a deal? I'll kill you."

"You're capable, no doubt about that," Bernie said, "but your killing days are over. The first question, Von, is how did you lure Chaz here?"

"I had Monk call him, say that some rando had spotted his reindeer."

"Why that day?" Bernie said. "Monk must have told you that Cuffy's case file was missing before you grabbed Rudy."

"Keep your mouth shut, Von," Drake said.

Von kept his mouth shut.

"Were you hoping Rudy's disappearance would distract Chaz, make him forget about Teddy? But when that didn't happen you lured him up here? Or had you just discovered that Nellie had ended up in La Plata, and it was only a matter of time until Chaz found out?"

Their eyes, Drake's and Von's, got inward looks at the same time.

Bernie nodded to himself. "How did you get him to bring the file? Or was that just luck? He had it on him?"

No answer from Drake or Von.

"Just luck then," Bernie said. "But luck runs out. Right now, a full confession is your only choice. Full and immediate."

They stayed silent. Then came that clickety click of the shotgun getting cocked, a sound that always gets my attention. But after that, even though I was paying strictest attention, things speeded up in a way that was hard to follow.

First, for some reason, or maybe none at all, Rudy chose that moment to make a break for it. Did he think he was no longer tied to the beam? Or now just tied up loosely, almost untied? No one will ever know. All I can be sure of is that there was a splintering crack and Rudy came bolting forward, a crazy look in his eyes. He ran straight into Bernie from behind, lifting him right off the ground. The shotgun went airborne, and also went off, an enormous blast in this small space. There was a cry of pain—I thought from Von—and perhaps a splash of blood, and then the light went out and the roof fell in.

My body takes over at times like that. It sprang—no thought on my part—sprang high and forward, in the direction of the mouth of the mine. The falling roof caught me anyway, driving me back down with enormous power and burying me. But not all of me, just the back end. I squirmed, I struggled, and finally burst free. Well, not burst. Let's say wriggled. And as I came free I noticed that it had gotten kind of light in the mine. I looked up and saw a big hole in the ceiling, daylight showing above. Down below we had a huge pile of rubble, dust and maybe even some smoke rising above it. To one side of the pile lay Von, motionless, a big red hole in his chest.

But no Bernie. I scrambled up the rubble pile, clawing and clawing, scattering rocks and dirt all over the place. Bernie! Bernie! Bernie! And then, all at once, sticking out of the pile, a hand! I dug and dug around that hand, finally exposing the top of a head and then a face. But not Bernie's. It was Drake's face, eyes closed, mouth open and packed with dirt.

Bernie! Bernie! Bernie!

I scrambled back and forth over the rubble pile, up and down, back and forth, out of my mind, and then from the back of the pile, where I hadn't even tried yet, I heard the sound of a rock rolling dink dink dink down over other rocks. I raced to the back side, and saw not a hand, but a single fingertip, poking free. I darted over and dug like many many Chets at once, way more than that, and dug my Bernie out of that rubble, his head, his shoulders, arms, all of him, and dragged him free.

He lay on the floor of the mine, eyes closed, not breathing. I licked his eyelids, licked his mouth, even stood on his chest, which made no sense, but maybe that was what did it. His eyes opened. He gasped. He choked. He puked. He breathed.

Meanwhile, the mine seemed to have come alive, was trembling a bit, trembling and rumbling. I helped Bernie sit up, helped him stand, helped him walk out of the mine, pushing from behind. He went down on his knees, took a handful of snow and rubbed his face with it, rubbed his whole head, even ate some.

"That's better," he said, putting his other arm around me. Breathing better than puking, choking, or gasping? There you have it. Bernie's brilliance: unstoppable.

Meanwhile, we had quite a snowstorm going on. Blizzard? Was that it? What a nice, peaceful moment, just the two of us in all this whiteness! From inside the mine came a deep crashing boom. It didn't seem to bother Rudy, who came strolling out of the woods, trailing the rope and chewing on a huge clump of green that hung from his chin.

Twenty-seven

"Do you think Chet likes Slim Jims?" said Stell, deputy sheriff around these parts, but also Timmy's mom, which was more important, at least to me.

"Only one way to find out," Bernie said.

He can be quite the jokester, as you must know by now. Stell took off her bulky glove, reached into the pocket of her parka and in a flash a Slim Jim was mine. This was all happening in the clearing by the mine, Bernie and Stell leaning on a snowmobile and me close by, with a few more snowmobiles from the county also around, with folks from the county, cop types and rescue types, unloading all sorts of gear and nosing around the entrance to the mine. The wind had died down, and the snow wasn't falling hard, although the flakes themselves had gotten harder.

"If he doesn't like them that's one hell of an acting job," Stell said. "I'd like to send him a lifetime supply."

Bernie laughed.

"I'm serious," Stell said.

They looked at each other. "How about just sending one of those eight packs every Christmas?"

"Done," said Stell. "Does Chet have any progeny?"

"One," Bernie said. "That we know of. Still a puppy. His name's Shooter."

"Does Shooter have a good home?"

"Yes."

"If any others should turn up please me know."

"Okay."

Shooter was suddenly in the conversation? Still a puppy, true, but an extremely large one, and a somewhat troublesome character in my life. Shooter, who lives with Charlie, Leda, and Malcolm, the husband after Bernie, in their big house in High Chapparal Estates, has something to do with events that followed some very insistent she-barking from across the canyon on a long-ago night. Let's leave it at that.

A cop unspooling crime scene tape at the mine called to her. "Sheriff? Got a minute?"

"Sheriff?" said Bernie.

"Acting," Stell said. "Monk handed in his resignation ten minutes after your call came in. Word is he's going on vacation."

"To somewhere extraditable, I hope."

Stell patted his knee. "I believe there are going to be problems with his passport."

Bernie smiled at her. "Congratulations on the promotion. You're going to be great."

They shook hands, Bernie also barehanded, his gloves gone missing during the recent . . . dust up? Close enough. Dust was certainly part of it. Stell rose, heading toward the mine, but passing me she leaned down and kissed my head.

Time passed. More snowmobiles arrived, one towing a sort of horse trailer on skis. Rudy strolled into the trailer without even being asked, then stood looking out from the back, eyes blank. Different folks asked Bernie questions and he answered. I didn't pay much attention. All I knew was how tired he was. I kept close watch. The wind fell off to almost nothing, and now there was only the odd flake or two, wafting down and sometimes up. The sky darkened. The helo with the red cross on the side flew in and Albie set it gently in the clearing. He climbed down from the cockpit, saluted Bernie, and helped unload some big lights, a generator, gas cans, and lots of other stuff. Full night fell and the stars came out, so many. Then all the lights started going on and the stars went away. Bernie's eyes kept closing and he kept opening them back up.

A cop came over. "You parked down by the oil drum?" he said.

"Yup."

"Sheriff said to take you back."

Sometime later we were back at Cratchit House. Bernie checked his watch.

"In twenty minutes it's the start of Christmas Eve day," he said. "How does going home for Christmas sound?"

It sounded great. Christmas Eve day sounded confusing, so I forgot that part right away.

We went into the bedroom and Bernie started packing. "Maybe I'll change out of these boots. They've brought the cold in with them." He sat on the bed and began untying a boot lace. Then he kind of lay down on the bed. Then he was fast asleep, one boot on and one boot off.

Bernie sat up. The room was full of light. He checked his watch. "Oh my God! Why didn't you tell me? It's almost noon!"

None of that made sense. Soon we were up and out of there. The red pickup with the wreath on the grille was parked outside, engine running. Hal, now in complete Santa outfit, got out and came over. He gave Bernie a big hug, and hugged me, too. In fact, my hug came first.

"I didn't want to disturb you," he said. "Headed somewhere?"

"Home," Bernie said.

Hal laughed. "Not today. Roads out of town are all closed. Meanwhile Ariadne would like a moment."

"Wouldn't miss that."

Bernie tossed all our gear in the Beast and then we got in the pickup and Hal drove us, not to the North Pole but to Dickens House.

"She's writing," he said.

"Yeah?" said Bernie.

"In torrents since the news came in, she said. Thirty-three pages before breakfast."

"She's something else," Bernie said.

Rudy was standing on the highest part of the Dickens House roof.

"Like the king of all he surveys," Hal said. Which made no sense at all. I went over the events of the night before, searching for a moment when grabbing Rudy by the pant leg would have worked. Meanwhile Hal knocked on the door. No answer. He opened it and we went in. "Ariadne?" he said. "Ariadne?" He checked the writing room and then headed toward the kitchen, which I could see down a short hallway. Bernie and I moved into the writing room, me because Bernie was doing it, and Bernie for reasons of his own.

He went over to the desk by the big window. The laptop was open. Bernie read what he saw.

"Trudi had never been so baffled. How could Brigadier Throckmorton have possibly been at Ascot for the races and Skye for the fishing on the very same day? And yet she had witnesses who swore to each. She entered the Snorting Pig in a very thoughtful mood indeed, took a seat at the end of the bar, and ordered a pint of bitter. In her mind she added, Make it your most bitter. But that wouldn't do, especially at Christmas, and she kept it to herself.

"She had taken a sip or two when a big man walked in. An American, as she knew at once. There were many indications. He had a dog with him, a mutt, but magnificent. The American sat several stools away.

"'Sir?' said the barman.

"'A beer, please,' the American said.

"'What would be your preference?'

"The American gazed at the beer taps and then glanced at Trudi, or rather, her pint.

"'What's that?' he said.

"'Bitter,' said the barman.

"'Uh, ma'am?' he said. 'Or, um, miss? How's that bitter?'

"'Very good,' Trudi said.

"'Then bitter it is,' said the American. And when it came he raised his glass and said, 'Cheers.'

"'Cheers,' said Trudi. At which the dog walked over and pressed his head to her knee, obviously wanting some scratching or petting, in which she was happy to indulge him. Quite oddly, she felt her dark mood lifting. 'What a fine creature!' Trudi said. 'What's his name?'

"'Champ,' said the American. 'And I'm Barnie. Barnie Small.'"

At that moment Hal stuck his head into the room. "I called her. She's gone to the hospital. Chaz is awake and sitting up. But she hopes you can drop by."

"Sure," Bernie said. "We'll check on Nellie at the same time."

"Ah," said Hal, and explained why that wouldn't be happening, which I already knew. After that he handed Bernie a check, which

Bernie stuck, rather absent-mindedly, I thought, in his chest pocket, meaning I'd have something to worry about all day.

We drove the Beast to the hospital, parked, and walked down the hall to Chaz's room. The door was open. We looked in. Yes, Chaz was sitting up, looking wide awake. Ariadne sat on the bed, her back to us. Their heads were close together. They were holding hands. We backed out of the room.

"All those books, drowning out that one bad Christmas," he said as we got in the Beast. "Or am I reading—ha!—too much into it?"

A complete puzzler. I let it go at once.

There was a roadblock at the edge of town. A cop came over. "Road's closed."

"We've got chains," Bernie said.

The cop shook his head, but in the middle of that he stopped and gave us a closer look. "You the guy who . . ." He called in. "Sheriff? Got the fella here at the South Bonanza fork, fella with the dog. Wants to go through, says he's got chains." On the other end, Stella said, "Help him mount them."

"Yes, sir. Ma'am."

Bernie told the cop he didn't need help, and I'm sure he was right, but in the end those chains got mounted pretty much by the cop on his own. After that the Beast took over, not in fast mode, but in strength and power mode. The Beast taught all that snow a lesson, and in no uncertain terms. We didn't see one other car until we were down out of the mountains and on the freeway ramp, no snow in sight. Bernie pulled over and took the chains off, all by himself.

It was dark by the time we got to the Valley. Bernie had been doing some singing—even trying out a new one I didn't particularly care for, all about chains, chains, chains, these chains of love—but now he was quiet. Somewhat to my surprise we didn't seem to be headed for Mesquite Road, but farther up the canyon, near the Rio Calor crossing. We turned onto a side street and stopped in front of a small lemon-colored house with a lemon tree in the yard and a nice shady porch, a house I knew well. Weatherly opened the door before we could knock.

"Hey!" Bernie said.

"The news outpaced you." Weatherly hugged and kissed him and hugged me, too, then pulled us inside, where Trixie seemed very happy to see us, her tail wagging faster than any tail I'd ever—no, that couldn't be true. I got my tail up and going at warp speed, whatever that was, and what was this? Trixie's tail had a warp speed gear, too? Possibly as fast or even—no, I refused to go there.

Meanwhile Bernie and Weatherly were laughing, at what I couldn't imagine. We all went into the living room, had drinks, sat in front of the tree, lit with blue lights and hung with silver bells.

"Beautiful," Bernie said. "And, um, so is the tree."

"My my," said Weatherly.

"I know it's not Christmas Day but want to see your present?"

"You first."

Weatherly handed him a flat but sizeable gift-wrapped package. Bernie unwrapped it and held up a big framed photo. Hey! Bernie! Out in the desert somewhere, a tall saguaro in the background. He had a big smile on his face and a tennis ball in his hand and was just starting to rear back and throw it for . . . for this big, rough and tough looking hombre to chase after and—and that was me! Chet! I was the rough and tough looking hombre! We were playing fetch, me and Bernie.

"I don't even remember you taking this," Bernie said.

"That's the idea," said Weatherly. "Merry Christmas."

"I love it. And here's—" Bernie fumbled around in his pockets, finally producing the velvet box. The next thing I knew he was down on one knee, handing it to her.

Weatherly took the box, opened it up. And there was the Desert Star. I won't be forgetting the look in her eyes at that moment anytime soon. She put the ring on her finger, held it to the light, and looking up her eyes became two desert stars themselves, only darker. Then she was also off the couch, the two of them, Bernie and Weatherly, kneeling and holding each other. It was a lovely sight and I almost hated to break it up but otherwise Trixie would have beaten me to it.

Here's one of those lucky breaks. On Christmas Day Weatherly's neighbors have a parade. My parade! At last! Leda and Malcolm brought Charlie over before the parade got going, and Nixon and Rui plus a bunch of the guys and gals from Championship Autobody—including Nixon's sister Mindy Jo, whose arms were pretty much covered with the tattoos of all her boyfriends—dropped in, all of them wanting to see Charlie's face when he opened his present. I won't describe that look—you had to be there—but on account of the size of the present the unwrapping took a long time. Good thing I was there to help. Rip and tear, rip and tear, and at last there it was. The Beast! Only smaller!

But exactly the same, down to those rippling black and white stripes!

"DAD!"

Charlie hopped right in, took the wheel, and started pedaling around the house. Of course he also rode it in the parade. Here's an interesting detail. Nixon and the gang had made a small motor that could be attached to something inside the Little Beast for when Charlie was older. But soon a vote—whatever that is exactly, apart from being noisy—got going on how old was older, and Charlie ended up driving in the parade instead of just pedaling. No one was injured, not seriously.

I know what you're thinking. Parades need a leader—for example, someone big and strong, wearing a red collar. Not someone not quite as big and strong, wearing a green collar and continually getting her nose out in front. I, Chet, was the leader. Why couldn't she understand that? But I handled the situation quietly, like a good, good boy. This was the Christmas Parade, after all, a big responsibility, so everything went smoothly until a spectator leaned out and offered antler treats, one for Chet and one for Trixie.

An antler treat was the last thing I wanted—do I have to explain why?—so I turned my head aside and Trixie ended up snagging both. That was when things went south.

ACKNOWLEDGMENTS

I am very grateful for the steadfast and cheerful support of the wonderful team at Forge—Kristin Sevick, Troix Jackson, Libby Collins, Jennifer McClelland, and Anthony Parisi. No writer is an island!